8/4/19

To Lauren & Denise,
  I hope you enjoy this
little read! ☺ Looking forward
to lots of adventures with you.

Love,
Cathy

Sarah's Gate

I could feel the sun's massaging heat and intense brightness bearing down on me through the blue nylon of our Kelty tent. A vague recollection of Liza unzipping the doorway and slipping out through the vestibule hung in my mind. The unmistakable exhale and burning of the Whisperlite stove and the clank of a camping pan woke me. I absorbed a final moment of the down sleeping bag snuggled around my naked torso, then stretched my legs and arms to their fullest length, my fingertips brushing the dew-soaked nylon.

"Good morning, Sunshine," I said, catching Liza's attention as I pulled the tent zipper to the right. The mountain view spread before us under a Robin's egg blue sky.

"Good morning," she replied, turning toward me. She wore a smile that easily consumed one-third of her face.

Liza's smile is like nothing I've ever seen. As her lips pull away from one another, the corners of her mouth veer up at an angle toward her ears. Her thin upper lip becomes more like a fine line as her plump lower lip underscores perfectly aligned milk-white teeth. Rippled skin forms a deep parentheses around her mouth. A dimple sinks into place on her left cheek. Her eyes, the way they squint, just a little, causing crow's feet wrinkles at the corner of each eye … search, then lock onto you.

"What time is it?" I asked, hoping I hadn't slept away too much of this gorgeous day.

"About seven-thirty," she said. "Are you ready for coffee?"

Such rhetorical questions are meant for humor and not to incur an answer, so I didn't bother giving her one. Instead, I offered an "Mmmmm" only loud enough to reach her if she was truly tuned in for a response.

I scooted back into the center of the tent to pull on my blue climbing pants and a T-shirt. The pants were still sort of warm, having spent the night under my fleece jacket which had served as my pillow. I opened the belly zipper of my backpack and identified a couple of T-shirt options for the day. The faded mustard yellow shirt I had picked up at the Dole Plantation in Hawaii felt right for such a sunny morning.

Although we were within sight of the Rocky Mountains, our elevation was still reasonable enough that we could enjoy the August warmth. My guess was a temperature of around 55 degrees, looking to climb into the high 70s by afternoon. My forecast for the rest of the day: nothing but clear skies.

"How long have you been up?" I asked.

"Probably a half-hour or so," Liza said, still monitoring the Whisperlite and the state of the pot of water balanced above it.

"Has anyone ever told you that a watched pot never boils?" I said, attempting to draw a little laughter. She barely acknowledged the attempt.

I worked my way into a kneeling position inside the tent so I could tuck in my shirt. My cycling socks had to be somewhere near the bottom of the middle section of my backpack among those things you think you might need, but might not. I found them right under my rain pants, which should have been accessible through the bottom zipper, packed with my other shoes. Well ... packing faux pas #7. *What* I packed or *how* I packed it wasn't important enough to snap me out of the daydream I was experiencing at packing time. The anticipation of my first camping adventure with Liza had led me into multiple scenarios. There are intense campers who like to stay busy all the time, then there are those who like to sit and contemplate life when they are surrounded by trees and mountains instead of people and high-rise buildings. I wasn't sure Liza would fit either of those molds. If I were lucky, she would be a combination of both, slightly leaning toward the intense traits, but only slightly.

Cycling socks and fleece donned, I maneuvered myself to the front of the tent. Feet first, I slipped into my Birkenstocks and crawled out from under the vestibule to join Liza.

"Come 'ere," she said, reaching out to me.

When I was close enough, she pulled me into her embrace, wrapping her strong arms around my body and locking her hands at the small of my back. Her chin and nose cradled into my neck and I heard her breathe in the scent of my hair and of me. Our bodies swayed slowly side to side like a buoy in calm water. Her dark hair, warm from the sun, brushed against my cheek. My hand slid up her back, past the collar of her pullover, and my fingertips gently began caressing her neck.

2

"Mmm." With that, her hands pressed against my lower back and directed my pubic bone to the top of her thigh. A sudden warmth rushed through me.

"Is that coffee ready yet?" I laughed, squeezing Liza until she also began to laugh.

We both took a deep breath and pulled ourselves away from each other.

"You are dangerous," Liza said, grinning and pointing her index finger at me.

"You were the one who said, 'Come 'ere,'" I responded, trying to say the command just as she had, rolling over the "h."

"Uh-huh. And the neck thing was just …"

"I was just exploring, letting my fingers follow where my mind was taking me."

"It felt nice, very nice."

The bubbles of the boiling water caught our attention. I snatched the clear, heavy-duty plastic cups, which she already had prepared with the appropriate amount of instant Folger's, and set them next to the stove. Liza used a folded handkerchief as a potholder to grab the handle and carefully tipped the pot over each cup. Steam and the smell of fresh-brewed coffee coiled into the air.

Here in the quasi-wilderness, there is no telephone that might ring, no television news, no noise from the neighbors. No distractions. Just us (and the birds and that glorious "whisp" of the wind as it passes through the trees). This morning differs significantly from the first morning we spent together, two weeks ago.

Those were the longest two weeks of my life.

We had met at The Fairmont, one of the city's many upscale hotels near Wacker Drive and the Chicago River, during the Chicago Foundation for Women's annual black-tie gala, "Make Today the Day." The Foundation, formed in 1986 to promote the activities and futures of girls and women, has done so much in its short history and boasts an admirable collection of women on its board. Impressed (or intrigued) with my background and drastic career change, the committee asked me to serve as keynote speaker for the evening.

As I later would discover, Liza always attended the gala. Friends were past board members, current board members. She had helped the organization several years ago develop an "interactivity" branch through which major donors could have direct contact with recipients of Foundation funds. Besides, Liza loved people. She had no celebrity status, per se, but she knew people all over town, in all types of circles. For the last three years, Liza's date for the evening was Callie Langston, a Lambda Legal Defense attorney in the Midwest office. They had dated but never lived together, never made a commitment to date only each other. Some people described them as the hottest-looking 30-something couple in town. Callie was 36. Liza was 43, but no one would ever guess it by looks alone. She and Callie had decided they were good friends who were intimate, but it held no promise for long-term, and they both were okay with that decision. At this year's gala, Liza shared a table with nine friends – some couples, some individuals. This all surfaced in conversations weeks after the event.

Red looks fantastic – stunning, actually – on Liza. For the gala, she wore a vivid, cherry red Liz Claiborne silk blouse with a charcoal gray tailored jacket and pants. I remember the outfit well.

When she first arrived to the event, I already had perused the silent auction tables. The brilliant color of her shirt caught my eye as I glanced over to the check-in area to see if there was anyone I knew. My eyes froze upon her. Quickly, I looked away, afraid of being caught staring. I had to look again. My head turned back toward the line to find her. There she stood, first talking to the two men in front of her, then making conversation with the man and woman in line behind her. I was so caught up in watching her that I didn't flinch when she looked directly at me, most likely in response to the feeling that someone was glaring at her. When our eyes met, she smiled that smile – at a complete stranger who was standing across the room in a near trance. I was embarrassed. I blushed. A wonderful nervousness raced through me and, for the moment, I completely forgot why I was attending the event. To meet this woman would be reason enough.

Within seconds, Liza's eyes were turned back toward the check-in tables where I could see her picking up a program book and a card with her table assignment. Was she with someone? Surely she isn't single and here alone? Why would she be single? She must be here with a date. What am I doing? I have a keynote address to give in less than an hour. Focus. Make Today the Day. Girls and women, their futures.

My tablemates for the evening included the Foundation's executive director and her husband (Marianne and Jack Kasten), the chair of the board of directors and her partner, the gala co-chairs and their respective dates, and a United Methodist female preacher (the Rev. Maggie Birmingham) from a Southside church, who was giving the invocation for the evening. The committee had encouraged me to bring a guest and I had considered inviting my mother, but that would have involved an airline ticket and airport pickup and dropoff and, besides, she has plenty to keep her busy back home during the summer months. A date instead? No. I considered it, but I didn't want to have to worry about entertaining someone at an event where I was speaking. There would be plenty of people with whom to socialize. At the table, the conversation with Rev. Birmingham would suffice.

Foundation volunteers shuffled guests toward the ballroom so we would take our seats for the first course. The normal get-to-know-you questions passed around our table along with the multi-grain dinner rolls and Fetzer Cabernet. I tried to pay attention to detail, remembering names and jobs and connections, but I was distracted, though not by the 22-minute speech I soon would be giving to this ballroom of 800. The red shirt. The smile. Our table was, of course, up front next to the stage, making it difficult to scan much of the room in search of anyone. Luckily, my seat faced away from the stage and out toward the rest of the ballroom, but there were so many people and so many tables between the boundaries of the room and me. As nonchalantly as possible, I strayed from table conversation and began looking, first at the tables nearest me, then moving in a calculated manner to the next row, then the next. Suddenly, the Reverend was nudging me, alerting me that the co-chairs were about to go on stage and I was next.

Speaking engagements, truth be known, are one of my joys. I view them as an opportunity to reach out to people, touch them and share with them. That evening's talk – "To the Morning" – stemmed from the Dan Fogelberg song that bears the same name. I use it regularly as a motivational tool, predominantly because the audience can relate to the words Fogelberg uses: "Yes, it's going to be a day.

There is really nothing left to say but come on, morning." Undoubtedly, it tied in well with the gala theme: "Make Today the Day."

I was about one-third of the way through my speech. The room was eerily quiet, having reached that point as I described the night I was told my sister had breast cancer. My throat tightened, as it normally does when I relive that experience, and I had to take a moment before continuing. The reason, the basis, for why I left a flourishing journalism career to start a breast health foundation was simple. I was unhappy with many of the existing breast cancer fund-raising events and how the money was being divided among service providers and researchers. I knew such events could produce higher net proceeds and I knew I would be accountable to donors.

My speech shifted focus from my experience to how the listeners can move forward to create their own experiences. The objective during this phase was to make direct eye contact with as many audience members as possible. Considering stage lighting and the size of the room, my direct eye contact possibilities were limited to the first three rows of tables directly in front of the stage. As words left my mouth, my eyes directed them to one individual, then another, then another, attempting to implant in them the inspiration that had fired me up four years ago. Then, in a clear line of vision, the woman in the red shirt sat completely still, staring up at me, two tables to my left. For a split-second, I wondered if I would lose my train of thought due to the overwhelming excitement of seeing her sitting there. Impromptu disturbances at previous speaking engagements had made me immune to that, however – thank goodness – and I continued toward my closing without missing a beat.

Typically, once I leave the stage after speaking, people approach me throughout the evening and introduce themselves, expressing compliments, feedback or objections. Tonight was no different; the cast included the new director of development for a breast cancer advocacy organization who would have kept me in a one-on-one, hour-long discussion had it not been for the kind interruption by … the red shirt. She stood directly in front of me now, having maneuvered herself into the thin vertical space between the development director and the pink ribbon and rose corsage pinned to the lapel of my jacket.

6

"Hi," she said, her dark blue eyes locking onto mine.

"Hi," I replied, almost too quickly, too appreciatively. I couldn't help but grin. I didn't know if she was pleased with my speech or ready to debate and I didn't really care. If she could just stand there for a few more moments, I could handle whatever followed.

"Your speech moved me. It was obviously heart-felt," she said, bringing her right hand to her chest. "You seem very driven to do what you're doing."

"I am." A couple of seconds passed before I continued. "Thank you." I wanted to say something else, something clever or funny. I really wanted to tell her how beautiful she is and that her smile could make someone forget everything I had just told them in my speech.

"I'm Liza Aplington," she said, floating her right hand toward mine. "I'm familiar with your writing and foundation work, but we've never met."

"No, we definitely haven't," I said, shaking my head, grinning more this time. I immediately raised my hand to meet hers. Once our palms had touched, she clasped tightly. I hoped she didn't detect the intensity that was surging throughout my body. The aura surrounding her was enveloping me as if I was 17 years old and feeling my hormones for the first time. For a millisecond, the practical side of my personality reminded me that as a fairly recognizable face around the city, I should muzzle my sexual attraction to this person and act as the general populace would expect. I knew nothing about this woman, who her partner might be, where she worked. In my position, I was treading on the proverbial thin ice at this point.

I couldn't deny sexual attraction was playing a powerful role, but my instincts led me to believe this encounter was, well, I guess I want to say … fate.

Our eyes remained locked on each other and I sensed hers trying to tell me something. Then she took a deep breath and exhaled through her mouth, as if she were blowing out a candle. It was a sigh, the good kind. We both smiled. We were still holding hands.

The gala had moved into the dance mode and many people already were calling it a night. We realized this only when the

Foundation's executive director tapped me on the arm. I quickly glanced around, but slowly released Liza's hand.

"Excuse me, we just wanted to say thank you once again before we head out," the director said, putting her arm around me. Her husband reached over to shake my hand and turned to Liza, insinuating he would like an introduction. His wife, however, took over.

"Liza, it's good to see you again. It's been a while," she said. "This is my husband, Jack. Jack, this is Liza Aplington. She was the mastermind behind the donor-client interactivity project at the Foundation a few years ago. It's so good to see you. If you have time, would you call me in the next few weeks and let me buy you lunch so we can catch up and discuss some new projects the Foundation is considering?"

"I would love to, Marianne," Liza said, her cordialness further winning me over. "It was a pleasure meeting you, Jack."

The rest of my tablemates followed suit, departing with a brief "thank you" and "good-bye." Liza stayed next to me the whole time, which felt so natural, particularly since everyone at the table except for the Southside minister knew Liza better than they knew me. I had gathered, by this point, she was not with a date, but I had to be sure.

"Would anyone be upset if I slipped you out of here with me?" I asked, trying to be coy.

After I had said it, I felt it had been too bold, but now it was too late. What was she thinking?

"I'd be upset if you didn't," she said, gently grabbing the front of my silk shirt between her thumb and two fingers. She looked down to where she was touching, then back up and into my eyes. "I'm valet parked. How about you?"

"I took a cab."

"Then I guess *I'm* slipping *you* out of here with *me*," she said, causing us both to laugh.

We beat the valet crowd and escaped within minutes, heading south on Lake Shore Drive. When we got to the Museum Campus – an architectural collection of the Field Museum, Shedd Aquarium, Adler Planetarium and Soldier Field (the Chicago Bears' home turf) – Liza exited and meandered her midnight blue Jeep Liberty toward the Planetarium. Since we'd left the ballroom, I had been grilling her for personal information. What do you do for a living? Where were you raised? Do you have siblings? Are your parents still living?

"I started out coaching and ended up associate commissioner of the Big 10 Conference," she said, attempting to sum up two decades in one sentence. "My family is all over the country, really. My parents are in Jacksonville, Florida. I have a sister who coaches in southern California, another sister who is working on a master's degree in zoology in Philadelphia, and another sister who works in the Mayor's office in Boston."

Her response was informative and concise. She hesitated, perhaps assuming similar questions were on the way. Although I wanted answers to all those questions, and more, I was hungry at the moment for the more intimate characteristics of this woman.

"Are you currently involved with anyone?" At age 44, I usually brought this question to the surface quickly. It seemed more difficult to ask this time, maybe because I really wanted the answer to be "no" and I wasn't sure what I might do if she said "yes." She was just pulling into a parking space that looked northwest at the Chicago skyline. When she had turned off the engine, she turned to look at me and smiled, shaking her head.

"I wanted to ask you the same question," she said, "but I wasn't sure where to slip it in."

"Former journalist, you know. No question is that hard to ask."

Some questions, I thought to myself, just don't get asked because we don't want to hear the answer.

The clear July night sky served a perfect backdrop to the city's famous architecture. The white-light fortress atop the building I always referred to as White Castle World Headquarters shined to our left. The Amoco/Standard structure appeared top-heavy that night with solid bars of its upper-floor office lights allowing maintenance crews to chip away at getting the behemoth clean by Monday morning. The patriotic Hancock Building still bore its headband of illuminated red, white and blue in observance of Independence Day. I'd been out here on the Planetarium point before, many times, looking back at majestic Buckingham Fountain, beautifully groomed Grant Park, and the way both merge into a frenzy of high-rises, traffic, the elevated train, construction.

I liked coming here alone sometimes, days when I'm exceptionally pensive.

"No, I'm not *involved* with anyone," Liza answered, with an emphasis on *involved*. "And you?"

"No, I've been waiting for you," I said, making her burst into laughter. Anxiousness played a part, I'm sure, in how funny she found that answer to be. As I had been, she was worried the answer might be "yes."

Instead of pursuing the reason she attended the gala without a date, I steered the conversation toward how we both landed in Chicago. Did she miss coaching? She asked if I missed journalism. How much travel was involved in her job now? We discovered we both held United Airlines Premier status.

We'd left The Fairmont around midnight. Her car clock radio now displayed 1:45 a.m. What had we been talking about for nearly two hours? Why am I not tired? She must have read my thoughts.

"Where to now?" Liza asked, reaching over to cover my hand with hers. She slid her fingers under mine and softly rubbed the back of my hand with her thumb. That surge again raced through my body.

I leaned forward, pulling her hand and mine to my side, pulling her toward me. She slipped her left hand along my face, my temple and through my hair. Before our lips touched, I stole a yearning glimpse into her eyes.

We couldn't stay there long. It was 2 a.m. and we were parked in an area the Chicago Police Department likes to see vacated about that time of morning. Besides, making out in a Jeep Liberty might be a fun date down the road, but it was an obstacle to how close we wanted to be right then. We backed away from each other, both taking deep breaths. Liza pulled the seatbelt strap over her shoulder, turned the ignition and headed back to Lake Shore Drive.

"Do you have pets that need attention before morning?" she asked, addressing an issue that would determine where we were going.

"No. I had a Husky mix named Lucca for 12 years. I had to have her put to sleep several years ago and have never gotten another dog."

Issue addressed, Liza need not ask where *I* lived. As we drove along the south entrance of the gargantuan Field Museum, she got into the lane for merging with north-bound traffic and we again passed by the downtown business district. At this late (or early, depending on your perspective) hour, the sidewalks appeared deserted except for a homeless young woman pushing a shopping cart packed with her worldly belongings, her mangy mutt keeping close to her heels.

"Twelve years. That's a long time," Liza said. "What happened that caused you to decide to euthanize her?"

Euthanasia. That *is* the term I should use. Why do I continue to say "put to sleep?" I know why. It sounds less medical, less technical, more humane. The day that decision had to be made is as vivid to me now as the actual day it occurred.

"A tumor must have burst in Lucca's chest cavity and she was struggling to breathe. Jen, a good friend of mine, is a vet and was actually at the title company closing on her house that morning. Unfortunately for her, I knew exactly where to find her," I said, raising my brow. "I picked her up at the "el" station closest to my house and she spent the rest of the day with us. We drove to her office where she could run blood tests and do X-rays. She explained to me the few options. Lucca's prognosis was very bad and, at Jen's suggestion, I agreed to euthanasia. So, we took Lucca back to my house and I laid her on her flowered blue comforter in the living room."

I caught myself. She hadn't asked for a blow-by-blow testimony.

"I'm sorry. Did you want to hear all of this?" I asked. Embarrassment started setting in. "When someone asks me, I sort of replay the whole day in my mind and the story line comes out with all the little details that are probably of interest to no one except me and, maybe, Dr. Jen."

"Yes, I want to hear all of it," she said convincingly.

Five miles north of downtown Chicago, she took the Irving Park exit and sailed through green-lit intersections all the way to Damen Avenue.

"It was still afternoon when Jen and I got back to my house and I wasn't able to ask her to give Lucca the shot until sometime that evening. At one point, I finally said to her, 'Jen, I'm never going to be ready.' She was so patient, so compassionate."

"She sounds like a great friend," Liza said, reaching over to again take my hand.

"Yeah, she's the best. And she's an excellent vet, the kind who reads all of her veterinarian magazines so she can keep up with studies and new developments. She's also involved with the Rainbow Therapy Dog Program where dogs are used in therapy for people with disabilities. She's a good egg."

"A good egg. I haven't heard that in a while," Liza said, looking over at me.

"Where exactly did that originate?" I responded, chuckling.

"I don't know, probably the farm, but I know exactly what you mean when you say it. Compliments are compliments, however they come out, whether they are a cliché or not."

My opportunity to express to Liza what I had wanted to say when she first approached me at the gala had presented itself.

"You are a very beautiful woman," I said more slowly than I normally speak. I wanted her to hear my sincerity in every word.

Her first response was another sigh.

"I don't know whether to thank you first or tell you how difficult it was for me to wait for that woman from the advocacy organization to stop talking to you so I could introduce myself," Liza said, her smile widening. "I don't think she *was* going to stop, so I had to cut in."

"My speech got to you that much?" I asked, fishing.

"Your speech, the way you presented yourself on stage, your devotion to what you're doing …" she said, pausing. "The physical attraction was icing on the cake, to borrow another cliché."

She turned south onto Hamilton and pulled over to park near the end of the block. The St. Ben's neighborhood had turned high-dollar a few years ago. Buyers couldn't touch a single-family home there for less than $375,000 these days. Two-flats, of which there were a substantial number in this area, listed for closer to $500,000. The real estate market showed no signs of depression despite the downward spiral of tech stocks. It was a transient neighborhood, though not transient in the "poor way" that might imply. Families who were second-generation, maybe even third, in these predominantly Catholic city blocks were selling and moving out. Some couldn't afford rising property taxes. Others were anxious to take the $500,000 for a lot their parents or grandparents had

12

purchased for a mere $25,000. Even though family names were being erased and replaced by new ones on the ward residents' ledger, the same alderman was starting his 21st year in office. I had rented the first floor of a three-flat years ago only a few blocks from where she parked. Lucca loved our walks through this neighborhood.

Curiosity had me guessing which building was hers. I hadn't gotten to my line of questioning that includes "Do you own a home or rent?" Directly to my right sat a brown brick two-flat, its front yard quaintly landscaped with what appeared to be yellow chrysanthemums and a multitude of snapdragons, though the available natural light at 2:30 in the morning is limited. On the north side of the brown two-flat was an older single-family home undergoing an obvious renovation, though its front yard was immaculate and smartly designed. South of the two-flat rested another single-family home: blue siding, big front porch, brick pavers leading to the steps. I was leaning toward betting on the blue house as we got out of her SUV.

"Mine's across the street," she said, motioning for me to come around the front of the car.

The anxiousness of that 17-year-old within me was revived as we started toward a two-story limestone house. Although it was dark, I could see how well manicured she kept her yard and the variety of flowers and shrubs strategically placed along the front of the porch. Eight stone steps led to an old-fashioned solid wood door that was accented at eye level with a gorgeous clear and cobalt blue stained-glass window.

"Have I mentioned how much I like cobalt blue?" I asked, motioning to the stained glass.

"I'm glad to hear it," she said, opening the door. "This is it. Welcome to my home."

Maybe I should have wandered around a bit, checked out the living room or kitchen and complimented her on the décor. Instead, I stepped toward her, putting my hands on her waist and letting them slide back along her silk shirt until my arms were completely around her. I ran my hands under the jacket and up to her shoulder blades, feeling each detail as if I were reading Braille. Kissing her without a console between us was long overdue.

13

Chapter two

The sun's fingers had awakened me inside the tent as gently as they had stirred me nearly two weeks ago on North Hamilton Avenue.

Morning rays pierced the east window of Liza's bedroom. If she had thought about closing the blinds three hours earlier, we might have slept in, but I was perfectly content to be horizontal and awake. Speaking at the CFW event had been something I looked forward to for months, though I had no idea just how fruitful the experience would turn out to be.

Rolling onto my back, I opened my eyes and began taking in my surroundings. The walls were burnt orange, a vibrant choice for a bedroom, capped with a white ceiling and white trim around the windows and door frames. Her Quaker-style furniture took a back seat to the dark walnut, rectangular floor mirror standing in the northeast corner of the room. It was an amazing, beautiful piece. The reflection of us lying there peered back at me. From the chain of the ceiling fan above us hung a curious string of beads, some of which looked like scrimshawed bone amidst spheres of lapis and amber.

Although the windows were each open about three inches – as high as they could be raised before hitting theft guards – the neighborhood was almost silent, like waking in the woods with no one around you for acres. The faint hum of cars on nearby Grace Street seldom reached the room. It was early. It was Sunday morning. We could expect peacefulness for at least another hour or so.

"How was your nap?" Liza asked, breaking into one of those enormous smiles so early in the day.

If I fell asleep, it wasn't for more than an hour. She knew that. She had dozed off only after I began creating words on her back with my fingertips, the way grade school girls do during sleepovers with friends. I would lightly drag my fingertip over her skin, making words, one letter at a time, then she had to guess what I had spelled. I find it very relaxing, in the same way my father would hold my hand during church service and rub my thumbnail with his thumb, like he was shining a silver coin. I knew Liza had given in to its calming effect when she failed to tell me I had spelled "sweet dreams."

We picked up in conversation where we'd left off driving down Irving Park.

"Do you have a pet needing breakfast sometime soon?" I asked.

"Not anymore. It's just you and me, kid."

Interesting that she would say "kid." I couldn't help myself and immediately pursued the path of potential age difference between the two of us.

"Since you brought it up, what year did you graduate from high school?"

"How did *I* bring that up?" Liza said, raising her eyebrows as she looked at me.

"Don't skirt the question," I warned, teasingly.

"If the underlying question really is 'How old am I?', the answer is 43, which means I graduated in 1977. I have you beat, right? I'm guessing we're pretty close in age, but I have you beat by a year or two."

"And you're basing that on what?" I asked, intrigued by how she might answer.

"Because when you smile, your face doesn't transform into a Rorschach abstract of wrinkles like mine," she said, rubbing her own cheek with the back of her fingers.

"I think you've used that line before," I responded, rolling onto my side to face her. "You don't have me beat. I graduated in '76. And just for the record, my friend, I love the lines on your face when you smile. You have the most amazing smile."

"Thank you," she said, leaning over to kiss my cheek, her lips brushing along my jaw and almost to my chin.

Around 7 or 7:30, the car doors of neighbors leaving for church began slamming and the sunlight reaching into the bedroom created the need for circulating air. Liza crawled off one side of the bed and headed toward the ceiling fan switch next to the bedroom door. I couldn't take my eyes off of her. When she turned around to return to bed, she caught me staring, just as she had at the gala while she was waiting in line to check in.

15

"Not until this moment did it strike me that you were the one glaring at me from over by the silent auction tables when I arrived last night," Liza said, a look of mild amazement on her face.

"I wouldn't call it 'glaring.' "

"And here I thought I was the one trying to catch *your* eye."

"It seems to have worked out well, regardless, don't you think?" I asked, reeling her toward me.

Over the next three hours, we managed to find time for toast and scrambled eggs, a nap and lots more conversation. An enviable Sunday morning, needless to say. We were back under the powder blue cotton sheets, coffee cups in hand. I had to go home at some point, but felt confident we could reunite in the afternoon.

"Will you have dinner with me tonight?" I asked.

"I would if I could," Liza answered. "I have a 6:15 flight to San Francisco."

It was an NCAA workshop for conference commissioners from around the country. From San Francisco, she was flying to southern California to visit her sister before going to another business commitment in Oregon. She would be back to Chicago in 13 days.

"Thirteen days?" I asked, my voice full of playful sarcasm, my lips forming a practiced pout.

She was visibly frustrated about our not being able to see each other for two weeks.

"I haven't seen my sister for several months," Liza said, trying to explain the weekend in California. "I'd postpone it or ask you to join me on the West Coast, but it might be awkward …"

I didn't let her finish that sentence. Of course it would be awkward for me to join her and her sister for the weekend. She and I still needed to learn so much about each other and we both knew better than to … well, we both just knew better.

"You need to go spend quality time with your sister," I said. "I'm sure she's excited that you're going out there to visit her."

I was making assumptions here since I was clueless about her relationships with her sisters. My frame of reference was the relationship I have with my two sisters. I don't get to see them often enough and they, for whatever reasons, don't travel to visit me.

"So you're hearing me when I say how much I'd like to stay here and spend the time getting to know you, right?" Liza wanted to be certain I knew how she felt.

"It easily could have been the other way around," I said, starting to laugh. "Listen to us, we sound like a couple of young girls who met at summer band camp and we're afraid we're never going to see each other again. I'll miss you, really miss you, but I'm hoping you'll be available for a date in about 13 days."

"It's a date."

Knowing she needed to take me home, pack and probably finish a couple of other projects before her trip, I initiated the separation. I stepped out of bed and began gathering my clothes.

"Hey, you don't have to put that outfit back on," Liza said, practically jumping off the other side of the bed. "Do you prefer jeans or shorts?"

"What size are you?" I replied, happy to not wear the Saturday night outfit.

"My jeans are 30 waist, 32 length. Most of my shorts are men's small."

"How about gym shorts or something like that?" I asked.

Liza pulled open a dresser drawer packed full of folded shorts and snagged a navy pair that read "Michigan" on the left thigh. She threw them toward me, then disappeared into her walk-in closet and returned with a white T-shirt.

"Today I'm promoting college athletics," I said, noticing the 2001 Women's College World Series logo on the back of the shirt.

"I'll make you a fan of the Big Ten before you know it," Liza said.

"I don't doubt it."

"Do you want to go barefoot or wear a pair of my sandals?" Liza asked, guiding me toward the closet where her shoes were neatly organized on the floor. "I wear an 8 or 8½ in most shoes. I think these Speedo pool sandals might work."

I slipped my feet into them, discovering a perfect fit.

"Will you be needing these back?" I asked, smiling.

Liza pulled on a pair of frayed, faded Gap jeans and a red University of Wisconsin T-shirt. I was drawn to her by an indescribable magnetism. We stood hugging in the center of the

17

room, feeling the rise and fall of our chests against each other with every breath.

"Okay. One of us needs to break this up," I whispered.

Before I could back away, Liza's warm lips were on mine, dancing in slow motion. The intensity grew and I closed my eyes as passion raced through me.

"You have to pack," I said, 20 minutes later, sitting up. Liza lay flat on the floor, smiling, lightly rubbing my back with her fingers.

Like an obnoxious alarm clock, the telephone rang.

"I'd better get that," Liza said, rising to grab the mobile phone next to the bed. "Hello. Yes, it was a fun evening. Yeah. Uh-huh. No, I think they left early. Hey listen, I was just headed out. Could I call you later or tomorrow?"

I didn't intentionally want to eavesdrop and started to get up to leave the room, but Liza reached over and grabbed my hand, signaling for me to stay.

"Oh, thanks for offering, but someone else is giving me a ride. Yep. No, near Portland. Yeah. I'm sorry, but I do need to get going. That's okay. Thanks again for the offer. I'll talk to you in the next couple of days. Bye."

"Sorry about that," Liza said, releasing my hand and replacing the phone on its cradle.

"My competition?" I playfully asked.

"No competition," she said, again taking my hand and leading me out of the bedroom and downstairs. "That was Callie Langston, a friend, former girlfriend, who was my date for the CFW dinner the past three years. She wondered if I had a good time."

With that, Liza looked back over her shoulder at me and shared an irresistible smile.

We ended up in the kitchen, snacking on grapes and potato chips while Liza threw together a couple of turkey and cheese sandwiches.

"This is the last of the turkey. If it's not enough for you, I can maybe make something else or we could stop somewhere on the way to your house." Liza realized, at this point, she had no idea where she would be taking me. "I can't believe I didn't ask you this earlier! Where *do* you live?"

18

"Not to worry, my friend. We had a lot of other things to talk about," I said, popping another grape into my mouth.

Liza placed each sandwich on a plate, then accented each with a small bunch of grapes and handful of chips. I followed her through a sliding glass door to a small, elevated deck overlooking the backyard. A glass mosaic-topped table and two wrought iron chairs sat in full sun.

"Is this going to be too hot?" she asked, setting the plates on the table.

"This'll be great," I said, choosing my chair.

"Now, where *do* you live?"

"I own a two-flat on Farragut in Andersonville. It won't take us long to get there."

"So you're a landlord."

"Don't you mean landlady?" I said, trying for a little humor. "That was my realtor's suggestion when I first went house hunting. Prices on two-flats were still reasonable in that neighborhood at the time and the rental market has been strong around there. People are willing to pay high rent to live in 'Girlstown.' I think I was lucky with the timing of when I bought."

In the past five years, the Scandinavian flavor of this sector of Chicago had been altered, like serving Swedish pancakes with strawberries instead of lingonberries – still good, but different. Small fitness centers now occupied square footage previously packed with cases of low-cost alcohol and wire stands of cigarette packs. Cleverly named restaurants with entrees priced no less than $9.95 had replaced many of the mom-and-pop deli shoppes where a person used to get a hot dog and fries for $1.50. Most of the changes were good, for most people, and new residents were choosing to rehab the old buildings, retaining their character, rather than level them and start anew.

"I'm anxious to see it," Liza said.

"I might have you just drop me off at the front door. I really wasn't expecting company and the house isn't prepared for visitors."

"No, I don't think so," she said, emphatically. "Do you think I was expecting company last night?"

She had a point, but I didn't want to give in so easily.

"I don't know. Were you?"

"Very funny," she replied. "No, bringing strange women home is not a habit or hobby of mine."

"Strange?" I asked.

"Ha ha. You know what I mean. I should've just said 'strangers' since it can be assumed they would be women. Should I have shown more restraint last night and left you standing there with the advocacy organization woman?"

"Okay, you can see my place."

The day was slipping away and Liza had a lot to do before leaving for the airport.

"If you don't mind me asking, who's taking you to the airport? I heard you telling Callie someone is giving you a ride."

"If you don't mind me asking, would *you* take me to the airport? When I was talking to Callie, I was being optimistic that you might be willing to take me."

"Safe bet on your part," I said, getting up from my chair and giving her a quick peck on the lips. "Let's get going."

Traffic was light between Liza's house and mine. I had her pull into the alley and park behind my garage instead of looking for a spot on the street.

"Sneaking me in, are you?" she said, razzing me for taking her in the back door.

"Yeah, the girls who rent the first floor tease me because it's a different woman every week, so I use the back door pretty often to avoid the jokes," I said, wondering if Liza was going to believe such fiction.

"You're a busy woman," was her first response. She needed a few seconds to conjure up a rebuttal. "Are you sure you're going to have time for our date in 13 days? Sounds like you might be booked for weeks to come."

We had reached the top of the back stairs. I unlocked the door leading into my kitchen, stepped inside and immediately turned to face her.

"No, you're on the calendar. You're definitely on the calendar," I said, leaning toward her.

Liza was the first woman I had kissed in my kitchen in more than four years. Don't misunderstand. It hadn't been four years since I had dated, but I had not brought women into my home. That's an incredibly involved story that will unfold, but now is not the time. I have not allowed myself to share the intimacy of even a kiss in this sacred space, my fortress, my refuge. With Liza, without a second thought, it just happened.

Still carrying my dress clothes, I excused myself to drape them over a chair in the next room. Liza was looking at pictures on the refrigerator door when I returned.

"I'll fill you in on who's who some other day, okay?" I said, leading her out of the kitchen.

A quick tour of my place gave Liza a glimpse into my personality. The living room featured a distressed brown leather couch and matching chair with ottoman. Mission-style coffee and end tables were covered with old and recent copies of *National Geographic*, *The Advocate* and *Time*. The round dining table, formerly my paternal grandmother's, and its ornate wooden chairs took up much of the space allotted for a dining area adjacent to the living room. The small bedroom nearest the kitchen and main bathroom served as my home office, with south and east windows giving it good natural light. Liza followed me up solid oak stairs to what once was an attic. With a bold rehabilitation plan, the space had been transformed into a master bedroom, complete with Jacuzzi tub, separate marble-walled shower and walk-in closet.

"Unbelievable," Liza said as we topped the stairs and she had a full-circle view of the room.

She stuck her head into the bathroom, then decided to completely walk in and check it out.

"This is amazing," she continued. "Did you do this after you bought the place?"

I hesitated. Glimpses of that time period flamed in my head.

"Yeah. It turned out pretty nice. I'm very happy with it."

"Did you design it yourself?"

I swallowed and turned away from her, shuffling some picture frames on the dresser.

"With some help from friends who were willing to fine-tune my general plans. And the contractor was fantastic to work with, asking me for explanations when he didn't understand some of the specifics as the project went on. If you ever need a general contractor …"

"I love it," Liza said.

We were only standing a couple of feet from one another and, all at once, I felt too far away. I stepped over to her and wrapped my arms around her, squeezing tighter than I had all morning.

"Is everything okay?" Liza asked.

"Yeah, I just wanted to hug you," I said, reluctantly releasing her and heading back down the stairs. "I don't want to push you out the door, believe me, but do you need to go home and pack?"

"Yes, yes, I need to pack. I also need to pull together some paperwork and make sure I have everything I need for Oregon. If we leave my house by 4:30, that should get me to the airport by 5:00. Can you be at my house at 4:30?"

"What if I come over at 4? Then we won't be rushed and, if you're still packing, we can chat while you finish."

"I like the way you think," Liza said.

We walked down the building's back staircase and I escorted her to the gate next to the garage. She initiated a hug and spent an extended amount of time pressing her lips against my neck.

"I'll see you around 4," she said, heading out the gate.

I watched her leave the alley, then turned to head back into the two-flat. Peering out the first-floor kitchen window were my tenants, Claire and Amy.

Although they had rented the first floor for only two years, it seemed to me they had lived there since I bought the building five years ago. They were nearly perfect tenants: paid rent on time, kept the apartment clean, always alerted me when minor repairs were needed instead of letting them turn into major repairs. They also had become friends to me, despite the 12-year age difference. Keenly aware that I had not invited girlfriends (of the romantic kind) into my home since they had moved into the first-floor apartment, Claire and Amy would be wondering "What's up?"

I sort of wondered myself.

They had left the window and were standing at their open kitchen door when I got there. They were grinning like two kids in a Toys R Us.

"Good morning," I said to them.

"It's afternoon in our world, Cate," Claire said, giggling, waiting for me to bring up the topic of "my guest."

"Oh, you're right. How are you two?"

"Good. We're doing good," Amy replied. "We're going to ride bikes to Hollywood Beach in a little while. Do you want to come with us?"

I imagined they knew my answer would be "no" and thought this might be an attempt on their part to gather information. Since I anticipated seeing Liza again – as soon as possible – after her return from Oregon, I saw no reason to keep them totally in the dark.

"Thank you for the invitation. That would be fun. It's a gorgeous day for it. I have other plans, though. I'm giving my friend Liza a ride to the airport."

"Friend from out of town?" Claire asked.

"No, she lives here," I answered. "She's leaving on a business trip."

I could tell they were craving more detail and, admittedly, I was enjoying leaving them in the lurch.

My journalism years had honed my skills at digging information out of people. Amy, who was completing a master's degree in sports psychology, could have been a great journalist.

"She doesn't look familiar to me. What does she do for a living?" she asked.

"She works for the Big Ten Conference," I replied. "To tell you the truth, I don't know a great deal about her yet. We met at the dinner last night."

"Oh, how was the dinner? How'd they like your speech?" Claire asked, getting an elbow from Amy.

"I want to hear about the dinner, too," Amy interrupted, "but first tell us how you met Liza. Come into the living room so we can sit down."

I followed them down the main hallway. As we passed the bathroom, I detected the aroma of Scrubbing Bubbles or something very similar. Claire moved the vacuum against the dining room wall so I wouldn't trip over the hose. Amy sat on the couch and waved for me to sit next to her.

"The brief story is all you're getting right now because I have a few things to do before I take her to the airport. Okay? She had just arrived and was checking in when I first noticed her. She was wearing this brilliant red blouse and I had a hard time taking my eyes off of her. At one point, she caught me staring and smiled, then went back to what she was doing."

"Did you go over and introduce yourself?" Claire asked.

"I'm guessing not," Amy chimed in. "That's not Cate's style."

"No, I didn't, and then they started directing all of us into the ballroom. Once everyone was seated for dinner, I didn't see her again until during my speech. Here I was, perched on a platform speaking to 800 people, and my attention totally honed in on this one intriguing woman sitting near the stage."

"Did you eventually walk around looking for her or what?" Amy probed.

"Actually, I was in the middle of a conversation with Kris Johnston – do you know her? – the new development director at Y-Me. Anyway, the next thing I know, this woman I had been glaring at before dinner was about six inches from my face, introducing herself."

"Look at her," Claire said to Amy, pointing in my direction. "She's blushing."

"Obviously, the two of you hit it off," Amy said. "So you made plans to meet for coffee this morning or a late breakfast?"

If I was blushing before, what were they thinking of the red tone my face was turning now?

"We had breakfast at her place," I answered, hoping to leave the explanation at that. "I need to get upstairs and get some things done. I'll be around until about 3:30 if you guys need anything, okay?"

The two of them knew me well enough to know I'd divulged enough personal information for now and did not press me with more questions.

"Have a great time at the beach," I told them. "Ride safely."

"Thanks, Cate. I hope you can join us next time," Amy said. "Maybe Liza could come."

"Maybe." I nodded my head in agreement.

As I walked upstairs and through the back door, I almost could feel Liza's presence as I stood where we had kissed in the kitchen.

"I'm happy for you." It was the voice of Sarah, my partner of six years.

Unable to hold back tears, I sank to the floor. Crying became sobbing.

"I miss you, Sarah. I miss you so much. I don't want to lose you, not again."

Sarah's death 4 ½ years ago nearly killed me. My salvation came two nights after her funeral.

"Dwell on the wonderful years you got to spend together," my mother had said to me when they pried me away from the cemetery. She continued hiding her own pain in order to console me. My family had to return to Missouri and their responsibilities, get on with their lives. "She'll always be in your memories and in your heart."

When they left that night, I was alone…truly alone. My listless body surged into uncontrollable tension, shaking with anger and grief.

"Why? Please tell me why. Why did this happen?" I begged my empty room for an answer.

"Cate, don't be afraid. I'm here."

"Sarah?"

Once I'd spoken her name, I wanted to scream. I wanted to turn back time. I wanted her there with me so badly that I thought I heard her talking to me.

"Cate, it *is* me. It's Sarah. Please don't be afraid. I wanted you to know I haven't left you, not completely."

"Sarah, am I losing my mind or are you really here?"

"Your mother's right, you know? We'll always have the memories of our six precious years together and you can carry me in your heart for as long as you need me."

"I need you *now*," I said, my words drowning in self-pity. "If you're here, let me see you. Let me hold you."

The room's darkness began to strangle me like a noose.

"Tonight, only tonight," Sarah's voice spoke again. "If you'll get up and go stand next to the bedroom door leading out to the deck, I'm there."

This seemed so real. I wanted it to be real. I peeled myself off the bed and slowly walked toward the door. Standing next to it, I looked out past the staggered rooftops jutting up between the faint city skyline and me.

"Close your eyes," she said. "Picture us here, together. When you hear my voice, watch my lips. I'm here. I'm really here."

With my eyes closed, a vision of Sarah emerged before me. She was healthy and beautiful. I thought I would begin to cry, but no tears came, just pure joy.

Sarah stayed and talked with me. I'm not sure how long. Hours, I think. Then she told me she had to go and I didn't question her or beg her to stay.

"I love you, Cate," she said, wrapping me in her arms. I could feel her embrace as completely as when we'd held each other five days ago.

"And I love you more than you'll ever know," I said softly.

"I already know," she said. "That's why I'm here."

Holding her ended too soon. She started backing away from me, the outline of her face and body beginning to fade.

"Physically, we've been separated, but we can talk to each other," she said. "Our lives are going to be different now, but I'm still here for you. We share an amazing connection and our love has moved to a new dimension."

As her image melted from my mind, I resisted opening my eyes and returning to reality. I kept standing there, trying to resolve how the impossible could be possible. Had grief driven my imagination to such an extreme? If what had just happened was not real, why do I feel so peaceful? I drew a deep breath and opened my eyes. The Chicago sky was graduated shades of indigo. Soon, the sun would break open a new morning.

Chapter Three

Telling Liza about my unusual relationship with Sarah would be difficult. Should I tell her while we're in Colorado? What if she doesn't comprehend it or, worse, can't believe me? Sarah's visit with me in the afternoon before I took Liza to the airport appeared vividly in my mind.

I was still sitting on the kitchen floor, feeling sorry for myself. It suddenly dawned on me that I'd completely lost track of time, and my eyes went searching for the oven clock. It was already 2:30 p.m.

"You're not going to lose me again if you fall in love with Liza. Whatever feelings that develop between the two of you, you'll still have me with you – always."

Sarah's voice calmed me, as it had the past four years when I emotionally would slip to a low point. The aching started to subside.

"What you and I have, Cate, should not exclude you from having the sort of life you could have with Liza. You deserve what she can give you. You should have someone in your life who'll sit and have coffee with you before work, someone to hike with, someone who might like your bland cooking."

Even now, Sarah enjoyed teasing me.

"I need to shower and get ready to take Liza to the airport," I said, rising from the tile floor. "She's going to be gone for almost two weeks and I think I'm going to want some company."

"Then I'll talk to you soon," Sarah replied. "Count on it."

Steam clouded the bathroom mirror as the showerhead rained hot water over me. As I ran the washcloth up my arm, I was more aware than usual of the cloth's texture against my skin. All my senses seemed on high alert. I took a deep breath through my nose – the smell of fragrant body wash filled the room – and bent over to stretch my back. With a relaxed exhale, I rolled back to a standing position and reluctantly turned off the water.

It's been an incredible weekend, I thought to myself. I am so lucky. Brunch on Saturday with some friends from Chicago Women in Philanthropy. An afternoon of catching up on magazine reading prior to the CFW dinner. Liza. Talking with Sarah today.

I *am* so lucky.

I quickly combed my hair, then proceeded into the bedroom to decide what I should wear. Hopefully, Liza would be thinking of me while she was gone. If she did, I wanted her to remember what I was wearing when she got out of the car at the airport. I picked up her Michigan gym shorts and softball championship T-shirt and dropped them in my laundry basket in the closet. Staring at the variety of shirts hanging in front of me, I finally reached for a white sleeveless V-neck. My tan was fairly deep by this time of summer and I liked the contrast between white and my skin tone. Gap khaki shorts and a two-toned blue web belt rounded out my attire.

My Birkenstocks were by the door leading out to the deck. When I was a few steps away, the city skyline popped into sight. Nearly eight miles north of city center, I had a crisp view of skyscrapers towering onto a baby blue canvas. This was the spot where Sarah first spoke to me four-and-a-half years ago. In this space near the door, I again found solace.

Shoes in hand, I jogged down the stairs and into my office. I wanted to send out a couple of emails so they'd be waiting for the recipients first thing in the morning. The next two months would involve key negotiations with a massive corporate sponsor I'd been courting for more than three years. They had contacted me less than a year after I had publicly introduced "A Sister's Hope," the breast health foundation inspired by my sister's bout with breast cancer. Although they were extremely interested at that time in partnering with the foundation, there was some inner-corporation education and cohesion that had to take place first. The next few weeks promised high activity and I needed to stay on top of communication with all parties involved.

The turkey sandwich I'd eaten at Liza's was good, but now was long gone from my stomach. A bowl of Breyer's strawberry ice cream, accented with a handful of raw pistachios, would hold me over for a while. I looked at the oven clock. It was 3:35 p.m. I ran back upstairs to grab earrings and a watch, getting myself out the door by 3:40.

On the way to St. Ben's, I listened to Fogelberg's *The Netherlands* CD. Only three songs had played by the time I reached

Hamilton Avenue. Liza was on her front porch when I stepped out of the car.

"You're already packed and ready to go?" I asked, meeting her on the top step.

"Yes, I am," she said. "Are you surprised?"

"Pleasantly."

"Come in."

She reached back for my hand and guided me inside to the living room. The sun now was coming through the west windows, giving the tan walls an amber glow. Before I thought about sitting down, Liza turned around to kiss me.

It had been so long since I felt like this, sensations pouring through me. I had unbelievable desire for this woman.

Liza backed her head away from me to say something, but my lips reconnected with hers before a word could escape. Minutes went by. The room got warm – very warm.

"My heartbeat is out of control right now," Liza finally said, turning toward the couch and pulling me down onto it next to her.

"That makes two of us."

Unwilling to resist, I repositioned myself to face her and let passion take over.

An alarm, like the one on a runner's watch, started beeping from what sounded like the kitchen.

"That's not good," Liza said, taking my face in her hands and staring into my eyes. "That means it's 4:30."

"You're right," I said, getting up from the couch. "That's not good."

Liza asked me to grab some bottled water out of the refrigerator for the two of us while she ran upstairs for a minute. When she returned, she handed me a canary yellow sealed envelope.

"You're not to open this until my flight leaves Chicago. Got it?"

"If you say so," I answered, taking it from her.

We grabbed her suitcase, carry-on and the water and headed outside. She followed me to the navy Saab convertible parked in front of her house.

"I wouldn't have guessed a Saab," she said, lifting her suitcase into the trunk, "but I like it."

"What were you expecting?" I asked.

"Either an SUV similar to mine, or something like a Camry."

"Not bad. I've had a Camry and I've been looking at the Ford and Honda SUVs. I bought this from a friend a few years ago after Lucca died."

As I pulled onto Irving Park, Liza reached over and laid her hand on my leg. Sometimes Sunday afternoon traffic near the airport can be heavy with people flying out after a weekend in the city, but we pulled up to United's curbside check-in about 20 minutes after leaving her house. I turned on my flashers and started to get out of the car, but Liza's fingers squeezed the top of my leg.

"Can we sit here a minute?" she said, an insistent look in her eyes. "Thanks for showing up to the house early."

We both laughed.

"I get the feeling you figured I might show up early."

"You didn't let me down either, did you?"

"If you get a chance to give me a call, we can talk about what we should do 13 days from now," I said, handing her a business card with my home number and email address written on it, trying to not sound like I was expecting her to call.

"*When* I get a chance to give you a call, that's definitely one of the things we can talk about," she replied, grinning. "I really do appreciate you bringing me to the airport."

With that, she opened the car door and met me at the trunk. A long hug and brief kiss sent her on her way into the terminal. When she had gotten through the automated glass doors, she looked back at me to wave good-bye. I was anticipating that. She didn't let me down either.

I stopped for groceries on the way home and picked out some five-day rentals at Blockbuster, thinking I might want some distractions during the next few evenings. I steered away from the sappy love stories that generally end up in my bag, instead choosing action and comedy: "Gladiator" and "Sister Act II." A simple pasta dish and steamed broccoli preceded my watching a special segment of *20/20* that focused on the rich and famous: "Are They Getting Away with Murder?" Just the sort of story to intrigue an investigative journalist. I'd always been awed by the crimes committed by big business and the hard-to-trace paths companies would take to escape conviction. The pursuit to unearth these wrong-doings and see that slimy chief executives paid for their betrayal of the public became my self-assigned responsibility. When the *20/20* segment ended, my shoulders felt tense, and I decided a 45-minute soak in the jet bath was in order. I poured myself a healthy glass of Merlot, turned off the downstairs lights and ascended for the evening.

The patchouli candle at the edge of the tub subtly lit the bathroom. Only my head lay above water level, the jets making bubbles that occasionally spritzed my face. Periodically, my arm emerged to accommodate a sip of wine. I remained long enough for my fingers to wrinkle like raisins, then it was time for bed. As I walked by the closet, I reached into the laundry basket and pulled out the white T-shirt loaned to me earlier in the day. I slipped between the sheets, holding the shirt against me.

All at once, my heart seemed to skip a beat.

"The card! I forgot to open the card!"

When I was unloading the car, I had dropped the yellow envelope into the bag with the movies and that's where it remained. The bag was now laying next to the VCR in the living room. I was out of bed, downstairs and back in bed within seconds. I leaned back on two pillows against the headboard, redirected my bedside light and caught my breath. Intrigue began eating away at me, and I tore at the yellow paper.

The cover of the card was a full-color photograph of a sunrise lifting over a field of wildflowers. I opened it to see she had filled the blankness inside with very few words.

"Beginnings offer exploration of the unknown."

I laid there reading it several times, imagining her as she sat writing it. With the card and T-shirt next to me, I drifted asleep.

My computer mailbox showed 27 new messages when I arrived at the office Monday morning. I set my coffee on the desk and got to work. It was nearly 11 a.m. when an instant message popped onto my monitor from screen name "Applelady."

"Good morning. Breakfast wasn't the same without you."

Hmmm. I couldn't stop my smile.

"Good morning. How was your flight?"

"Fine. By the time I checked into the hotel, it was late, too late to call, even though I wanted to."

"I like the card. Thank you."

"I was hoping you would. Busy week ahead?"

"Luckily the next two weeks look pretty busy."

"This conference involves dinner meetings every night this week, so I'm not sure when the best time will be for us to catch up."

"It's the unknown."

"Cute. It was ironic you were online right when I added your name to my buddy list. Lucky me."

"Lucky me, too."

"I'd rather stay and chat, trust me, but I need to get to a meeting. I hope you have a fabulous day."

"Thank you. Same to you. Thanks for putting me on your buddy list. Does that mean we're buddies?"

"So funny so early in the day! Yes, we now are buddies. Bye for now from California."

"Good-bye from Chicago."

Work made the day fly by. I was home by 7:00, sitting in front of the living room television with a microwave-cooked dinner in my hands. The well written comedy of "Sister Act II" pulled me into Whoopi's world for a couple of hours. I persuaded myself to push through my 20-minute home workout routine, then showered and made it into bed before 10 o'clock.

Tuesday morning's emails included a brief note from "Applelady," written at 12:20 a.m. Pacific Standard Time.

"Do you camp? If so, what would you think of a three-day camping trip in Colorado? Could your schedule allow you to be in Denver a week from Friday?"

That's odd, I thought. Liza isn't scheduled to get back from Oregon until a week from Saturday. What's she planning?

"Yes, I camp. Love it, actually. With whom would I be camping since you'll still be in Oregon? Yes, I can arrange my schedule so that I'm free that Friday. Signed, Curious."

It was another full day of returning phone calls and preparing for Wednesday's long-awaited meeting. Tomorrow, my four-year courtship with an interested corporate partner would pay off – or not. I'd just turned off my bedside light when the telephone rang. It was 11:10 p.m. and I hoped I knew who was on the other end of the line.

"Is it too late for me to be calling?" Liza's voice asked softly.

"Absolutely not," I replied. "How are you?"

"Great. And you?"

"A little tired. I spent most of the day in the office, then went to dinner with a woman who works part-time at the foundation. We didn't leave the restaurant until 9:30."

"Yeah, we just got back from dinner and I thought I'd take a chance and see if you were still awake. So you love to camp. That's good. Your message was quite funny: 'with whom would I be camping?' "

"Well, you have my curiosity up. Are you cutting your trip short?"

"If you're game, it looks like I can get into Denver around 10:30 that Friday morning, taking a flight right after my breakfast meeting. My friends Sue and Julie live in Boulder and I occasionally borrow their camping gear when I'm passing through on business trips. If you'll come, I'll call them and see if that would work out."

"I already cleared my schedule and tentatively reserved a flight for that morning," I said, proud of having gone ahead and done that. "American has a fare special for $159 round-trip."

"I was going to use some of my United miles for your flight since I'm asking you to meet me there," Liza said. "$159 is unbelievable. Are you sure that's on a real plane?"

"So funny so late at night?" I answered.

"Then let me pay for the ticket," she said.

"No, I don't think so. *I* want to go and *I'm* paying for my ticket. It sounds like an adventure."

For a moment, I thought we'd been disconnected. Liza said nothing.

"Hello?" I queried.

"I'm here," she said.

Then neither of us spoke. Several seconds, maybe a minute, passed. I thought I heard her sigh.

"I'm going to call Julie and Sue tomorrow and get this going, okay?" Her voice sounded excited.

"Okay. What can I do?"

"Just plan on packing clothes and toiletries. They'll loan us everything else."

"Wow, good friends, huh?"

"Great friends. I've known them for about 15 years. I'm anxious for you to meet them."

"I'm looking forward to it myself."

"Should I let you get to sleep?" she asked.

I looked at the clock. It was 11:30. If I didn't have an 8 o'clock meeting in Northbrook, I could sleep in tomorrow.

"I do have an early meeting in the morning in the suburbs," I said. "Otherwise, I might keep you on the phone all night."

"Oh, would you? Then I'll say good night."

"If this time of night works best for you," I said, "it's okay to call."

"Are you sure?"

"Yes, I'm sure."

"I hope your meeting goes well and have a good day tomorrow."

"Thanks. You too."

"Sweet dreams," she whispered.

"Good night."

The conference room at Baxter Pharmaceuticals overlooked a reflection pond and freshly mown grass that seemed to be a strolling park for dozens of Canadian geese. A table in the corner had been set with fresh pastries, sliced fruit, ice water, juice and coffee. I was putting Half & Half in my coffee when a man and woman walked into the room.

"Good morning," the woman said, walking over to me. It was Cynthia Pruitt, Baxter's vice president of marketing.

"Good morning, Cynthia," I responded, shaking hands with her.

"This is Francois Courteau. He's our worldwide director of public relations," Cynthia said, introducing me to her co-worker.

"Bon matin, Francois. It's a pleasure to meet you."

"Et tu, mademoiselle," he replied, seemingly pleased with my gesture of French.

"Our Director of Human Resources will be joining us briefly this morning," Cynthia said, forking slices of honeydew and watermelon onto a plate. "When she comes in we can get started."

Francois took a cup of black coffee and a pastry to the conference table and sat down with his back to the windows. I selected a seat directly across from him and Cynthia soon claimed the end of the table to my left. I had heard of Francois and knew he was the company's public relations guru, but we had never met. Both of them had been with Baxter in their senior positions for more than four years, thus were fully informed on the potential partnership with A Sister's Hope. The company was approaching the sponsorship from a business perspective rather than philanthropic, though both goals could be obtained from the business angle if the correct strategy was laid out. I wondered why the Director of Human Resources had been invited to this morning's meeting.

"How have you been?" Cynthia asked.

She had a knack for keeping conversation going in any room, with any crowd. I liked that about her.

"Fantastic, thank you. Busy. How about you?"

"Well, I was forced to go on a 10-day business trip to Brussels and got to spend a weekend in Paris," she said, laughing at her good fortune. "It was a nice change of scenery. Lately, it had been Houston, Nashville, Philadelphia … And things here are going very well. We're expecting some FDA approvals soon, the market's strong and no one is questioning our accounting practices."

She was alluding, of course, to the unfortunate criminal allegations related to Enron, the Houston-based energy conglomerate that misled investors, employees and the stock market with its fictional financial statements. The three of us laughed at her comment, though none of us found Enron's conduct amusing.

"That's good," I replied. "A Sister's Hope doesn't need anyone like Enron in the family."

The conference room door opened and the woman I assumed to be director of human resources walked in. She wore a dark skirt suit, which hung a bit too much on her thin frame, and a gold-toned silky shirt that added color to her pale skin. A gold and black patterned scarf wrapped around her head.

"Come in, Leslie. Good morning," Cynthia said, getting out of her chair to greet the woman. "Leslie Carvalho, I want you to meet Cate McGuire, the founder of A Sister's Hope. Leslie is Director of Human Resources for Baxter International."

"Hi Leslie, it's nice to meet you," I said, beginning to assume why Leslie was joining us.

"All right then, I guess we can get started," Cynthia said, taking command of the meeting. "Cate, I think what I'd like to do is update you on where Baxter stands with this partnership and then we can start addressing specific steps that need to occur and paperwork that needs to change hands. Okay?"

Cynthia's introduction sounded more promising than any over the past three years. She was a straight-shooter in the business world, direct with her messages and confident in her delivery. She was the one who made initial contact with me regarding a partnership after researching A Sister's Hope. It was her belief that Baxter could greatly benefit from associating itself with a non-profit organization that was addressing a high-profile medical problem – in this case, breast cancer. She believed the company needed to partner with a young organization that did not already have major ties with a large corporation, an organization that Baxter could take pride in helping to build.

"I suppose I first should ask you if the opportunity still exists for Baxter to be your title sponsor," Cynthia said, wanting to avoid being presumptuous. "Has another corporation gotten to the finish line ahead of us?"

"You're still in the race," I replied, staying with her sports analogy. "As you know, I've actively been pursuing substantial partnerships since the foundation's inception. There *is* interest from other companies, but nothing has been contracted."

"Good, I'm glad to hear that," Cynthia said, quickly making eye contact with Francois. "Cate, Baxter senior management is convinced your foundation is a good fit for us and we would like to finalize over the next few weeks a five-year partnership with a right of first refusal on a new contract when those five years have expired."

She looked directly at me for a reaction. Although I was pleased, Cynthia had not yet mentioned a dollar figure.

"What are the numbers, Cynthia?" I asked, stoically.

"Two million dollars in year one, a majority of that earmarked for research, the recipients determined by you and your board of directors. A minimum of one million for each of the following four years with the possibility of an increase if a Baxter review committee determines it appropriate."

She again looked directly at me, waiting for my reply.

"I'm thrilled, absolutely thrilled," I said, trying to maintain my composure.

Cynthia, despite her business approach to this project, was keenly aware of the foundation's importance to me. We had shared long conversations during numerous breakfast meetings over the past three years. She had witnessed my commitment to the foundation. She had seen me cry.

I wouldn't cry now, though releasing tears of joy would have felt wonderful. Instead, I got out of my chair and went to hug Cynthia. She was out of her chair, arms open wide, when I reached her.

"Thank you," I said softly, fearing my voice might crack at that moment.

"Thank you for being so patient with us," she said. "Sometimes I wondered if this day would ever arrive."

When I returned toward my chair, I looked at Leslie Carvalho. She hadn't held back her tears. I walked over and hugged her, too.

"In case you hadn't figured it out, I'm going through chemotherapy treatments," she said. "Stage II, a couple of lymph nodes affected."

"How are you feeling?" I asked.

"Aside from being tired most of the time, I'm doing pretty well," she said, pulling a tissue from the pocket of her jacket.

Francois might have felt a bit alienated, but he arose from his chair and came to hug me, then Leslie.

When we all were again seated, Cynthia continued.

"I see we're all in agreement that this is a good thing," she said, smiling, lifting the heavy emotion in the room. "One of the reasons I asked Leslie to join us this morning was, ironically, to discuss Baxter's decision to support a breast health organization as opposed to one that addresses colon cancer or child leukemia or whatever else might be of concern to our employees worldwide. When the partnership is announced, questions definitely will surface from our employees and we want to be prepared with answers."

"Particularly now that I've gotten my diagnosis, senior management has to be crystal clear on our reasons for choosing A Sister's Hope," Leslie added. "Through Francois's department, we will deliver the information with enough detail so that our 45,000 team members know this has been in development for three years, that I was diagnosed just four months ago and that the leaders making this decision thoroughly reviewed other potential partnerships.

"Because of Baxter's size and worldwide presence, we have numerous employees who have diabetes, multiple sclerosis, other cancers … the list is long. As a company, we want to be diligent in making sure this partnership is accepted and supported by the employees. Realistically, that's nearly impossible, but it's the ideal situation."

"I completely understand," I said. "What can I do to assist in that effort?"

"That's a generous offer," Francois said. "At this point, we're still finalizing our in-house strategy so it would be premature of me to ask for your help. If and when that time comes, however, be sure I'll be calling you."

Initiating an embrace with me and with Leslie, at such a sensitive time, had scored him points in my book. Working with him was going to be enjoyable.

"Then shall we go through the next steps?" Cynthia said, not really asking for or needing an answer. "Cate, you and I will need to schedule several meetings over the next couple of weeks with my marketing staff, Francois and, of course, Baxter's legal department. Once you've met with your board of directors and given them our proposal, our senior team would like to meet with them and start developing a familiarity with one another."

"Cate, after you have met with your board members, could you call me immediately so that my department can get press releases out to the media?" asked Francois, making notes on the pad of paper in front of him. "We plan to move fast on this once everything is in place."

Although it had been three years in the making, this process all of a sudden seemed to be racing. I felt the need to steal a few minutes of privacy.

"I sure will, Francois. Would it be all right if we took a break for a few minutes?"

Cynthia was quick to respond. "Absolutely," she said. "I'm going to run to my office and check on a couple of things. Cate, if you need anything, just ask the receptionist near the elevator. Do you want to convene in 10 minutes?"

"That'd be great. Thank you."

"I'm going to take off then," Leslie said. "It was nice to finally get to meet you. I've heard so much about you from Cynthia."

"Just do me a favor and don't believe *everything* she tells you," I said, drawing a playful glare from Cynthia as she left the room. "I hope we'll be seeing each other again soon. If you don't mind my asking, how many more chemo treatments do you have?"

"I don't mind you asking," she said. "Three more, and, hopefully, that'll be it. As you probably can tell, I'm not fitting into my clothes these days. The anti-nausea drugs haven't been as effective for me as they are for some people. But I'm confident I'll put the weight back on, maybe even grow some hair, when I've finished the treatments."

Her attitude refreshed me and I felt totally comfortable giving her another hug.

"Good luck," I said to her as she headed out the door.

"Thanks," she answered. "Take care."

Francois had excused himself while Leslie and I were talking, so I had the conference room – and view of the strolling geese – all to myself. I wanted to clear my mind, then evaluate the morning's discussion.

Cynthia startled me when she re-entered the room about 15 minutes later. I was reliving the moments when my sister reluctantly pulled the baseball cap from her head so I could see her baldness. The thought of losing her hair during chemotherapy had scared her, maybe more so than the chemicals roiling through her body. When the cap was completely off, I had laughed, causing her to begin laughing, and my nephew and I stood in agreement telling her she looked just like Dad.

That image in my mind, Cynthia's voice broke in.

"Sorry I'm a little late getting back," she said.

She must have noticed the slight jump in my stance as she spoke.

"Where were you just then?" she asked, giggling.

I laughed.

"Missouri," I said, "the Show-Me State."

"Francois asked me to tell you that he'd be in touch," Cynthia said. "He thought you and I should get our schedules aligned and items finalized before we involved him any further. I think he's right."

"Yes, that's fine."

Comparing calendars, the two of us found common openings over the next several days and took turns choosing a rendezvous that would be convenient. When just she and I would be meeting, she picked a place in Old Town near where she lived. We'd also meet in my office at Dearborn and Polk. I now would be making more trips to Northbrook.

On the drive back into the city, the sun's heat coming through the window soothed me. It was such a gorgeous day, I decided to head east and hit Lake Shore Drive so I could stop in Lincoln Park. A corn dog tasted best in one of two places: the Southeast Missouri District Fair and the Lincoln Park Zoo. Lunch that day would be spent sitting across from the seals, watching them swim while they watched me roll my dog in a pool of mustard.

I'd just taken my last bite when my cell phone rang.

"Hi Michelle," I said, seeing the name appear on my phone. "What's going on at the office?"

Michelle Cianfrini, with whom I had eaten lunch on Monday, works at A Sister's Hope three days a week. She's the second youngest of four girls in her family. Her mother and three sisters all are breast cancer survivors.

"Hi Cate," she said. "I couldn't wait any longer to find out how the meeting went with Baxter. So how did it go?"

"Incredibly well," I answered.

"Really?!"

"Really. I'll be into the office within a half-hour. Do you think you can wait that long for details?"

"It'll be hard. Hurry and get in here."

"Okay. I'm at the zoo, so it won't take me long,"

"You have incredible news and you went to the zoo before coming here?" Michelle said, being humorous with her impatience.

I was going to respond with "I came to get a *seal* of approval," but it even sounded corny in my mind, so I didn't bother.

"I'll see you soon, okay? Good-bye."

Passing by the Starbucks in the lobby of the Dearborn Station building, I got the urge for a mocha Frappucino. I walked into the office to find Michelle standing there with one in each hand.

"Ahhh, I was going to surprise you," she said. "If the news is that good, we needed drinks for celebrating."

"I'm sorry, Michelle." I had to laugh. "I'll bet between the two of us we can easily drink all three of them. What do you think?"

"No doubt. So fill me in."

When I gave her the outline of Baxter's proposal, she was ecstatic. I could envision her wanting to tell the world, or at the very least, her family. I made it painstakingly clear to Michelle that none of the partnership – not even the company's name – could be discussed with anyone until all the paperwork and Baxter's marketing plans were complete. She could be trusted. And she, by no means, would do anything that might jeopardize the deal.

"Meanwhile, we have other issues needing our attention," I said, moving toward my office. "Is there anything you needed to discuss with me before I check my messages?"

"No, we're all set."

"Thanks for the Frappucino," I said, taking my half of the third beverage and setting it on my desk.

Despite wanting to check my personal email, I opened the foundation's general mailbox and started chipping away at responding to those messages. Sometimes I'd ask Michelle to handle this, but often the questions required my attention and I'd found it more efficient to look at them first. Formal thank-you notes from Cynthia, Francois and Leslie, saying how much they appreciated my driving to Northbrook to meet with them, already had arrived. Leslie's included a "P.S."

"Cate, after meeting you this morning, I feel much more at ease asking this. I think I'd like to become part of a support group – to receive support right now, and hopefully be supportive to others in the future. Could you recommend someone to contact in the northern suburbs? I would truly appreciate it. Thanks again."

She had listed her home contact information at the bottom of the message and I transposed it into my address book and Rolodex, then searched for the number of a wonderful woman in Deerfield whom Leslie could call. The fact that Leslie had reached the point where she wanted to talk with other breast cancer survivors was a healthy sign.

Once the foundation emails had been pared to the few Michelle could answer, I pulled the folder from my briefcase containing information Cynthia had compiled for my perusal. It was no wonder Cynthia had earned a post as vice president at well-respected Baxter. My observations were that she had an uncanny ability to motivate and manage people. She had common sense, could articulate whatever was brewing in her head and loved things to be organized.

The folder lying before me had colored tabs stuck to the edge of some pages. A makeshift legend of the color-coding was drawn on a post-it note on the cover. Red tabs meant Cynthia believed I'd want to look at those more closely than others. Yellow tabs were areas of the partnership agreement that were unresolved and needed the board's and my input. Green tabs designated pages containing financial arrangements, including dollar amounts and timeframes. Was she like this in her personal life? Probably. I began to read.

"Cate?"

I looked up and found Michelle standing in the doorway.

"You have a call. Would you like to take it or do you want me to take a message?"

My heart rate rose as I anticipated Liza's call on hold.

"Yeah, I'll take it. Thank you."

Then it dawned on me. Why did I immediately think the call was from Liza? I guess I was anxious to hear from her.

"Hello, this is Cate."

"Hi Sis. Are you busy?"

It was Casey, my little sister, catching me completely by surprise. Calls from family members were irregular, at best. We talked often, but I usually initiated the contact.

"Hey Casey! How are you? What are you doing?"

"I'm off today and am trying to stay outside to enjoy the beautiful weather. I went for a run this morning and I've been working in the yard since lunch. I was getting kind of hot, so thought I'd take a break and see if I could reach you."

"I'm glad you did. Good timing. I was at a meeting all morning. So how are you?"

It had been five months since we'd seen each other. I try to make it back to southeast Missouri three or four times a year. Ruth, our older sister, lives a few miles from our parents. Casey's a firefighter in St. Louis, two hours north of our hometown. Anytime I'm back there, we all get together. Usually the most light-hearted of the three of us, Casey had been going through some challenging times lately.

"A run always helps," Casey said, her voice remaining cheerful. "I've decided it's time to train for a marathon. I didn't know if I'd ever feel like doing one, but I think I'm ready. Want to run one with me?"

Casey knew I loved to run. What she didn't know is how out of shape – for a runner, anyway - I had gotten over the past year. I was still working out, but not running.

"Oh, I don't know. It would be fun to run one with you. How long would I have to prepare?"

"Some friends told me about the Cowtown Marathon in Fort Worth, Texas. They said it's a lot of fun and ends at an area called The Stockyards where they serve you beer and barbecue."

That seemed to be a smart move on the part of organizers. How much barbecue can a person actually eat so soon after running 26.2 miles?

"I also should tell you," Casey said, "that most of the last mile of the run is an incline."

Challenge. Casey always loved a good challenge. This marathon sounded perfect for her.

"I'll seriously consider it," I told her. "So you didn't tell me when it is."

"February 22. That gives us plenty of time to train. Come on. Do it with me."

"Can I think about it for a few days?" I asked.

"Sure. In the meantime, I'm going to print entry forms off the web and mail one to you."

Casey could be persistent. It is one of her best qualities and probably was a great asset when training for the firefighter's exam. Whether dealing with professional or personal conflicts, it was her persistence to overcome that always kept Casey going.

"How long before you go back to work?" I asked.

"Two days. I originally was off until Saturday morning, but one of my buddies needed someone to pick up his Friday shift."

"Let me know when you have a full weekend off again and I'll try to schedule a trip to Mom and Dad's," I said. "Would you drive down?"

"Sure. Bring your running shoes when you come!" Casey said, further pressing me to commit to the marathon. "I probably should let you get back to work, huh?"

"Yeah, maybe," I answered. "I'm glad you called. It was a really nice surprise."

"I'm glad I caught you. Think about the Cowtown Marathon and let me know, okay?"

"I will. Hey, how's everything else going?"

The last time we'd seen each other, Casey confided in me about problems she was having with her husband, Tom. Married nine years, they had struggled for the past five to overcome Tom's fits of jealousy. Lean and muscular at 5-foot-9, Casey was an attractive and confident woman working in a male-dominated profession. In the early years of their marriage, Tom would say how proud he was of Casey's job. Then somewhere along the line, he decided he would prefer she change careers – a request not well received by Casey.

"If you need to get back to work, we could talk later," Casey said.

"No, I have time to talk to you. What's going on?"

"Tom moved out in April and it seems he has moved on."

I was expecting more of an explanation, but Casey said nothing more.

"What do you mean 'moved on?' Is he seeing someone else?"

"Yeah," she answered, her voice sounding strained. "I don't know how long it's been going on, but a divorce is already in the works and should be finalized in a few months."

"Casey, I'm sorry. How are you feeling about all of this?"

"Actually," she said, "I'm relieved. I'm sad, but relieved. I did not want our life to continue the way it was. We would argue the days we both were off work. We'd argue when I'd get home from a shift because he'd wonder which one of my station brothers was putting the moves on me. Isn't that a trip? And he was the one out there putting moves on someone!"

"So you're going to be okay with this? Is there anything I can do?"

"For starters, you can fill out that entry form for the Marathon."

I should've seen that coming.

"You're relentless," I said.

Casey laughed and I felt reassured she *would* be all right.

"I haven't told Mom and Dad yet, but thought I'd tell them in person next week. I'm going to drive down on Tuesday and spend the night, see Ruth and the kids."

"Promise me you'll call me if you need anything," I said, a big sister firmness in my voice.

"I promise. Listen, I'm going to let you get back to work. We'll talk in the next few days, okay?"

"Okay," I said. "I love you."

"I love you, too. Good-bye."

Once she'd hung up, I sat at my desk staring at the screen of my computer monitor. The million thoughts racing through my mind were interrupted by Michelle walking in with a Federal Express box.

"This just came for you," she said, handing me a next-day delivery package.

"Thank you, Michelle."

As she left my office, I checked the sender's name. My thoughts returned to the past weekend. Liza had mailed the package from the West Coast last night. Curiosity overwhelming me. I pulled the tab and reached inside, retrieving a gift-wrapped box the size of a deck of playing cards.

Interesting, I thought to myself, trying to imagine why I now was holding a thin, stainless steel-plated travel alarm clock. Why did it need to arrive today? I wondered if she had sent an email that might explain, so logged into my personal mailbox to see. Several new messages had arrived, but none from Applelady. My new clock read 3:30 p.m., which meant I needed to return to my review of the Baxter materials and begin getting in touch with board members.

Hard as it was, I soon redirected my thoughts to the Baxter proposal and Cynthia's color-coded tabs. It was nearly 5 o'clock when Michelle once again knocked on the frame of my office door.

"Did you have anything else you'd like for me to do before I take off?" she asked.

"No, I don't think so. Are you coming in tomorrow?"

"Yep," she said. "I think the family's going to Michigan for the weekend, so I'll be heading up there Friday morning."

"Remember, not a word about the Baxter deal until it's signed," I reminded her.

"Don't worry. I won't say anything to anyone until you tell me it's okay. Okay?"

"Thanks, Michelle. I'll see you in the morning then."

"Good night, Cate."

Over the next hour, I succeeded in reaching each board member and we were able to nail down a time everyone could come to the office to discuss the proposal. Lindsay, an energetic bank vice president who joined the board last summer, had asked if I had dinner plans. She suggested we meet at Dearborn Street Oyster Bar, a short walk for both of us from our respective offices, around 6:45. I checked my personal email once more before leaving the office: nothing from Applelady.

I could see from the sidewalk through the restaurant windows that Lindsay already was seated in a booth. As the hostess approached me, I pointed to the table where I would be joining my friend.

"Thanks for the dinner invitation," I said, sliding into my side of the booth. "You saved me from a microwave frozen entrée."

Lindsay laughed.

"Good," she said. "I've been wanting to do this for a long time. I'm glad you were free tonight."

Since the two of us had never spent time together without other board members around, Lindsay and I found much to talk about, steering clear of board of directors "stuff." She had grown up in Knoxville, Tennessee, the U.S. city where most athletic little girls dream of playing basketball for the legendary Coach Pat Summit. Her father was a biology teacher at the high school she attended; her mother, a Certified Public Accountant, had built a successful accounting business. All I truly knew about her before that night was her professional background and how appropriately she fit with the board of directors. I'd always thought her southern accent was cute.

As we unveiled our family histories, I was surprised to discover she had no siblings. She seemed the caretaker sort, mindful of others' needs before hers.

"Did you develop the stereotypical traits of an only child?" I asked. I was half-kidding.

"One of the most valuable skills I learned as an only child," she said, "was how to handle being alone."

I wasn't expecting a statement so profound and, witnessing her complete honesty, it nearly brought tears to my eyes. Lindsay seemed to notice I was struggling to produce my next comment.

"I didn't mean for that to come out so heavy," she said, starting to laugh. "It's a *good* thing. I know so many people who feel they have to be with someone, even if that someone is not the right person for them. At least they're not alone, right? I always believed if you are going to share time with another person, it should be someone you choose, not simply accept."

"I can see I've been missing out on good conversation the past year," I said, smiling. "Why didn't you suggest having dinner last fall?"

My question was meant to be playful, but it gave Lindsay an opportunity to share more personal information.

"I was dating a woman who has a nine-year-old daughter, so my schedule was pretty full," she said, watching me as she spoke, waiting for a reaction.

Instead of responding, I stared back at her until she began to provide more detailed information.

"The short story is that she and I realized we were not a viable combination. We stopped seeing each other romantically in January. I still spend time with them occasionally, but she's met someone else and I think they might be a good match. I hope so, anyway. Would you like to get out of here and take a walk?"

Enjoying the evening, I was game for it to continue. We turned east on Congress Parkway and found ourselves leaning against the copper railing that surrounds Buckingham Fountain. Lindsay's story-telling entertained me and she didn't seem to mind carrying the conversation. As the wind changed course, we stood there, the fountain mist pluming us.

"I hope you don't mind that nice outfit getting wet!" Lindsay said, her eyes scanning the suit and blouse I'd worn to the Baxter meeting.

Kids standing around the fountain were screaming and running as the water fell upon them. Couples, young and old, were safely seated on the dry park benches 50 feet away. Lindsay stepped forward and, for a moment, I thought she was going to kiss me. Her movement was more like holding a hand out to a cat, allowing it to evaluate the imposition, then decide if it would run or invite further attention. I stood completely still, looking at her.

"You know, until you told me tonight about the woman you were dating in the fall, I wasn't sure if you were straight or gay," I said, fighting a nervous grin. "My gaydar isn't what it used to be, I guess."

"You have to remember, the banking world is still very white male," she said. "Some of the guys are perfectly fine with my being a lesbian, but some are not, and some of our clients are blatantly homophobic. As much as I might want to make a political statement to those clients, I choose to focus on the business relationship and keep personal matters, shall we say, in the closet. They don't need to know who I'm sleeping with, anyway."

I stared at the underlit fountain water, spewing from the brass dragon's mouth turned green with age.

"My situation is quite similar," I finally said in response. "Companies like Baxter that have been around since the early 1900s still look at some things the old-fashioned way. Unfortunately, I believe there are still a lot of corporations who would reject partnering with A Sister's Hope solely because they did not want to associate with a foundation created by a lesbian."

"We find a way to work around it," she said. "We always have. We always will."

After a minute or so of being mesmerized by the running water, Lindsay looked back toward me.

"I need to think about heading home," she said. "Are you parked at your office?"

"Yes, I am," I answered. "Where are you parked?"

"I take the 'el' unless I have meetings that require me to drive," she said. "I'll walk back that way with you, though."

"Can I give you a ride somewhere? Where do you live?"

"On the southern edge of Andersonville, on Winona, just east of Clark," she said.

"No kidding? You live just a few blocks from me. I'm giving you a ride home."

"I should've paid for dinner then," Lindsay said. "I'm picking up the check next time."

Dinner and the walk had consumed the entire evening, though I wasn't unhappy about that. It was 10:15 when Lindsay directed me to pull over in front of her building.

"I didn't know a Wednesday night could be so fun," she said, turning her shoulders to face me. "I've been wanting to do this for a long time."

I thought she still was referring to getting together for dinner because she had made the same comment when I first arrived to the restaurant, but Lindsay's lips were against mine before I could react. Although I did not push her away, neither did I encourage a longer kiss. When she retreated, we remained silent. She dropped her chin just a little, then slightly cocked her head to the side.

"Being shy is not one of my personality traits," she said, grinning and raising her left eyebrow.

"That's okay," I replied.

The kiss was sensitive, non-threatening, but inquiring. I surely would have kissed her back had this night occurred a week ago.

"I just started seeing someone," I said, intensely looking at Lindsay.

"I should have asked," she said, acting a little embarrassed. "Since you didn't have to call anyone to check in or anything, I was banking on you being single."

"Well, I *am* single, but the woman I'm seeing is out of town and, even if she were in town, we're not at a point where I'd be *checking in* with her before having dinner with someone."

"Good," she said. "Then dinner again sometime is not out of the question?"

"Dinner again sometime sounds great. Besides, you already said you're buying."

Realizing how late it was, she reached for the door handle.

"Lindsay," I said, touching her arm, "this was a very fun, unexpected evening. Thank you."

My instincts guiding me, I leaned forward and lightly kissed her cheek. She appeared pleasantly surprised.

"Good night, Cate."

Once she had closed the security gate behind her, I drove away. Thoughts of Liza emerged from where I'd been holding them down. I don't remember driving from Lindsay's to my place, parking or walking up the back stairs. It had been years since this much emotion consumed me. Keeping feelings like these locked away made life easier.

Too late to soak in the tub, I quickly shuffled through the mail, then climbed the stairs to get ready for bed. I hadn't heard from Liza today, except for the package. I set the new alarm clock on my nightstand and got undressed, followed by a 10-minute shower to cleanse my mind and body. Lying down, the softball T-shirt still nestled on the other pillow, I closed my eyes and began imagining what surprises the morning might bring.

Chapter Four

Folger's instant coffee somehow tastes amazingly flavorful when you're camped out on the skirt of a mountain range. While Liza and I sat quietly, admiring nature's majestic high-rises around us, my thoughts drifted back to eight days earlier, the Thursday I learned why she'd sent me the clock.

When the coffee grinder had finished reducing hazelnut-flavored beans to a fine ground, I heard Claire and Amy clacking down the back steps as if they were wearing tap dancing shoes. I unlocked and opened the kitchen door to catch them before they left, noticing immediately their cycling clothes and clip-in shoes.

"Going for a ride this morning?" I asked.

"Yeah. We're riding over to Caldwell Woods and are going to take the trail up to the Botanic Garden," Amy answered. "You're welcome to come along."

I stood there in a T-shirt and underwear, dumping coffee grounds into the filter, anxiously awaiting a fresh-brewed cup to start my day. Morning exercise is fine, as long as I plan for it the night before.

"I'm going to pass," I said, stepping inside to flip on the coffee pot. I looked at the oven clock and saw it was 6:25. "Is this early enough that you'll beat morning rush hour?"

"Yeah, that's why we're leaving so early. Some people have a real hard time waking up in the mornings and some of them drive like they're still asleep," Claire said, her voice straining with frustration toward the end of her sentence.

"Well, don't let me slow you down," I said. "Be careful and have fun."

With no scheduled meetings, I decided I'd work from home all morning. Michelle could handle things at the office, then she and I could have a lengthy conversation in the afternoon outlining priorities for the Baxter deal. There were specifics I needed her to take care of before next Wednesday's board meeting, but I wasn't fully prepared to assign them to her.

I carried my coffee, a black pen and pad of yellow paper upstairs. I pulled on a pair of roomy camping shorts, opened the deck door and transported coffee, pen and paper to the glass-topped patio table. Clear on the sequence of events needing to take place, I began to make notes for Michelle.

This partnership with Baxter – or another large corporation – was vital to A Sister's Hope. In four years, the foundation had grown as much as it could without budgeting for additional full-time staff. For six months out of the year, Michelle and I comprised the entire foundation directory, assisted by the highest caliber of volunteers. When we were in production for our special events, two temporary event managers joined the team and day laborers were hired as needed. Michelle worked for a pittance, a fraction of what she could make working elsewhere, but the money held little importance for her. Breast cancer had clouded her family's future and, in doing so, had enlightened them on the things in life they feel truly matter. She chose to work only three days a week so she'd have more time to spend with her family.

When I started the foundation, a salary was non-existent. Seed money from wealthy acquaintances, small companies and the minimal grants I could scrape together covered basic expenses of a phone, stationery and postage. I had convinced a printer to produce – pro bono – our first marketing piece for getting word out about the organization and the first benefit cross-country run. Michelle contacted me almost at the beginning, begging to be involved and help however she could. A board of directors was intact four months into the project and within the next five months, my salary and a staff pay scale were established. Michelle and I officially were on the payroll.

Springtime, as unreliable as the Chicago weather might be, was the season we had chosen for the annual cross-country run. Other breast cancer organizations hold popular fundraising walks/runs on Mother's Day weekend in May and during Breast Cancer Awareness Month in October. We did not want our event to conflict with those, and June through September is packed with Chicago summer festivals, so a late March/early April weekend made the most sense. Temporary event managers worked mid-October through the end of April, taking off a week at Thanksgiving and a week for Christmas or Hannukah. The race was slated for the

Sunday before Easter and, in four years, we'd experienced a wide range of weather conditions. Growing from 1,200 participants in the first year to more than 5,000 this past April, I was encouraged by the public's participation and the support we received from the running community.

I laid the pen on top of the notepad, having comprised a detailed guideline for Michelle and myself, accomplishing my morning objective. Four hours had passed and the sun was almost directly overhead now. A steady northwestern wind neutralized the high-80s searing temperature and, for some unknown reason, I decided to go for a run. Maybe Casey was sending vibes from St. Louis or subconsciously I had committed to registering for the Cowtown Marathon. Whatever the impetus, I soon found myself in turquoise runner's shorts and a white tanktop, jogging toward Lake Michigan.

Traffic on the bike path was mild compared to evenings when I'd run after work. You might as well forget using the path on weekends, trying to share the popular trail with cyclists, rollerbladers, baby carriages and walkers. A runner friend of mine sustained serious facial fractures when she and a cyclist collided a couple of summers ago. I preferred today's sparse crowd.

As I weaved south past Lawrence, Wilson and Montrose Avenues, downtown high-rises cut into a faint blue sky. Winds rolled the lake westward, splashing against the rocks. My turn-around point would be the totem pole at Addison. I hadn't run five miles in over a year, having switched to Spin classes and Stairmaster as aerobic alternatives. Nonetheless, I was feeling good on this run, mindful to keep a steady, comfortable pace. Running had always been an outlet for me, a way to release excess energy while my brain paddled down an endless river of thoughts. On this particular run, I attempted to tone down my feelings for Liza and considered being receptive to Lindsay's interest in me. Yes, Saturday night and Sunday revived parts of me I thought had died with Sarah, but I told myself that intensity couldn't be sustained. "Don't put all your eggs in one basket" – the old saying rang clearly in my self-protecting state of mind.

When I turned west on Farragut, sweat trickled outside my eyebrows and along my cheeks. Claire and Amy were walking their bikes toward me and waited in front of the building until I reached them.

"Did you ride your bikes or push them to the Botanic Garden?" I asked, stepping onto the porch to stretch my calves.

"That's why we love you, Cate. You're always the comic," Amy replied. "Starting to run again, eh?"

"We'll see," I said. "Casey has asked me to run a marathon with her in February and that could be fun, running one together."

"We were talking about going to Ann Sather for lunch as soon as we're showered," Claire said, referring to the Swedish diner around the corner. "Why don't you come with us?"

"I can't, but thanks anyway. I need to get into the office. Are you around this weekend?"

"Some gals are going rock climbing at Devil's Lake and invited us," Amy said, "but we haven't decided if we're going or not."

"You should go," I said definitively. "Are they experienced climbers?"

"A couple of them have been climbing for years," Amy said. "They've climbed all over the country. If we do go, do you want to come with us? We'd leave really early Saturday morning and drive back Sunday night."

"That might be an invitation I can't turn down," I replied. "Let's talk tonight. I need to get upstairs and shower. Stop by this evening, okay?"

"Okay," they said, almost in unison, "see you later."

As I walked into the bedroom, my eyes fell upon the clock on the nightstand. Liza. What is it about this woman that summons me? Although I actively try to clear her from my mind so she's not showing up somewhere in the middle of the Baxter proposal or standing next to me at Buckingham Fountain while I'm with Lindsay, she persists.

Serving its mechanical purpose, the clock told me it was time to shower and go meet with Michelle. When I arrived at the office just before 2 p.m., three pink "While You Were Away" telephone notes in the center of my desk snagged my attention. That generally means whoever was trying to reach me wanted to be certain I got the message since I might not check voicemail as soon as they would hope.

"Lindsay. 10:30 a.m. Weekend plans? Please call," read the first one I picked up.

"Liza. 11:45 a.m. On break. Will try you later."

"Applelady. 1:50 p.m. Are you in today?" Her cell number was precisely printed across the bottom.

I stood at my desk, holding the third pink slip of paper, an excited tension filling my chest.

"Cate?" Michelle said, taking a step into my office. "What time do you want to meet to go over the things you need me to do for the board meeting?"

"Does 2:30 work for you?" I asked.

"Sure does. By the way, I think the woman who called herself Applelady is anxious to get hold of you," Michelle said, pointing toward the note I held in my hand. "At least, she sounded like she was."

"Okay. I'll give her a call. Thanks, Michelle."

When she left the room, I had to laugh. Could Applelady possibly be more anxious to reach me than I was to reach her? I sat down and picked up my phone.

"Is this Chicago calling?" Liza asked as she answered her cell phone.

"Yes, I'm trying to reach Applelady. She apparently was trying to get in touch with me this morning."

"Yes she was," Liza said, keeping the third-person reference going. "And the more times she tried, the more frustrated she became."

"Well, we can't have her getting frustrated, now can we?"

"I'm so glad you called back," she said. "Not talking to you yesterday was tougher than I expected it to be."

"Yeah, I kept checking my email for some clues as to why I have a new travel alarm clock. Then I thought, well, maybe you were going to call before you went to bed. It's sitting on my nightstand. You might be happy to know it was the last thing I looked at before going to sleep and it was the first thing I looked at this morning when I woke up."

"I *am* happy to hear that," she said. "That's a special clock, you know. That little jewel woke me up in Barcelona, Honolulu, Baltimore … everywhere I've traveled over the past four years."

"So did you oversleep the past couple of mornings?"

"Remember that triathlon watch that startled us at 4:30 p.m. Sunday? It now has a new purpose in life."

I sat at the desk, grinning like a 16-year-old girl who was taking Mom's car out for a drive on her own for the first time. I felt pure, simple pleasure bantering like this with Liza.

"I hope you're not thinking I'm crazy. I wanted to send you something that would make you think of me while I'm out here, but I couldn't figure out what to send," Liza explained. "Then I went up to my hotel room after lunch and, for whatever reason, the first thing I looked at when I walked into the room was my travel alarm clock. I knew right away that's what I wanted you to have. It and I have spent many nights together. I imagined the clock being on your nightstand, there to wake you up since I can't be."

"You wouldn't believe the possible reasons I came up with for your sending me a clock, but that was not one of them. I like your reason much better. That's a very clever way to ensure I'm thinking of you, but I have news for you: it's been hard trying to get you out of my mind."

Liza was completely silent again. I could have counted to seven before she said another word.

"I'm glad," she finally said. "So now you have no excuse for oversleeping and missing your flight next Friday."

"You must have talked to Julie and Sue, then."

"I spoke with Julie and she's very excited about facilitating our trip," Liza said. "She'll drive to the airport Friday morning to pick us up and we'll go back to their place to hook up with Sue. They'd like us to have lunch with them, if that's okay with you, then they want to send us off in their SUV."

"Where did you find friends like that?" I asked, amazed by their generosity.

"There aren't too many around like those two," she said. "So did you have a good day yesterday?"

This was an opportunity to discuss my evening with Lindsay, but I chose to leave that conversation for another time.

"Yes, and today is even better. I worked at home this morning, which is why you didn't reach me here, and I went for a run before I came into the office."

"You're a runner. I should have guessed. I've been using the fitness room at the hotel instead of battling the San Francisco hills. Do you want to run together sometime when I get back into town?"

"We'll have to see," I said. "I haven't been running this past year and it might take a while to whip myself back into running condition. Dare I ask about your pace?"

"We can go at whatever pace you want," she said. "Mine varies between 7½- and 9-minute miles, depending on how I'm feeling that day. I really just like to get out and run. It's good for clearing my head."

"Me too. We'll talk about it when you get back. How's the conference going?"

"Fine. The best part of it is getting to see some folks I rarely see throughout the year. Speaking of which, I'm supposed to meet a friend in the lobby in a couple of minutes."

"I guess I'll let you go then. I was happy to see that you called."

"I wanted to hear your voice and make sure you got the package," she said.

"Well, have a great afternoon. And thanks for the clock."

"Thanks for putting it on your nightstand. I'll talk to you later."

Our call ended just as Michelle walked into my office and took a seat across from me, eager to start our meeting. I had to shove thoughts of Liza into a corner brain closet so I could concentrate on the business at hand. We spent the next two hours mulling through the notes I'd made, double-checking ourselves to make sure we weren't missing any "bridges" – our term for vitally important issues that needed to be addressed to bring the Baxter deal to fruition. If a bridge was missing, A Sister's Hope and Baxter could not come together.

Michelle's detail-oriented personality made her the perfect office manager. When she reached a point in our discussion where she felt comfortable with the volume of work, she suggested we end the meeting so she could get started on key tasks that would require more time.

"I'll come in Monday, Tuesday and Wednesday next week to finish everything else for the board meeting," she said. "What time will they start showing up Wednesday night?"

"As early as 6:15, but the meeting is scheduled for 7," I answered. "We'll set up beverages and snacks to keep them occupied in case you and I need that last 45 minutes to finish up."

"I'd like to have everything pulled together by Wednesday lunch," she said.

"That would be ideal, Michelle. That would give me plenty of time to look through the board member packet before we make copies. How long are you staying today?"

"Until traffic clears, maybe around 6:30."

"Well, I'll be here if any questions come up," I said, knowing that Michelle would try to save all of her questions until she hit a true roadblock. She excelled at time management and had taught me numerous valuable tips during the past four years.

That first pink "While You Were Away" slip I had picked up when I got to the office was laying at the top of my desk. It was nearing 5 p.m., so I reached for the telephone.

"Lindsay Cuvier speaking."

"Lindsay, it's Cate. I'm sorry it took me so long to get back to you."

"Hi there. Could you hold on just one moment?"

"Sure."

She would be presenting the question that was written on the note: weekend plans? My indecisiveness about joining Claire and Amy at Devil's Lake began to clear.

"Cate, thanks for calling me back. I figured you were caught up with the Baxter project, so I wasn't holding my breath," Lindsay jested. "Sorry I had to put you on hold. The new vice president of the trust department invited himself into my office about 10 minutes ago. He finally got around to asking me out for a drink right before you called."

"Do you need to go?" I asked, unsure of her response to him.

"Not hardly," she said, laughing. "Your timing was perfect. He apparently asked around the bank to find out if I'm married. He certainly didn't waste any time. I think his first day at the bank was last Monday."

"Popular among male bankers, huh?" I asked.

"A couple of women have been in my office with the same mission, but I don't mind *that*."

I was laughing hard enough to cause Michelle to look toward my office.

"So what did you tell the V.P. of the trust department?" I asked.

"Thanks, but no thanks. I'm sure he'll eventually hear from a co-worker that I'm gay. Then I'll discover whether he's homophobic or not based on how he treats me once he knows why I won't go out with him. If he ends up being a good guy, *then* we can go out for a drink."

It wasn't surprising that Lindsay dealt with dating propositions on a fairly regular basis. Shoulder-length blonde hair topped her 5-foot-6 frame, a thin physique you might find on the point-guard of the Tennessee Lady Vols basketball team. She probably weighed around 125 pounds, though I'm really bad at guessing people's weight. Square shoulders, lean arms and muscular calves had caught my attention earlier in the summer when she showed up to a board meeting in a sleeveless dress. Her fun and aggressive personality accented her physical attractiveness. She had learned how to effectively use those nickel-sized, chocolate brown eyes and southern accent to her advantage.

"How was the rest of your day?" I asked.

"Typical; nothing special," she said, offering no details. "I love my job, but other people don't find it nearly as exciting. I always said the only exciting thing that happens at a bank is a robbery."

She had me laughing again. I'm sure Michelle wondered who had me so entertained.

"The reason I had called was to see if I could get on your weekend schedule for brunch or dinner or something," Lindsay said. "Is the person you're seeing still out of town?"

"Yeah, she is. I was considering leaving Saturday morning, though, to go rock climbing at Devil's Lake, Wisconsin, so I don't think I'm going to be around."

"Any time Friday for a quick dinner or drink?" Lindsay persisted.

I stopped to think for a moment and didn't answer right away.

"Hmmm," I said in a low tone. "I think you're used to getting what you want."

"No, but I always try," she said.

As she had told me the night before, shyness was not among her characteristics. Her confidence amused me.

"How about this: let's meet at the Hopleaf around 7:30 for a beer. I won't want to stay out late because I'm leaving really early Saturday."

"You can leave when you need to," she said. "I'll be there at 7:30, then."

"All right. Well, have a good day tomorrow."

"Thanks. You too," Lindsay said. "I'll see you tomorrow night."

As I hung up the receiver, I realized I was shaking my head. Why had I come up with the Hopleaf suggestion? I have plenty of things to do before leaving Saturday morning without socializing on Friday evening with a woman who wants to date me when I've just met an amazing woman who happens to be out of town. I suppose I know why. Those self-preservation driving forces are pretty strong. Mine grew much stronger when Sarah died and I knew that my feelings for Liza put me in a terribly vulnerable position. My self-defense mechanisms were saying, "What's the harm in getting to know Lindsay? She's gorgeous, smart and generous with her time to A Sister's Hope. You like her. Roll with it."

There was nothing wrong with my spending time with Lindsay. I knew I shouldn't feel guilty. I'd been out with Liza once; one date certainly did not qualify as a relationship.

I stopped worrying about the Hopleaf and redirected my energy toward loose ends at work. Cynthia Pruitt had emailed to check in with me, so I composed a response and hit "send." I also had received a thank-you note from Leslie Carvalho for the contact information I'd sent her about a suburban support group. My pal in the Mayor's Office of Special Events mailed an envelope full of permit applications to me a couple of weeks ago and I pulled it from my "To Do" stack to get started.

In the special events sector, obtaining all the proper permits can be a harrowing experience in some cities, but Chicago has Matthew O'Reilly. Matt and I were introduced to each other by the city beat reporter while I was still working for the newspaper. I ran into him on numerous occasions after that and we developed a great rapport. His patience and high energy are a flattering combination

60

for the post he holds under Mayor Daley. The only drawback to the permit process for me is the time it takes to fill out the dozens of pages of questions. I was not even halfway through the permit packet when Michelle stuck her head into the office to say good-night.

"I'm taking off, Cate," she said. "Any special weekend plans?"

"I think I'm going climbing with Claire and Amy," I said. "Have a great time with your family in Michigan."

"You know I will," she said. "Be careful climbing. We have a big week next week, you know."

"Did any questions come up while you were working on Baxter this afternoon?" I asked.

"Nothing that can't wait until Monday," she said. "Maybe we can go over stuff during lunch. We'll have Potbelly sandwiches delivered. How's that sound?"

"Delicious. I just realized how hungry I am. I think I'm going to get out of here, too."

"Do you want me to wait and walk out with you?" Michelle asked.

"No, that's okay. I'll see you Monday morning."

Speeding north in the far left lane of Lake Shore Drive, I sensed that Sarah was waiting at home for me. The sun's scorching heat had been reduced to a mere simmer now and the lake shore bike path looked like an army of ants streaming north and south. Although the air conditioner might have been cooler, I had retracted the convertible top and allowed the summer wind to tango with my hair.

"Welcome home," Sarah's voice greeted me as I walked in the kitchen door.

"I'm glad you're here," I responded. "I thought I'd be talking to you earlier in the week, but … "

"But you've been a busy woman," she said, interrupting me and giggling. "How did I ever keep up with you?"

While Sarah and I were together, my journalism career demanded much time outside of the normal workload. There were social engagements to attend in order to develop relationships with sources. There were seemingly endless meetings and spur-of-the-moment deadlines on breaking stories that took precedence over our personal social life. One evening's events that still knotted my stomach was the night I'd taken Sarah out to dinner for her birthday – her last birthday. We had just finished a Caprese salad appetizer at Trattoria No. 10 when the news editor paged me. Rumors were flying that the Republican state senator had scheduled a press conference for the next morning during which he promised to reveal shocking background information on his Democratic challenger for the upcoming election.

"Couldn't the political beat reporter cover this?" I pleaded with the editor. No. He insisted I research the rumors and determine – rather quickly – whether there was a real story or not.

There wasn't. But I didn't know that until after I'd dropped Sarah back at our place and spent four hours in the office tapping every source imaginable. A press conference at the State of Illinois Building did happen, but the Democrat's name never surfaced.

I've regretted how that night transpired ever since, feeling the greatest remorse each year on Sarah's birthday. She didn't complain that night. Not the next day. Never.

"I should have spent more time with you and less at work," I said, risking a fall into the cave of guilt. "We've gone over that a million times or more, though, right? So I won't go there. Yes, I've been busy. I get the feeling you're referring to my whereabouts on Wednesday evening. Am I right?"

"I was hoping you'd bring that up," Sarah said, her hesitation inviting me to continue.

"Lindsay caught me a little off-guard. She's always been a fun person on the board and – I can admit to you because I know you're not going to tell anyone – I had a tiny crush on her. I didn't see this coming. Hell, I didn't even know for sure that she was a lesbian."

Sarah knew it all, about my life anyway. Although we could actually speak to each other only within the walls of our Farragut home, her eyes followed me everywhere. There were no secrets in this relationship.

"When she kissed you, how did your feelings then compare to how you felt when you first kissed Liza?"

"Totally different dynamic," I said, easily recalling the sensation of Liza's smooth, trembling lips. "I can't say it wasn't exciting having this attractive woman sharing her lip gloss with me, but it definitely did not overwhelm me. Last Saturday night, I felt out of control. My guilt-ridden alter ego that normally pulls me back to the life of borderline boring had no effect. It always feels nice, though, to have someone show an interest in you."

"What's in store for tomorrow night at the Hopleaf?" Sarah's probing was genuine concern for my mental health.

"One microbrew tap beer with a board member," I said, unclear if I was trying to convince Sarah or myself of that.

Our conversation continued as I went through the mail and started making a list of what to take to Devil's Lake. Lindsay, Liza, the Baxter deal … we jumped topics like a kid playing hopscotch. When Sarah and I were "visiting," as I called it, in my mind she always wore a faded mint green shirt that never started out as mint green. She had it for years, long before I met her, and its many wrestlings in the washing machine had worn the color and cotton thin. Her face was summer tanned and the light green in her hazel eyes complemented the shirt beautifully. Of course, I only got to see her once after she died, the first night she spoke to me. It was the last time I felt her physical being, warmth from her arms around me. Visions of her now emerged from a vast library of memories.

At a little after 9 p.m., Amy knocked on the back door. Sarah would hold her comments while I chatted with Amy.

"What's the verdict?" Amy immediately asked.

"I've decided to join you," I said.

"Whoohoo, she's coming!" Amy yelled down to Claire. "We were really hoping you would. We're thinking of leaving around 6 a.m. Saturday. What do you think?"

"Yeah, that should work. Assuming your pals will be ready to climb when we get up there, we could have ropes set before lunch. What do you need me to bring?"

"Just your climbing gear, sleeping bag and pad, unless you mind sleeping in our tent," she said. "It's huge, though. Claire's parents gave it to us and I think it sleeps the entire Brady Bunch!"

This would be a fun weekend; the fun already had started.

"If either of you start snoring, I'll start punching," I joked. "Are you sure you don't need my campstove or lantern or anything?"

"No, I don't think so," she said. "That's all covered. I'm excited you're coming. We'll touch base tomorrow when you get home. Enjoy the rest of your evening."

"I intend to. Good night."

Once I had pulled my climbing bag out of the spare bedroom closet, confirming my harness, shoes, rack of Friends, camelots and tri-cams, and my chalk bag and rope were accounted for, the bathtub was my next stop. That five-mile run had converted my hamstrings into violin strings. Nothing that a long, hot soak (and stretching) couldn't cure. The water was almost too hot. I laid a folded towel on the edge of the tub and sat down, slowly slipping in my feet, then up to mid-calf. As I squatted toward the water, bubbles tickled my thighs, triggering memories of the many times Sarah and I made love here.

We had designed this upper floor – every inch of it – together. We wanted it to be a space that encouraged our intimacy as we grew older, a master bedroom and bathroom most people experience only on vacation. We planned a home that would be nurturing for us and inviting to friends and family.

For the few months Sarah and I got to live here together, the Jacuzzi tub was an aphrodisiac. We would lie together in the water, relax, then an unassuming caress would lead to unbridled intensity. Tonight, I wanted to make love with Sarah.

"Cate," Sarah's voice whispered as if her lips were brushing my ear. "Is this going to confuse how you feel about Liza?"

"Sarah, I don't want to think about that. I'm thinking about you. Just talk to me. Be with me."

Her words guided my hands.

Friday morning I awoke with a full heart, and sore calves and hamstrings. I guess the hot soak didn't help as much as I had hoped. Following a rigid list of stretches and morning hygiene, I pulled on tan pants and a blue paisley pullover shirt and left for the office. It was a quiet day, allowing me to work on a new corporate solicitation packet for a product donation. An afternoon scan of personal email included a short note from Liza, sent apparently just before she checked out of the San Francisco hotel to go visit her sister. Basically, it said to not expect a call or message over the weekend and to be "emphatically pleased :) " if it did, by chance, happen. About 4 p.m., I decided to call it a day and beat the traffic. The Saab was sauna hot when I slid onto the driver's seat and I opted for air conditioning on the way home.

A rendezvous in the basement with Claire and Amy cleared up questions on my packing list. As I laid my weekend clothing choices on the bedspread, I reminisced about early climbing years. When I glanced at the travel alarm clock and saw that it was 7 p.m., a quick evaluation of packing showed I was nearly finished. It would take me no more than five minutes to walk to the Hopleaf. I walked into the bathroom and peered into the mirror, as if it could tell me if I should change into shorts or not. Jeans sounded like a much better idea and I pulled on a pair of faded Carpenter's pants. My hair had been pulled back in a ponytail all day, so I decided to leave it as is. Besides, this wasn't a date.

I walked into the Hopleaf at 7:35 and thought for sure Lindsay would be waiting. That's more in line with her personality. To my surprise, she was about 10 minutes late meeting me.

"Hey, Cate. I'm so sorry I wasn't here on time," she said, walking toward me and apologizing again when she reached the booth where I was sitting. "My mom called from Knoxville and I didn't want her to wait up until 9:30 or 10 for me to call back, so I made you wait."

She grinned as she finished her explanation and sat down across from me. The light brown, short-sleeved shirt she was wearing blended well with her eyes and banker's mild tan. Her blue jeans were more faded than mine and had started fringing at the ankles.

"Perfectly all right," I said. "When my mom calls, everything else has to wait. Isn't that a written rule somewhere?"

"Absolutely. Have you started a tab?" she asked, seeing I'd consumed almost half of the pint in front of me.

"Yes, I did. Just tell him to add yours to the McGuire Visa card."

"I don't think so," she said in a playful, scolding sort of way. "Tonight's my treat and it does *not* count as the dinner I owe you."

She got up and headed toward the bar. I was betting with myself which tap beer she'd choose – if a tap beer at all – and settled on two possibilities. When she placed the amber-colored pint on a coaster and sat down, I presented her with my guesses.

"One of them is correct," she said, enjoying my game. "Which one are you putting your money on?"

"Oh, there's money involved now, eh?"

"Or it could be a different wager," she said, her facial expression causing me to blush. "Sorry, I couldn't resist saying that. No, let's make it something like coffee at the bagel shop one morning before work. If you're right, I buy. If you're wrong, you buy. C'mon, it's $1.75. What do you say?"

"You're not a gambling addict or anything, right?" I asked, getting her to laugh as she had me laughing the day before. "Okay. You're drinking the Big Shoulders firefighter ale."

I looked at her, waiting for a nod or side-to-side head rotation. She picked up her pint, held it up to the light as if she were looking for something she'd lost in the bottom of the glass, then took a healthy swig.

"You're good," she said, smiling. "Beer aficionado, eh?"

"No, I just like beer and playing stupid little games like that."

"I found it to be fun, though I'm out another dollar-seventy-five now. I'm going to have to set up a spreadsheet to keep track of what I owe you."

Like most Friday nights at the Hopleaf, the regular locals packed in and the noise level soon had risen to the point where we were having trouble hearing each other. Our conversation had turned philosophical and Lindsay's perception of the "after-life" had piqued my curiosity. My watch said it was 8:30 and I was not yet ready to go home. Lindsay caught me checking the time.

"Do you need to leave?" she asked.

"No, but I think there's probably a better place to talk where we actually could hear each other."

"Did you eat dinner?" Lindsay asked. "If not, you could come to my place and have leftover lasagna and a salad. I haven't really eaten since lunch and I'm starving."

My mind quickly processed what was happening. Her place was close by. We had just gotten into an intense discussion about what she believes happens to a person's soul or spirit when that person dies – a topic that, obviously, I find incredibly interesting. Before I left home, I told myself this was not going to happen.

"Vegetarian lasagna?" I asked, basically responding that her place would be fine.

"Spinach," she said. "I'll go settle the bill."

Walking to her condo took only a couple of minutes. Her flat was the first floor of a three-flat yellow brick building on the south side of Winona. She keyed us through the front gate, then the front door of the building and, finally, the door of her place. A simple, clear glass vase of fresh flowers sat on an old sewing machine cabinet in her entryway. White and yellow carnations, purple aster, baby's breath and salmon-colored snapdragons stood out beautifully against the pale lemon wall. Although the evening air had cooled substantially from the hot afternoon, the central air conditioning felt like I'd just stepped into the refrigerated section of the grocery store.

"Oooh, it's gotten almost too cold now," Lindsay said, reaching over to turn up the thermostat. "When I got home, it was almost 80 degrees in here, so I cranked up the air. I think I went a little overboard. Come on."

She led me down the hallway and into her kitchen, a modernized working space that would have pleased Martha Stewart. Glass-paned cabinets revealed a collection of alphabetized spices and herbs, several bottles of various cooking oils and a set of blue and tan stoneware that had to have been handmade.

"Do you mind if I look at your dishes?" I said, already reaching for a plate.

Lindsay laughed.

"Help yourself," she said. "I had them made in New Braunfels, Texas, by two women who have a shop there. I love them – the plates, not the women."

Now I was laughing, too.

"They're gorgeous."

I placed the plate back on its stack while Lindsay pulled a foil-topped casserole dish from the refrigerator. She reached back in to grab a bag of prepared salad greens and bottle of dressing.

"The bottom drawer on your left has croutons and sunflower seeds we can put on the salad," she said. "Would you mind getting those out?"

Within 10 minutes, we were sitting at her round dining room table with a full meal in front of us. The conversation we'd been having at the Hopleaf picked up where we'd left off as I chewed her scrumptuous home cooking. She was nearly ranting about how traditional religions disregard any possibilities other than heaven and hell, how the theory of past lives is based in the ancient beliefs of many countries and how the general public refuses to allow itself to experience the "sixth sense." (That was a topic we'd have to save for another night.)

We continued sitting at the dining table long after we'd finished our spinach lasagna, pushing our plates to the center so we could occasionally rest our forearms on the table. As I finished sharing one of my profound thoughts for the evening, Lindsay pointed to her watch.

"I don't want you to leave, but it's almost 11," she said, smiling. "What time are you getting up?"

"Five," I said, frowning as I backed away from the table and started to pick up my plate and glass.

"Leave those right there," Lindsay said, placing her fingers on top of my arm as if to push it back toward the tabletop. "I'll take care of this. You need to get to bed, right?"

"Yeah, I do. Luckily, the women I'm going with will be driving so maybe I can sleep a little on the way up there. Thank you for dinner and the invigorating conversation."

She followed me down the hallway, then stepped ahead of me to open the door.

"I'm really glad we could get together before you left for the weekend," she said, looking directly into my eyes. "I respect the fact that you are seeing someone, so I'm not planning to kiss you good-night, even though I would like to."

"Thank you, Lindsay," I said, relieved that she was so open about the discomfort of the moment.

As we hugged each other, I felt like I was embracing an old friend. The Clark Street crowd was rocking as I headed north toward home. Late-night diners filled the sidewalk cafes, and dance club patrons spilled out to the parking meters for fresh air. I finished the minimal packing that needed to be done and decided to shower in the morning. It would help wake me up.

"Sarah, are you here?" I asked, crawling into bed and setting the alarm of my new clock.

"I'm right beside you, Cate."

Exhausted and knowing the weekend offered no sleeping in, I tried clearing my mind and imagined a deserted beach, one white lounge chair sitting near the water's edge. As I strained to hear the waves washing in, I dropped into a heavy sleep. Morning lay a few short hours away.

Chapter Five

Hiking through Roosevelt National Forest with Liza brought back humorous memories from the previous weekend's climbing adventure with Claire and Amy at Devil's Lake. Not true campers, they did their best to blend in with their outdoorsy friends.

Before the alarm clock had a chance to awaken me, Claire stumbled coming in the back door of the building, and the hard "thud" snapped me from my dream. I remained in bed another five minutes, then realized Sarah was there with me still.

"You stayed the night," I said, the words coming out in a segmented morning voice. "No wonder I slept so soundly."

"Actually, you were quite restless," Sarah replied. "I'm glad you feel rested. Otherwise, how are you feeling?"

"Good. I had another fun evening with Lindsay. She is extremely open-minded about life after death. I think she'd understand yours and my relationship, but I'm not planning on telling her about it."

"So you have two wonderful women in your life now: Liza *and* Lindsay," Sarah said in a teasing tone.

"Three," I quickly responded, grinning as I sat up in bed. "Or are you planning to step out of the picture?"

"Okay. Three it is."

Sarah and I talked while I showered, sipped my coffee and placed everything I was taking with me by the back door. At 5:45, Amy firmly knocked.

"Have fun climbing, Cate," said Sarah, who had excelled at the sport. "Try some F9 routes for me, will you?"

In our six years together, she advanced from beginner climbs – F4, F5 – to those rated F9 and some F10. We both could enjoy the F7 and F8 routes, however, and those generally were more accessible to members of the climbing club when we'd be out with a group. Pushing me to try to dissect the more difficult climbs was one of Sarah's ways of saying "I believe in you" and "I want to help you be the best you can be." I never resented the challenge. I also never knew how much I'd miss someone pushing me like that.

"Maybe I'll give Pine Box a go," I said, referring to one of her favorite F9 adversaries.

With that, I felt her presence leave the room. I walked over to the kitchen door and opened it to find Amy standing there, staring at me with a child-like grin on her face.

"Ready to go?" she asked.

"Let's go," I said.

She helped me get my gear to their car and we were on the road before 6 o'clock.

Devil's Lake sits amidst a bracket of quartzite faces protruding from the thick hills, partially hidden by the trees grown up around them. The climbing guide book includes a multitude of routes on the east and west ends, but we most likely would tackle the more popular eastern bluffs today. When we pulled through the admission gate, Amy turned right into the parking lot designated as our meeting place and backed into a spot close to a picnic table. Their friends pulled in next to us before we had time to get out of the car.

"We thought for sure we'd beat you guys here," the driver of the Ford Explorer yelled toward us.

Amy exited the car and stood next to the Explorer while five women spilled out of its doors. They were a cute group. Young. Two, I guessed, might be close to my age, but the other three definitely were part of Amy and Claire's generation. The driver, Tori, looked like a woman you'd see on a Colorado billboard inviting "granola lesbians" to come live in the Rocky Mountain state — and they likely would accept the invitation. She was tan, almost leathery looking, but her skin was taut, particularly around her quadriceps, hamstrings and upper arms. As Tori took my hand to introduce herself, the strength of her fingers assured me she was one of the experienced climbers.

"I'm Cate, landlord of these two wild women," I said, pointing toward Claire and Amy.

"Hi, I'm Tori and this is Laney, my partner," she said, motioning toward a sandy brown-haired woman not shaped like your stereotypical climber. "You've climbed here a lot, we hear."

"Used to," I said. "I haven't climbed much the past four years. A few outings with the Chicago Mountaineering Club each summer is about it."

While Tori looked like she could easily hike a canyon or throw green hay bales onto a wagon, Laney had the figure of Renoir women, rounder with broad hips. I knew from watching climbers over the years that some physiques will fool you. I was curious to see the variety of climbing styles I was bound to see today.

Amy and Claire briefly chatted with the three younger women, but Tori interrupted them to get us all headed toward the rock face. Our drive had taken more than three hours and, though we had plenty of daylight hours left for climbing, the best scenario would involve getting on the rock soon. By mid-afternoon, the less experienced climbers' muscles would be burned and it would be time to set up camp, eat dinner and relax. We reloaded our vehicles and drove to the lot nearest the eastern bluffs.

"Unless you had a specific area in mind you thought we should go to, I was thinking Balanced Rock Wall looked promising," Tori said when we arrived at the lot where we'd leave our cars. "Lots of fives, sixes and sevens, plus some eights and nines for the daring and adventurous."

"That *is* a good area, but since it's right along the path, it can get a little irritating with hikers walking on your ropes," I said. "Have you ever climbed Leaning Tower Gully?"

"No, but we're game to start wherever," Tori said. "We'll follow you."

I draped my favorite blue and purple climbing rope over Amy's head and shoulder, then pulled on my pack and crossed the road to get on the Civilian Conservation Corps path leading up to the Gully. Seven women trailing me, I kept the pace slow so no one felt rushed on the steep hike. Tori and Laney stayed near me; the younger group fell behind, distracted by their conversation. Although it was only 10 a.m., the sun already was beating down on us as we trekked through the exposed rocky portions of the path. When we reached a good vista, I stopped and looked back over the railroad tracks and lake, taking in a full-circle view of my surroundings.

"This is amazing," said one of the young women as their group caught up to us. "I had no idea a place like this existed so close to Chicago."

"Don't tell too many people, okay?" I joked.

By 10:30, we stood facing the 31 climbing routes of Leaning Tower Gully and Four Brothers, an area offering easier F5 climbs such as The Balcony and The Mezzanine that the less experienced among us could conquer. Foreplay (an F6), The Green Bulge (F7) and Out of the Woods (F8) would keep the rest of us occupied for a couple of hours. Since there were eight of us, Tori and I concurred that we should set two ropes. A couple of the women who had come with her and Laney had never climbed before, so we took a few minutes explaining "top-roping," the type of climbing in which you place three points of protection – laid out like a chicken's three toes – above the top of the climb. Each point is independent of the others, so if one piece of protection would come loose, two more remain. If two come loose, one remains. All three points of protection converge at two carabiners at the vertical peak of the climb. The climbing rope, hooked to the climber's harness on one end and hooked to the person belaying the climber at the other end, goes through these carabiners. This is the safest type of rock climbing.

"It sounds like you guys know what you're doing," one of the new climbers said. "What are we waiting for?"

Tori took the two inexperienced climbers up the back of Leaning Tower Gully so they could learn as they watched her set the first rope. Claire came with me as an assistant to set the second rope.

"Rope!" Tori yelled as she launched a faded green and yellow tether toward Laney.

I soon repeated the same with my blue and purple rope, completing our preparation stage. We all congregated at the bottom of the climbs and selected who would get started on the rock. Amy and Laney were chosen to climb first, giving the newcomers an opportunity to watch while Tori and I fulfilled belaying duties. They stepped into their harnesses and carefully attached themselves to their respective ropes. Tori, as a safety measure, doublechecked both climbers' connections and harnesses.

"Ready to climb," Laney said.

72

"You're on belay," Tori responded, following official verbal climbing protocol. She had settled in against a small tree with the belay device secured near her waist.

"Climbing," Laney said, wrapping her chalked fingertips around a rocky nub.

"Climb on," Tori said, giving Laney the go-ahead to begin.

Amy and I then went through the same process and she nervously stepped up on her first foothold. She and Claire had climbed before, but only a few times. The sport was still new and challenging and a little scary for them. Like most inexperienced climbers, Amy hated relying on her feet and felt much more confident when her fingers were draped inside a "bucket," a spot on the rock where your hand actually can wrap over the quartzite lip.

"Trust your feet," I called to her. "Your feet are your arms' best friends. Don't make your arms do all the work."

She need not worry about falling off the rock. Belaying her, I kept the rope as tight as possible without making her feel as though I were pulling her up the climb. As she moved to a height about 20 feet from the ground, she paused for a long time.

"There's a foothold about six inches above your left foot," I said. "Once you're on that, you can step up and reach with your left hand to a great bucket. I know how you love those."

If she stood there much longer, the climber's sewing machine leg – an unconscious twitching of the calf muscles that makes your leg go up and down like a sewing machine needle – would strike.

"Go for it," I coached. "I've got you."

I saw Amy draw in a deep breath as she lifted her left foot to blindly find the ledge I could see from below. She found it and I watched her exhale that same breath.

"Now step up on it and find that bucket almost directly above you. Your entire left hand will practically fall into the bucket."

Without further hesitation, Amy shifted most of her body weight onto her left foot and grasped toward the handhold. From there, she easily proceeded to the top and, on her command, I lowered her back to the ground.

"Great job, Ame," Claire said, smiling at her accomplished partner.

"Thanks for the coaching, Cate," Amy said, untying the rope from her harness. "I sort of got stuck at that spot, didn't I?"

"You got out of it, though," I said. "Nice climbing. Claire, you're up."

Our pals on the other rope had gotten ahead of us due to Laney's quick, masterful climb of The Green Bulge (F7). With a minor adjustment to the rope positioning, one of the new climbers already was experimenting on The Balcony, a non-threatening F5 route. Claire tied onto the rope and walked over to me for a second opinion on her knot and secured harness.

"That's perfect," I said. "Are you ready?"

"Ready to climb," she answered.

"You're on belay."

"Climbing," she said.

"Climb on."

Not counting a lunch break, we climbed where those ropes were set for about three hours, each of us completing two or three routes. We then shifted left to the routes called Foreplay, an F6, and Orgasm, an F8 that appealed only to the three older, more experienced climbers. These names, of course, encouraged discussion among the younger generation.

"All we get is Foreplay?" they asked, chuckling.

"We're not sure you know how to handle the F8," Tori barked back at them.

Laney and I joined in Tori's laughter.

Although I felt a tad rusty on my first climb that morning, I approached Orgasm with a fury. My confidence completely reinstated, I knew tomorrow I had to challenge a route rated F9.

"Make it look easy, why don't you?" Tori complimented me. "Laney, the pressure's on."

I relieved Laney of supervising the younger crew so she could take a shot at Orgasm. Stumped briefly during transition from under a ceiling, she calculated the rest of her route and moved smoothly to the top. As I'd said earlier, some physiques can fool you. Laney's plump, feminine figure worked well for her on the rock wall. Once Tori had taken her turn, steadily ascending without interruption, Amy decided she needed to give the F8 a go.

"Expect the holds to be much smaller and a little more challenging to find," I told Amy as Tori helped attach the rope to her harness. "Let me know when you're ready."

The rest of the group, now satiated with climbing for the day, collected around me to fire up Amy for her feat. It would not be easy for her. More likely than not, she'd slip off the face a few times, but I was willing to assist the effort as much as she required or wanted. Amy spent a solid five minutes studying the start of the route, analyzing a possible second move after she left the ground. Little did she know, the first move was one of the more difficult sections of this climb. Tori, Laney and I took turns offering tips and eventually we coached Amy about one-third of the way toward her destination. When she'd had enough, Amy requested to be lowered.

"Okay, I need a lot more practice before trying that again," she said, laughing at herself.

"You get points with the old girls for trying," Tori said in a flirtatious tone and wearing a catty expression.

Laney lightly punched Tori in the arm, casting her a "watch yourself" jealous look. Tori enjoyed triggering that nerve.

With six people removing the pieces of equipment and webbing from the top of each climb while Tori and I packed the gear, it didn't take long. We were back at the parking lot within 30 minutes. Tori and Laney wanted to camp in an isolated area they'd discovered a couple of years earlier. Only once had they found someone else housed there on a Saturday night. The Ford Explorer led us to the northern edge of the park where Tori turned left onto a faintly tread road. She rolled forward about 10 mph toward the middle of nowhere. Then to my surprise, the trees opened to a clearing that could comfortably accommodate five or six camping tents.

"There aren't any picnic tables back here, but the outhouse is just down that trail," Tori said, getting out of the Explorer and pointing.

The site suited us splendidly. For much of the evening, Amy, Claire and their three young friends kept us laughing almost incessantly. Since my tentmates brought the tent, I assumed they might have set it up once or twice before. Assumptions never did get me too far. The extra-large tent had many, many poles and many possibilities – in their minds, at least – of how those poles might attach to the nylon body.

"We never really had to set it up by ourselves," Claire admitted, collapsing to the grass as if in a physical comedy routine.

Amy plopped down perpendicular to Claire and laid out flat on her back, her head resting in Claire's lap.

"All that time you spent on Foreplay wore you out, eh?" Tori shouted to them as she finished staking down the rainfly of hers and Laney's tent.

A joint effort preparing dinner made that experience a joy. I had feared we "older gals" might have to take the lead, but as it turned out, one of the women who had come with Tori and Laney is a chef at one of the Lettuce Entertain You Restaurants in downtown Chicago. It was one of the most flavorful meals I've ever consumed at Devil's Lake.

As the sun crawled behind the treetops and camp fell dark, I had the urge to wander far enough away from my companions where I could have some quiet time. All day I wondered, despite the activity around me, how Liza was spending her day. Was she enjoying the time with her sister? Was she catching herself thinking of me throughout the day? I hoped so. The tugging around my heart reminded me how alive she'd made me feel last weekend.

I slowly stepped along the path dimly lit by my headlamp, absorbing the night noises of nature and the serenity of this space. A sawed-off stump came into view on my left, practically calling my name to come sit down for a little while. I took a seat and leaned forward so that both elbows rested near my knees, my hands clasped together and protruding past my legs. My eyes searched downward as if I was looking at my hands, though the darkness hid them from me. This was a common position of deep thought, I concluded.

Walking in the woods behind our Missouri home or sitting in a secluded spot of my dad's hay-filled barn were two of my favorite escapes from ages 10 through 18. At the time, I wasn't aware of why I really needed an escape or wanted to escape, but maturity eventually revealed that answer. Although I felt that I "fit in" with my peers, something always was missing. Once I came out and accepted my sexual orientation, my desire to escape dissolved (until adulthood introduced new reasons to want to escape). My hours in the woods or in the barn were some of the most pensive of my life, self-evaluation and diagnosis ad nauseam. Those were the growing-up growing pains that translated into great television comedies like "One Day at a Time," "My Three Sons" and "Family." (I still wonder if Kristy McNichol had a crush on Meredith Baxter Birney when "Family" was being taped.)

While I sat on the stump, my imagination brought Liza to the woods, standing before me and reaching for my hands. Next week I would see what she actually wears on a camping trip, but for now, I pictured her in a black fleece vest, zipped up the front, with a white T-shirt showing at the neck and its short sleeves sticking out around her beautiful, strong upper arms. Her legs were covered by sand-colored, durable pants and she wore lightweight tan and blue hiking shoes almost identical to mine. In my mind, she was there.

"Cate? Is that you?" I heard Amy say a moment before the light from her headlamp came into view on the path.

"Damn, you found me," I said, knowing she'd realize I was kidding.

"Am I disturbing you?"

"No, that's okay."

She now was standing next to me, the beam of her headlamp spotlighting my bare knees.

"Aren't the mosquitos getting you out here?" she asked.

"They know better than to bother me," I said, "which is more than I can say for you."

She began to laugh.

"Really, would you rather be alone?" Amy said, the sports psychologist in her coming out.

"No, really, it's fine that you're here. I just came out here to get a little time to myself. Is everyone heading to bed?"

"Tori and Laney already went to their tent and, by the sounds coming out of the tent, we're guessing someone was getting a massage," Amy said, giggling. "Claire and the others wanted to stay and listen, but I felt like I was intruding, so figured I'd come looking for you. I guess I'm intruding on *you* now, huh?"

I didn't answer. I knew Amy well enough to know she'd further pursue why I'd slipped away from the group.

"Contemplating anything in particular?" she asked after a minor pause.

"Liza."

"Why didn't you ask her to come with us?" Amy asked, not knowing how long Liza was going to be out of town.

"She won't be back from her business trip until next Friday. I'm actually flying to Denver that morning to meet up with her."

This information undoubtedly would send Amy's inquisitive mind into a whirlwind. I said not another word, waiting for her response.

"You're waiting for me to say something, aren't you?" she asked. "You're good practice for my psychology skills, Cate. You two must have really hit it off last weekend. What's happening in Denver?"

"We're going camping in Roosevelt National Forest. She has a couple of good friends who live in Denver and they are acting sort of like outfitters for the weekend since Liza will be flying there directly from Oregon."

"That sounds fun," she said. "Any anxieties about spending a weekend together so soon?"

Amy didn't know how Liza and I had spent the previous Saturday night and most of Sunday, therefore she had no clue that this weekend would be only slightly different: we'd get to spend an additional day and night together. I had absolutely no anxieties about that, only impatience.

"I'm looking forward to it with great anticipation."

"Well then!" Amy exclaimed, taken back a bit by my certainty. "It sounds like we might be seeing a lot more of Ms. Liza around Farragut Street. I'm happy for you, Cate, and I'm anxious to meet this woman and get to know her."

I was anxious to get to know Liza, too, intimately and in every other way. Each time a picture of her emerged in my mind, my entire body experienced a pleasurable twinge. I couldn't wait to see her. I would *have* to wait, but didn't want to.

"Should we call it a night?" I asked, starting to sense hovering mosquitos. "Do you think Tori and Laney are asleep yet?"

Amy laughed as we both headed up the path toward the campfire and tents. Our headlamp beams danced along the path until we stopped near the fire. Claire and the other young women were still corralled around the orange crackling logs.

"Is all quiet on the homefront?" Amy asked, directing her question to Claire.

Giggling bounced around the circle.

"Cate and I are headed to the tent," Amy said. "Are you coming, Claire?"

"Good night, ladies," Claire said, rising from her cross-legged position on a blanket.

We walked away from the flames and Claire stopped to shake dust and grass off the blanket, then haphazardly folded it and shoved it under her arm. Like Three Musketeers, we simultaneously brushed our teeth a few feet from the tent, sharing the water bottle for rinsing. Amy took the middle position inside the tent, but curled in a spooning position around Claire with her back toward me. I laid on my back, envisioning my trip to Colorado the next week.

Stop thinking about Liza or you'll never get to sleep, I thought to myself.

As I began drifting off, my thoughts had turned to where we should climb the next day. Somewhere in the middle of conquering Out of the Woods, an F8 climb, sleep set in.

Sunday morning, we awoke to an unexpected rain shower. Once I'm awake, I can only wait a limited time before my bladder needs relief, so I tugged the raincoat from my bag and proceeded into the light downpour. (That term might seem like an oxymoron, but in reality, there exists a *heavy* downpour that affects visibility; this rain, heavy as it was, did not hinder my finding the outhouse.)

Walking back, I noticed that Tori and Laney had a pot of water heating on their campstove. The rain started letting up and I made a bee line for the place I sensed could produce the quickest cup of coffee.

"Good morning," I said softly as I neared their tent.

"Good morning," Tori said as her head popped out from the vestibule. "How did you sleep?"

"I climbed all night long," I said, referring to my active dream. "I was on Darcy's Buttress when the rain woke me."

Tori laughed.

"Well, it's a good thing you decided to climb overnight because I'm not sure we'll get any climbing in today," she said. "If the rain stops in the next half-hour or so, we can hike up and see how wet the rock is, but we're just going to have to wait and see, I think."

"Yeah, I think you're right."

"I don't smell coffee yet," Laney's voice rang from inside the tent.

"Working on it, dear," Tori said with submissive sarcasm. "Cate, are you a coffee drinker?"

"I'll be your best friend for the day if you make me a cup of coffee," I replied, smiling.

The light rain wasn't enough to force us inside a tent and Laney crawled out from theirs just in time for java. The two of them camped a lot, I assumed, observing the array of gear, their clothing and the way the rain didn't appear to affect their moods in the least. Laney seemed to like purple camp clothing, this deduction made from seeing her wardrobe both days. Tori leaned more into the greens and tans, though her rain jacket was bumblebee yellow. We combined to make a colorful trio with me in my steel blue pants and royal blue rain jacket.

"So Cate, do you have a partner or girlfriend?" Laney asked, sipping her coffee.

Tori threw a warning glance her way, then noticed that I had seen her do so.

"That's okay," I said. "I don't mind people asking personal questions."

"There's nothing Laney won't ask, just so you know," Tori said, grinning at her partner.

"I guess my answer would have to be 'no,' though I did meet someone last weekend," I answered.

"Does it look promising?" Tori asked.

"Based on the one week I've known her, I'd say 'yes,' but it's pretty soon to say."

"Well, I have a theory," Laney said, drawing another interesting look from Tori. "When the soul of the person you're meant to be with steps into your line of vision, you know. Some people are more perceptive than others and can more easily sense it, but everyone, if they'll just tune in to themselves, has that ability. There are many reasons why people don't end up with their soulmate and a lot of couples make it work, even though they're not a perfect fit, but I truly believe you can recognize the right one."

"Laney's also an idealist," Tori said. "She was smart enough to hold on to me nineteen years ago and that's the basis of her theory."

"Who was smart enough to hold on to whom?" Laney bantered back.

"And does your theory allow for a person to have two soulmates in a lifetime?" I asked.

"Do you mean if the first one you meet dies, can there be a second?" Laney asked for confirmation.

"Uh-huh."

"Well, I loved the movie *Sleepless in Seattle* and the way the screenplay showed viewers how much Tom Hanks loved his first wife, then how he fatefully found Meg Ryan," she explained, "but I can't say Meg was a second soulmate for him."

"C'mon, Laney," Tori chimed in. "They were meant to be. Did you sleep through parts of the movie?"

"Okay, I didn't mean to start an argument between the two of you," I said, feeling like a referee. "The reason I ask is because my partner died four years ago and I believe we were what you call 'soulmates.' So, is it possible there's someone else out there for me?"

Laney looked over at Tori. I could tell neither of them knew what to say.

"I also love that movie," I said, easing us out of the uneasiness. "Whether or not Meg is his second soulmate, Tom looks like he's going to be very happy with her in his life."

"I'd be happy with her in my life, too!" Tori belted out, effectively getting Laney and me to laugh.

Our noise level was enough to wake the younger members of our group and we dropped the conversation.

"Who needs a rooster to wake you up when we have you cackling hens?" said the woman I now called Julia (the chef), though that wasn't her real name.

"We were getting hungry and decided you needed to wake up," Tori replied. "What's for breakfast?"

Julia stuck her head out from the tent and saw it was still misting rain.

"How far is the nearest restaurant?" she answered.

Eventually, all three campers emerged from that tent wearing shorts, sandals and bright-colored raincoats. I walked over to my tent to make sure Amy and Claire were still among the living.

"Would the two of you care to join us?" I called to them from outside the tent.

"Is it still raining?" Claire asked. "Is everyone else up?"

"Yes and yes," I said.

"We'll be right out," Amy said, her struggling morning voice making me smile.

Once all eight of us collected around Tori's campstove, we evaluated our options for the day. Since the rain showed no signs of ceasing any time soon, the chances of our doing any rock climbing were slim. If we went to "The Barn" in Baraboo for breakfast, we possibly could climb later for an hour or two, *if* the sun came out and dried the rock face.

"I vote we go for breakfast and, if it's still raining when we're finished, we come back here and pack up and head home," Tori said.

"That works for me," I said.

At the suggestion of Julia, we all piled into Tori's Explorer with Amy and Claire offering to clamber into the cargo area in back. I claimed a window seat behind the driver and shared the row with Julia and her two young, lean friends.

"Quit breathing for a minute, you guys," Tori yelled back at all of us. "You're steaming up my windows."

She carefully maneuvered the SUV out of our campsite and headed for The Barn, a mere five-minute drive away. The restaurant already was filling up with climbers when we arrived, but a long, rectangular table toward the back sat empty and the hostess headed in that direction. As crowded as it was, the kitchen did its best to fill orders in a timely fashion, but we waited nearly 30 minutes for our food. Not that we cared. While the rain took turns misting, then pouring, then back to misting, our group wasn't short on topics for conversation. The point arrived, however, when we started talking about packing up and returning to the city.

"We just have to come back again very soon," Tori said, the SUV guided back toward camp. "At least we did a lot of climbing yesterday. That will have to hold us over."

Taking down a wet tent never is a lot of fun, but I've rolled up plenty of drenched nylon over the years and the task went fairly fast with Claire and Amy managing breakdown of the poles. Even at our relaxed pace, we were ready to roll out of the state park within a half hour.

"Do you want to stay with each other on the way back to Chicago?" Tori asked Amy.

"We can start out that way," Amy said, "but if we get separated, don't worry about it."

"We'll follow you then, if that's all right with you," Tori replied.

Another learned behavior that comes with age: caravan in case one car has any trouble. I was glad Tori had made the suggestion.

By early evening, I had unpacked my gear, soaked in the tub and made a meal of leftovers scattered throughout the refrigerator. I felt good, very good. The physical drain from climbing invigorated me and, at the same time, calmed me. Although I knew Sarah was present, an overwhelming curiosity to get online and check for an email note from Liza drew me into my home office.

"Sender: Applelady. Subject: REALLY missing you." I double-clicked on the message and read one of the most charming letters I've ever received. Her words were subtle, but unmistakable. The tone was patient, but yearnful.

Liza ended the note with "Tonight, your head rests on the pillow of my chest where you can hear my heart telling happy stories of the days that lie ahead for us. Sweet dreams, Cate."

"She *is* a romantic, isn't she?" I said aloud, not meaning to initiate a conversation with Sarah, but pleased that it did just that.

"I don't know if I could compete with that," Sarah said, playfully, though I'm sure she was fairly certain I would never fall for anyone the way I'd fallen for her.

"I don't think I'm at a point where I can joke with you about Liza and me," I said, feeling a queasy churning in the pit of my stomach. "Some days I feel like you're going to call me at work and ask me to meet you somewhere for dinner or have me check my calendar for possible vacation dates so we could finally make that trip to Venice. And then I realize that's never going to happen and I …"

All of a sudden, a knot formed in my throat. I fought the desire to break down and pity myself, though the painful memories seared through me.

"Cate, if you feel like you need to let out those emotions, it's okay. You know it's okay."

My clinched fists finally began to relax and I took three or four ocean-depth breaths before trying to speak again.

"Those days might never completely disappear, but time helps dull the pain," Sarah continued. "I won't joke about Liza anymore. I promise."

"That's okay, my love. You know, I haven't told her about you yet. I still haven't decided when would be a good time. If the opportunity presents itself on the camping trip, I might do it then, but I think I want to wait until we're back in Chicago, you know, in case she doesn't take it very well."

"If she truly cares for you, she'll understand," Sarah said. "Be prepared, though. She might need some time."

"Time?" I asked. "Time for what, exactly?"

"Cate, this is *not* a typical situation that you and I are in," she said.

"If she's as open-minded as I think she is," I said, "we'll talk through it and ..."

"And what?" Sarah asked.

"It's going to be fine. Besides, worrying about it now won't change a thing, so I'm not going to worry about it. You know, I was thinking about watching 'Sleepless in Seattle' tonight. Care to stay for the show?"

Sarah's laugh rang through the room.

"Anxious to have a good cry, are you?" she asked.

"And to be reminded that maybe true love *can* strike the same person twice," I said, walking toward the television/VCR with the video in hand.

As Tom Hanks' character returned to the top of the Empire State Building, where he momentarily would meet his second true love, I stopped the movie and stared at the blank screen. Tonight, I didn't want to see the ending. I wanted to fall asleep imagining how my own story was going to play out.

The alarm had not been set, but the sun raining through my east windows the next morning awoke me to find a white softball T-shirt wadded under my cheek like a pillow.

Chapter Six

Liza and I hiked miles of trails in Roosevelt National Forest, occasionally stepping aside for a group of mountain bikers cruising through. We settled into a secluded spot along a racing mountain stream, an ideal setting for intimate conversation between two people who had been "close," but who knew little about one another. Would this be the time I told Liza about Sarah? Although I mentally began preparing for that conversation, Liza steered the day in another direction, asking me about the Foundation.

Wednesday's Potbelly sandwich lunch sat in front of me while Michelle walked to the break room refrigerator to grab two canned lemonades. Monday and Tuesday had flown, but Ms. Cianfrini had met her goal: everything for the board meeting was ready by noon.

"How was the weekend with your family?" I asked, unwrapping my hot turkey and cheese.

"We finally got to meet lil' sis's boyfriend," she said, seemingly pleased with youngest sister Christina's choice in men. "He's a keeper. We all loved him."

"How long have they been dating?"

"Seven months," Michelle answered. "It's too funny how they met. She went with her friend Mary to Mary's work Christmas party – one of the law firms downtown – and this guy, Mitch, works there. They started talking and, at some point, he asked her how long she and Mary had been together. Mary turned to walk away, laughing, but Christina decided to string him along a little and she asked him, 'How could you tell we were a couple and not just friends?' Basically, the poor guy didn't know what to say and admitted he just wanted them to know he wasn't some uptight, homophobic, conservative, big firm attorney. He told her he had noticed two good-looking women who looked like they might be good conversationists and thought he'd introduce himself. She let him believe she and Mary were a couple all night. It wasn't until Mary ran into him the next week that he found out they were both straight and he called my sister that night."

"I'm assuming the topic of breast cancer has come up," I said.

"Like I said, this guy's a keeper," Michelle reiterated. "Christina told him the first night they went out because she wanted that out on the table at the start. You've heard the story a hundred times how guys don't want 'damaged goods,' right? Well, Mitch's mom is a survivor – seven years after a late stage II diagnosis. And get this: his pro bono work at the firm primarily is representing cancer patients who have been dropped by their insurance carriers."

"You're not serious!"

"I am!" she exclaimed. "What'd I tell you? We already told Christina she'd better propose before someone else tries to put the moves on Mitch."

"I'm really happy for Christina. Would you tell her that?"

"Absolutely," Michelle said. "I'll tell her to put you on the wedding invitation list."

We laughed, commenting how sisters can be so opinionated about our choice of partners and protective of one another. Our sandwiches were gone and I got up to throw away our rubbish.

"Hey, how was the rock climbing trip?" Michelle asked. "Did you go?"

"Yes, I had a great time, but I'll have to fill you in on details later. I want to look through the board member packet and accomplish a few more things before the meeting tonight."

"No problem," she said. "Just give a yell if I can help with anything."

Around 4:30 p.m., I walked out to the reception area.

"Michelle, can I get you anything from the coffee shop?"

"Let me go, Cate," Michelle said. "What would you like?"

I handed her a $10 bill and requested a venti coffee of the day with almond syrup.

"Take your drink out of that $10, too. Thank you, Michelle."

She wasn't out the door five seconds before the telephone rang. I could have waited to let it go to voicemail or see if it got transferred to my extension, but I decided to pick it up.

"Thank you for calling A Sister's Hope. How can I help you?"

"Demoted to the receptionist's desk, huh?" Liza's voice came across the line.

"Actually, the receptionist runs this organization," I said, toying with her. "How *can* I help you?"

"Do you think you could beam yourself to Portland right this minute?" she asked.

"I'd love to," I said, "but I have a very important meeting in about two hours, so I'm going to have to stick around Chicago. Are you on a break or something? Why don't you come see me?"

"There's nothing I'd like better," she replied. "However, our meeting reconvenes in about 10 minutes, so … How are you?"

"Much better now that I'm talking to you. How was the weekend with your sister?"

"We had a lot of fun. We got together with some of her friends I've met before, went running both mornings, did a lot of hanging out at her place," she said. "She has a great place. How about your weekend?"

"I decided sort of last minute to join my tenants for a rock climbing trip to Devil's Lake."

"Is there going to be anything about you I *don't* like?" Liza asked.

"You like rock climbing, eh?"

"Actually, I've only ever tried it on a climbing wall at a gym," she said, "but I liked it and I like the whole concept of the sport."

"We'll have to go together, then. We left early Saturday morning and climbed all day with friends of Amy and Claire. It was a good group, fun women. When we got up Sunday morning it was raining, so we drove into a little town for breakfast and hoped it might clear up. It didn't, so we packed up camp and were home Sunday afternoon."

"Did you happen to check your email when you got home?" Liza asked.

"As a matter of fact, I did."

This time, it was my turn to remain silent, leaving her to wonder what I was thinking and what my reaction was to her rather mushy message. Three or four seconds passed. She didn't say a word.

"I'm smiling now just like I was when I read it the first time," I finally said.

"Smiling like you found it to be humorous or smiling because you felt good?" she asked.

"I said I was smiling, not laughing. Yeah, you could say I felt good."

"Good."

Michelle walked into the office carrying our hot drinks.

"Guess what? I need to go," I said.

"Let me guess: the receptionist has returned to her desk and is cracking the whip for you to get busy," Liza said, making me grin again. "Can I call you tonight?"

"That'd be good, but make it later. This meeting could go until 10 p.m."

"Okay," she said. "I hope the meeting goes well. I'll talk to you later."

"Okay. Bye."

"I'm not going to ask who that was, but I will say that you're grinning like a five-year-old on Christmas morning," Michelle said, handing me a large coffee and my change.

"That obvious, huh?"

I departed the area, still grinning, and returned to my office. When I heard voices an hour or so later, I came out to find Michelle had prepped the conference table, complete with a bouquet of fresh flowers at the center. She was greeting Tom Mansell, a three-year board member whose first wife passed away from breast cancer five years ago. Remarried last year, Tom remained extremely active on the board and seemed to have amazing support from his new wife. As I approached Tom, Michelle was welcoming another board member at the door. When I heard the voice, my head turned toward them while I was mid-sentence with Tom. Lindsay, looking straight at me, was wearing a cream-colored suit – pants, not a skirt – with a mocha-toned silk shirt and flat dress shoes of the same color. I couldn't deny I was pleased to see her and I knew she could tell.

"Hello, Cate, Tom," she said, walking toward the two of us. "Tom, how have you been?"

I stood and watched the two of them as they delved into conversation, then quickly excused myself to talk with Michelle. Occasionally, I'd catch Lindsay looking my way and she, in turn, noticed I was paying attention. Tom decided to snack, so Lindsay meandered in my direction.

"You look great, as usual," she said to me in a voice too low for anyone else to hear.

"Thank you," I replied. "I have to say, that suit looks good on you."

"Do you think so? I'll have to wear it more often," she said, keeping the volume of her voice down. "I'm anxious to hear about the climbing adventure, but maybe you could fill me in *after* the meeting."

As she was finishing her last sentence, I turned toward my office and motioned with my head for her to follow me.

"I thought you might call over the past couple of days," I said. "Friday night was a great time, good food, good conversation."

"I thought you might appreciate my backing off a little," Lindsay said. "Notice I said 'a little.' And I knew I'd be seeing you tonight."

"I *do* appreciate the thought, but you don't need to make a conscious effort to do that. I enjoy the time we spend together."

"Well, I did notice how happy you seemed when I arrived," she said, sounding a little cocky (and rightfully so). "Does that mean we can go somewhere after the meeting tonight?"

"You make me laugh, do you know that?" I said, snickering. "Yes, we should go somewhere, but I turn into a toad at midnight."

"A toad, huh? They're kind of cute. I hope to be in the depths of a good dream by midnight anyway, so I'd miss the transformation," Lindsay replied. "Let's make this a concise meeting."

As the clock neared 7 p.m., the rest of the board members arrived and filled small plates with snacks, taking them to the conference table as members claimed their seats. I always placed myself at one end so I'd have good peripheral vision of everyone present. Tonight, Lindsay sat near the opposite end, the farthest seat away from me on my right. Only Tom, who took the seat directly opposite me, had a clearer line of vision.

As business meetings go, this one was fairly painless. We perused, as a group, each line of the multi-page Baxter partnership agreement and discussed questions as they arose. By 9 p.m., we all had come to a consensus that the partnership proposal should move toward the signature stage. I would call Cynthia Pruitt in the morning to discuss minor changes in verbiage the board members had suggested and then notify Francois so he could light his public relations torch. With congratulatory hugs, board members said goodnight and headed home.

"Michelle, you're out the rest of the week, right?" I asked as Lindsay and I helped clean up.

"Unless there's something you need me to do," she said, never surprising me with her conscientiousness.

"No, no," I said. "You did an incredible job getting everything together for this meeting. Thank you very much. Why don't you go ahead and take off? Lindsay and I will finish putting this stuff away."

"Are you sure?" Michelle asked, quickly taking the hint. "I won't argue with that. I will see you on Monday then."

She grabbed her bag and was out the door within two minutes.

"That was smooth," Lindsay said. "Are rumors going to fly about the two of us being left here alone?"

"I wouldn't care if they did, but no, Michelle is the most trustworthy person I know," I said. "No matter how badly she wants to, she won't mention a word to anyone. Besides, what's there to tell?"

I looked up at Lindsay and she passed me a provocative glance.

"Are we going for a walk or what?" I asked, barely acknowledging her efforts.

"We could walk to Buckingham Fountain again," she said. "The Navy Pier fireworks will be going off at 9:30."

"That's a good idea. We'd better get going if we want to see the fireworks."

I turned out the office lights while Lindsay stayed near the front door. When I got to where she was standing, her hand cupped around my forearm and she held still until I looked into her face. The streetlights cast dim glows into the room. I could see only half of her face and the glistening strands of her hair.

"Shhh," she whispered. "Take in the moment."

Were the two of us lovers, I would have seized the moment, not just taken it in. Instead, I brushed the edge of my thumb along her cheek.

"We'd better go," I said softly, leading us to the door.

The fountain crowd had wandered closer to the lake, leaving open park benches, one of which we claimed. On the walk over, we had revived our conversation from Friday night and Lindsay began telling me of the powerful relationship she'd shared with her grandmother. Lindsay said she awoke from a deep sleep one night to what she thought was the telephone ringing. As she sat there, waiting for the continued ringing, no sound came. She went back to sleep, then got a call from her mother the next morning to say that Grandma had passed away in the middle of the night.

"I believe I'm tuned in to more senses than the basic five," she said. "People in the South seem to be more open to those beliefs or superstitions than elsewhere in the country. What do you think?"

"I'm from the Midwest, not the South, though a lot of people think southeast Missouri is formally the South. I definitely believe we have avenues through which we can communicate with those we love who are not physically still on Earth."

"You mean talking to the dead," Lindsay said, attempting to simplify my statement.

"If I can talk to them, I don't consider them dead," I clarified. "You can call it the after-life, or ghosts or present souls, but I wouldn't use the term 'dead.'"

As we discussed the topic, I could tell Lindsay had contemplated these theories often in her life.

"Did you or do you talk about this sort of thing with your parents?"

"My father, mostly," she said. "Mom is more into tangible things. She's an accountant. Remember?"

For 15 minutes, fiery red, gold, silver, green and blue flashed into the air just south of Navy Pier. When I turned away from Lindsay to watch the spectacle, I felt Lindsay's arm lay across the top of the park bench along my back. I didn't react until the fireworks had ended.

"I can tell you are above average in the category of courtship," I said, turning toward her and smiling.

"Graduated at the top of my class," she said, brushing the nape of my neck with her fingers as she lifted her arm off the bench. "Would you be up for splitting a sandwich or something? I should have grabbed a bite before coming to your office, but I was anxious to get there. Are *you* hungry?"

"Am I giving you a ride home tonight?" I asked.

"If you're offering, I accept," she replied.

"Can we get fast food on the way home or do you not eat that?"

"When convenience is more important than nutrition," she said, "I'll eat just about anything."

"That'll work. Should we head to the car?"

On the way toward Andersonville, I pulled into a Taco Bell near Wrigley Field and ordered at the drive-thru speaker.

"Just get me whatever you're getting," Lindsay said. "I trust your judgment."

Between bites of my Gordita, I managed to tell her about the weekend in Devil's Lake before we pulled down her street.

"Any chance of you coming in for a drink: wine, beer, water, cranberry juice?" she asked, her body language urging me to say 'yes.'

"I need to get home," I said, grinning and shaking my head. "I'm expecting a call."

"Okay, then," she said. "Thanks for spending part of the evening with me. And congratulations again on the Baxter deal. That's a big step for us."

I couldn't help but think her last sentence carried a double entendre, but I didn't pursue the issue. It was nearly 11 p.m. when I walked into the kitchen and looked at the oven clock. By the time I'd changed into shorts and a T-shirt, the telephone was ringing. My heart rate increased rapidly.

"Hi," Liza said.

"Hi."

"Did I wait too late to call?" she asked.

"No, not at all. Actually, I just got home and got changed."

"How did the meeting go?"

"Couldn't have gone smoother. We wrapped it up around nine, and then I hung out with one of the board members for a while. Did you have a working dinner this evening?"

"Sort of. Some coaches from the Southeastern Conference wanted to fill me in on some issues that are going on in their conference. Pretty interesting evening, as it turned out. But I don't want to talk about conferences or foundations tonight, okay?"

"Okay. What do you want to talk about?"

"Tell me more about you. Tell me about your first girlfriend or how you came out to your parents. You have come out to your parents, right?"

"Twenty-four years ago. I hope they're getting used to it by now."

"How did it come up? Did they ask or did you initiate?"

I carried the mobile phone upstairs and propped two pillows against the headboard of my bed, beginning the saga of that most memorable weekend. Liza asked for details on everything: where I was in my parents' house, how they were standing or sitting, what the first words were out of their mouths when I said the word 'homosexual' ... We laughed as I made the story much more comical than it was in reality. Nothing about that weekend 24 years ago was humorous. My family initially thought I'd fallen in with the "wrong crowd" at college and had been, in essence, brainwashed. They asked the family doctor to evaluate me and requested I visit with the preacher at their church. There were raised voices, crying, blame; there was little understanding. When retold, however, the story now made good material for a stand-up routine. That's what the years can do, dull the pain, just like Sarah said. Liza and I talked for more than an hour and when she mentioned we should think about going to sleep, I asked her if she was planning to beam herself to Chicago for the night.

"How I wish I could," she said. "Do you know how much I'd like to be there next to you right now?"

"I'm trying to imagine."

"Hold that thought for the next 34 hours, okay?"

That's about the time we would rendezvous at Denver International for our camping adventure.

"Is that it? Just 34 more hours? I might just make it."

I reached over and wrapped my hand around the travel alarm clock. I felt stupid getting ready to say what I was about to say, then I said it anyway.

"My fingers are touching the clock, so they're touching you, right?"

"Exactly."

Neither of us wanted to end the call, but it was getting late in Chicago.

"I'll be thinking about you," I told her.

"Me, too," she said. "Good night."

Thursday morning, the warm weather stepped aside for a comfortable, cool, overcast day. The first thing I did when I climbed off the bed was open the deck door. A refreshing breeze blew through the screen, causing my arm hair follicles to pucker like a recently plucked chicken. I walked to the dresser and pulled out a pale blue cotton sundress that I usually took on vacation to wear over my swimsuit. A hundred washings had worn the fiber to a softness comparable to the white tuft of a bunny's tail. The dress fell over my shoulders and draped freely around my thighs.

As I started down the stairs to make coffee, the telephone rang.

"You might last until tomorrow morning, but I'm not sure I will," the voice on the other end said. "I hope I didn't wake you."

"What are you doing awake at 5 o'clock in the morning?" I asked, turning to look at a clock.

"I actually had to make myself wait to call you," Liza said. "At 4:30 this morning, I woke up thinking about you and felt this need to hear your voice."

"Mmmm," I said, practically moaning with pleasure like someone had just set a slice of warm apple pie in front of me. "That's a nice thing to hear."

"So it's okay that I called?"

"Anytime," I assured her. "What's on your agenda for the rest of the day?"

"Meetings all morning," she said. "Lunch actually is a picnic about 20 minutes east of the city in an area that is known for its windsurfing. Our afternoon workshops all will be out there, so that might be fun."

"Will you be windsurfing?" I asked, half kidding.

"Ha! That would be a great workshop, but I don't think that's on the itinerary," she said, laughing. "I hope to try that sport some day, but it won't be on this trip. Do you know how to windsurf? Have you ever been?"

"No, I haven't, but I also want to try it sometime. Maybe that's something we can do for the first time together."

"That's just what I was thinking," Liza said. "What do you have going on the rest of the day?"

"Nothing in particular," I said. "I'll be in the office, probably on the phone with the folks at Baxter."

Thirty minutes into our conversation, I forced myself to think about getting ready to go to work. Liza and I created a plan for meeting at the Denver airport the next morning and, reluctantly, ended our call.

Since the weather forecast predicted temperatures remaining in the 70s all day, I packed a bag with my running shoes, shorts and a tank top. A run along the lakefront after work would help relieve some of the anxious energy that had been building all week. A little after 8 a.m., the telephone rang again.

"Good morning. It's Lindsay."

"Good morning," I said, curious why she might be calling so early in the morning. "Is everything okay?"

"Oh yeah, everything's fine," she said. "If you haven't had breakfast, I wondered if you'd meet me at Svea this morning. I'm taking the day off."

I checked my watch and quickly figured how long breakfast would take and what time I might arrive at the office. Lindsay's invitation was not out of the blue. We had discussed doing this the night we found out we lived only blocks from one another. Admittedly, I didn't think the invitation would come so quickly, but I wasn't surprised either.

"If we made it soon, I think I can swing it," I said. "I was just about ready to leave the house."

"Why don't I walk over to your place and we can walk to Svea together?" she suggested.

Lindsay didn't know that I don't invite "girlfriends" into this house. Well, except for Liza. Although I didn't consider Lindsay my "girlfriend," she had made her intentions quite clear.

"I'll be at the front steps watching for you in ten minutes," I said. "Does that give you enough time?"

"I can make it," she said. "See you soon."

After talking with Liza, I had exchanged my sundress for khaki summer-weight pants and an olive-colored, sleeveless golf shirt. Sitting in a wicker fan-backed chair on the front porch, I saw Lindsay walking up Farragut Street. She had her hair pulled back in a ponytail and I could see her dangling earrings dart back and forth as she neared me. Her baggy, off-white painter's pants and untucked blue scoop-neck shirt hid her physique, but she looked cute in the outfit.

"Hey there," she said, grinning as she reached the bottom of the steps. "I guess I called just in time, huh?"

"You almost missed me," I answered, getting up from the chair and starting toward the sidewalk. "I'm glad you called, though. I haven't been to Svea in quite a while and just thinking about it is making me very hungry."

"Good," she said, initiating the move toward Clark Street.

We claimed the last open table inside the small restaurant, packed with Andersonville regulars who frequented the place often enough that the wait staff could guess what they were going to order.

"Good morning, Lindsay," said a waitress, the front of her apron brushing my arm. "You're a little late this morning, aren't you?"

"Good morning, Val," she responded. "No, I'm actually taking the day off. This is Cate."

"Hi, Cate," Val said, finally looking my way. "Can I bring you both some coffee?"

Two affirmative responses sent Val toward the kitchen.

"I take it you eat here often," I said to Lindsay.

"Usually once a week, sometimes twice if I come in on the weekend," she said. "Val has been working here a long time. She remembers everybody."

Val returned with our coffee and a cream pitcher.

"Swedish pancakes with lingonberries?" she asked, smiling down at Lindsay.

"Too predictable, aren't I?" Lindsay said, looking over at me instead of at Val.

"I wouldn't say that," I answered, smirking. "I'll also have the Swedish pancakes."

I glanced up at Val to ensure she'd heard my order and, with a simple grin, she walked away. Lindsay and I simultaneously reached for the cream.

"You first," I insisted, pushing the small stainless pitcher toward her.

"I took after my father," she said, pouring a substantial amount of half 'n' half into her cup. "I drink a little coffee with my cream."

"And sugar?"

"No, I get enough sugar elsewhere in my diet."

"Did you leave me any?" I asked jokingly, looking into the pitcher. "So are you taking the day off for any particular reason or did you just need a break?"

"A friend asked me to go with her to the doctor this afternoon," she said, "so I decided to take the whole day."

"That's nice of you to go with her. It's none of my business, but is it anything serious?"

"We hope not," Lindsay said. "She's had some problems and the doctors are trying to figure out what's causing them. Hopefully, a few more tests will pin down the culprit."

"Since I reached my forties, I've seen a lot of my friends deal with all sorts of health issues: endometriosis, breast cancer, miscellaneous cysts … I guess all we can do is pay attention to our bodies and, if something goes wrong, catch the problem early."

"Yeah, it doesn't do any good to worry about it," Lindsay said. "We take care of ourselves and hope for the best. Any big weekend plans?"

I swallowed too fast and started coughing. I reached for my water glass and took an ample mouthful.

"Sorry about that," I said. "Some went down the wrong pipe. Yes, I'm going out of town tomorrow morning on a camping trip."

"Another camping trip?" Lindsay asked. "I never would have guessed you were such an avid outdoorswoman."

"I don't know if you could say I'm an avid outdoorswoman, but I do like to sleep in a tent and wake up in the morning someplace where I can't hear cars driving by or planes overhead. I have to say that it *is* unusual for me to be going camping two weekends in a row."

"Back to Wisconsin?" she asked.

Now I began feeling a tad uneasy, though it should have been no issue for me to tell her where I was going or who was meeting me at the Denver airport. I sipped my coffee and took my time responding to her question.

"I'm meeting *the woman* in Denver," I said, quickly looking up at her for a reaction.

"That qualifies as big weekend plans," she said, a big smile breaking across her face. "You'll have a great time."

Val was back at the tableside, placing identical plates of food in front of us.

"More coffee?" she asked.

"Please," each of us answered.

She brought a fresh, steaming pot to our table and filled both cups.

"You first this time," Lindsay said, handing the cream pitcher to me as if she was making an offering.

Those brown eyes were trying to work their magic, like a warm hand wrapped around M&M candies, attempting to dissolve the protective shell. She held the pitcher so that my fingers would have to brush hers as I took possession of the cream. I didn't say a word about it.

"Thank you," was my only response. "What are *you* doing this weekend?"

"I'll probably ride my bike to Belmont Rocks to watch the Air & Water Show one day," she said. "I might come back here for brunch, go to a movie, who knows?"

We found plenty to talk about while we ate, despite a mild awkwardness about our individual weekend plans. We had both finished eating and I was on a third cup of coffee when I checked my watch. It read 9:15 a.m., signaling me to get downtown.

"You need to go, right?" Lindsay asked, a tinge of disappointment in her voice that she did not try to hide.

"Yes, I do, but I'm really glad you invited me for breakfast."

Val identified our need to leave and rushed over with the bill. Lindsay snatched it from the table as soon as Val placed it there.

"My treat," she said, grinning. "It was my idea."

"I graciously accept," I said. "Thank you."

We were nearly back to my two-flat when Claire bolted out the front door. She glanced up the street and saw me coming.

"I'm running a bit late for work; could you tell?" she said, stopping at the bottom of the steps and waiting for us to reach her. "I was halfway to the office when I realized I'd forgotten the portfolio we're using for a presentation today, so I had to come back for it."

"Claire, this is Lindsay," I said, motioning with my head toward the blonde standing next to me. "Lindsay is on the board of A Sister's Hope."

"Breakfast meeting?" Claire asked.

"No, actually I live just a few blocks from here on Winona and hate eating in a restaurant by myself, so I asked Cate to join me this morning," Lindsay said. "She's not bad company."

As Lindsay made the "not bad company" comment, she ran her hand down my shoulder blade to my waist in a friendly, non-intrusive manner.

"Well, I know both of you have to get to work," she continued, "so I'm headed south. Claire, it was nice to meet you."

"Nice meeting you," Claire answered.

"Thanks again for breakfast," I said, opening my arms for a hug.

Lindsay took a step forward and embraced me, holding on a second or two longer than a traditional friendly hug. I was okay with that.

"Have a really fun weekend," she said, starting down the sidewalk. "I'll talk to you next week."

"Be careful at the Air & Water Show," I shouted to her. "If you see a plane wobbling, don't stay to watch!"

I could tell she was chuckling as she continued down Farragut.

"You have some very cute girlfriends," Claire said, raising her eyebrows at me.

"She's just a friend," I said.

"A single friend?" she asked.

"At the moment, yes."

"You go, girl," she said, continuing her insinuation.

"She's just a friend," I reiterated. "I don't know about you, but I need to get going. Drive carefully."

"Yes, Mom," Claire replied in her playful, sarcastic way.

I went into the house to get my briefcase and running gear bag, which I had left on the bed upstairs. As I grabbed the bag straps, my eyes fell on the alarm clock Liza had sent me.

"Tell me you're not feeling guilty about spending time with Lindsay," Sarah's voice said. Her tone was calm, not judgmental. "You've spent less than 24 hours in the same room with Liza. I know how you feel about her. I also know that spending time with Lindsay is good for you."

"How's that?" I asked.

"Cate, it's been a long time since you allowed someone to get as close to you as Liza has," she continued. "Lindsay puts Liza in perspective. Besides that, Lindsay seems like a wonderful woman, too. At this point, it's perfectly okay to have both of them in your life. You're a single woman, remember?"

"You make it sound so simple."

"Don't make it more difficult than it really is," she said. "If Liza is *the one*, your confusion about Lindsay will go away. In the meantime, I would enjoy the attention if I were you."

"I am, in case you hadn't noticed. Thanks for being here and being so rational."

"I'm here when you need me," she said. "You'd better get downtown."

As I suspected, most of the day was spent on the telephone with Cynthia Pruitt and Francois Courteau. I asked Cynthia about Leslie Carvalho, who she said had been out of the office all week.

"Is she all right?" I asked, recalling she was still undergoing chemotherapy treatments.

"I think she's doing very well, considering the circumstances," Cynthia said. "Leslie has put together such a dynamic team that she can work from home about half the time. Since several of our directors are located across the world, it's not unusual for our meetings to be conference calls. Honestly, we all think she's working too much, but that's for her to decide, not us."

"I'm guessing she prefers the normalcy in her life," I said. "When a woman is going through this, stability and routine help to keep her sane. When you next talk to her, please tell her I said hello, will you?"

"I certainly will, Cate," she said. "You know, you and I need to get together and look at some of the graphic pieces Francois's team and mine have designed incorporating your logo and Baxter's. Are you available tomorrow morning?"

"I'm flying out of town in the morning," I said, giving no details. "How about Monday?"

"I have a 9 o'clock appointment on Washington," she said. "Can we meet at the West Egg Café around 7:30?"

"It's a date."

"All right," she said. "Have a great weekend and I'll see you Monday morning."

The day dragged on. I'm sure it felt that way because I was ready to be in Denver. When 5:30 p.m. arrived, I changed into my running clothes and jogged to the lakefront. My instincts guided me north, toward Millenium Park and Buckingham Fountain. I stayed on the west side of Lake Shore Drive until I reached Monroe, then cut east and set my sights on Navy Pier. The constant cool breeze in my face invigorated me.

It was close to 6:30 p.m. by the time I got back to the office and gathered my things. I rushed home to finish packing, a project I'd been working on a little each day.

My backpack stuffed and sitting by the front door, I opted for a long, soaking bath, the patchouli candle melting down as it emitted an essence I find amazingly pleasing. As I lie there, my mind reviewed the packing list of all I wanted to take with me to Denver. The hot water relaxed me, but each time I envisioned seeing Liza at the airport, my heart began racing, flooding my body with excitement. I doubted I would get much sleep, anticipating the next morning's reunion. The water turned tepid, indicating my bath was over. I slowly stood up in the tub and pulled a thick white towel off the tiled edge, swaddling myself in the cotton. Double-checking my special clock to make sure the alarm was set properly, I shut off the lights and tried imagining scenes that calm me. Some scenario between floating in a pool and swinging in a shaded hammock must have worked; the next time I was coherent was 5:45 the next morning, the clock singing its wake-up call.

Chapter Seven

The sunset in Roosevelt National Forest Saturday night sent waves of tangerine and lavender across the sky. We parked the borrowed Subaru at a scenic overlook along the road, then laid a blanket on the ground next to the guardrail. Of the few cars passing by, some could have pulled in and spoiled our privacy, but none dared. So far on this trip, Liza had asked no questions about my past relationships. I followed suit, choosing to focus on the future. We could get by with that, at least for the weekend.

I called Wolley Cab Company as soon as I got up and requested a 7 a.m. ride to O'Hare. If my calculations were correct, I would be checking my baggage no later than 7:45 for a 9 a.m. flight. Although the airlines request that passengers arrive 90 minutes prior to departure, there are some unwarranted rules I simply can't follow. I took my coffee upstairs and sat on the side of the bed, carefully sipping while I contemplated the three days ahead. As if she felt me summoning her, Sarah's voice whispered behind me.

"Colorado is beautiful in the fall," she said.

Vividly colorful memories of a mountain biking trip we had taken the first year we were together flashed through my mind. Riding the frigid rapids of the Cache de la Poudre River in a guided, oversized rubber raft had added further adventure to our trip. We both loved the Rocky Mountains, the majesty they add to the terrain and the challenges they present to hikers, bikers, rock climbers … nature lovers from many walks of life.

"What are you feeling right now?" Sarah asked.

"I thought you always know what I'm feeling," I responded, avoiding a direct answer.

"I generally have a fairly accurate idea," she said, "but you fool me sometimes."

She obviously recognized my attempt to cloak the self-doubt and anxiety welling up inside me.

"You may not always know what I'm feeling, but you always have known how to pry open my head," I acknowledged. "How *do* you do that? Honestly, I'm afraid of this weekend, afraid of being disappointed or overwhelmed. I'm afraid of how Liza's going to respond when I tell her about you."

My face suddenly felt warm and flush. I caught the knot forming in my throat and began untying it mentally.

"Actually, this nervousness is a good thing, right?" I asked, not giving Sarah time to answer. "It's normal. It means I truly do care about her."

"And it reminds you that you didn't die when I did," Sarah said, her voice delivering those words as if she were tiptoeing into a sleeping infant's room.

Silence surrounded me.

Perhaps Sarah was waiting for me to speak, but my tongue lay still.

"Cate, you are so full of love. I think you'd better start letting some out or you're going to burst."

Sarah practically was giggling as she finished that sentence. She regularly teased me during our early years together about my persistent show of affection, physically and verbally. I insisted that the feelings had to be expressed or I would "burst."

"Very clever," I responded, giving a half-hearted laugh. "Using my own words against me."

"I'm not using them against you, Cate. You know that. All I'm saying is open the flood gates and let the love flow."

I tipped the last swallow of coffee into my mouth, sat the cup on my nightstand and headed toward the shower.

"Right now, the shower is what's going to flow. I have legs to shave and a plane to catch. Shall we continue this conversation in the bathroom?"

As I proceeded to get ready, keeping an eye on the clock as it neared 7 a.m., Sarah's encouraging words trailed after me … into the closet, down to the kitchen, back upstairs to the bedroom as I chose a favorite pair of Patricia Locke earrings to wear on the plane. At 6:56, a taxicab rolled to a stop in front of my two-flat.

"Your being here this morning soothed some of my anxieties," I said. "But you already knew that, didn't you?"

Sarah did not respond and I assumed I was alone, lifting my backpack to my knee and swinging it over my right shoulder. I slipped my left arm through the strap and readjusted how the pack was situated against my lower back. Reaching for the house keys on the window ledge, I drew in a deep breath.

"You're going to have a beautiful time." Sarah's words filled the entryway. "I just know it."

A smile overcame my concentrating face as I locked the door behind me and walked down the steps toward my ride.

Flight attendants passed through the aisles collecting empty beverage cups and reminding those who had reclined their seats to return them to the upright position in preparation for landing at Denver International Airport. I glanced at my watch and decided to set it back an hour to mountain time. It looked like we'd be landing early, which was ideal for me because I might be able to make it to Liza's gate before her flight arrived. A brief vision of her coming out of the passenger walkway and seeing me there, waiting for her, awakened the butterflies in my stomach.

Although my aisle seat was on row 22, it seemed I was off the plane in seconds and standing at Liza's America West gate just a few minutes later. I would postpone claiming my bag until my camping companion and I reunited. A medium-sized jet rolled down the tarmac toward me, then made a sharp left turn toward the airline employee waving his small orange flags in a directional fashion, guiding the pilot toward the appropriate berth. The nose of the plane came toward the gate where I stood. My heartbeat began to sprint. Middle-aged men began filing out of the walkway. Then, like a yellow daisy shining in a field of Texas bluebonnets, Liza emerged.

No longer could I hear conversation around me or intercom announcements overhead. Just as I was mesmerized by her appearance that night at the Fairmont, I could not take my eyes off her now. Since she was not expecting me to be at her gate, I suspected she would head directly toward our pre-arranged meeting spot at the main terminal, so I started toward her. Before I had taken a second step, she veered away from the line of passengers trailing behind her and turned my way, her eyes locking on to me as if she was expecting me all along. I stopped, trapped in a pleasing trance, while the rest of the world twirled around me like a colorful mobile above an infant's bed. Liza raised the brow above her left eye, silently inviting me to approach her. My body again began to move, somehow maneuvering through the waiting crowd, and when I reached her, the magnetism drew us into a powerful embrace. Her right arm went over my shoulder and that hand cupped the back of my neck, her warm palm pressed against my skin. The fulfillment and comfort I experienced at that moment felt wonderfully familiar, though Liza and I had spent so few hours together.

"I missed you," Liza said, her words coming out in a breathy whisper.

"Mmmm," I responded, squeezing her tighter. "Can you tell I feel the same?"

My eyes were closed and my right cheek rubbed against her ear and dark hair. The sweet scent of her perfume curled around my nose.

"Let's get out of here," she said, releasing her grip on me. As she backed away, a few strands of her hair lightly tugged on my earring.

This time, my eyes captured hers. Slightly cocking her head, Liza's look questioned me. I knew she wondered why I wasn't moving, why my gaze was so intense. I had waited nearly two weeks for this moment. As gently as a butterfly lights on a flower, my lips met the warmth of Liza's. The kiss was brief. A tease. A promise.

We exchanged grins with one another all the way to baggage claim, talking sporadically, walking mostly without conversation. When I noticed an attractive female about our age whose legs gave her away as a master cyclist, waving at us, Liza was oblivious.

"Is that your friend Julie?" I asked, nodding my head toward the woman.

Liza's face illuminated when she saw her.

"Oh, my God! I totally forgot you were meeting us!" she said, shouting toward Julie.

"It's great to see you, too," Julie answered sarcastically. She threw open her tan arms and engulfed Liza in a formal Colorado hug.

"Julie, this is Cate," Liza said, pulling away from Julie and stepping over to me. Liza lightly touched the back of my upper arm as if to alert me she was again within reach.

"Cate, I've heard more about you in the past two weeks than Liza talked about her past seven lovers combined," Julie said, making herself chuckle.

106

"Okay, Julie," Liza said. "You're not allowed to say anything else until we're in the presence of Sue. She's the only one who can control you."

Their bantering confirmed the long-term friendship between them. Liza quickly changed the subject to questions about mutual friends, some of whom lived near Vail, and another couple who both teach at Colorado State University in Fort Collins. Liza seemed to have friends everywhere. I suddenly had a recollection of the black-tie dinner and how Liza knew more people within the Foundation than I did. My half-laugh, simply a reflex from the thoughts passing through, caught Liza's attention.

"And what are you snickering to yourself about?" she asked. "You're thinking I probably never shut up when I'm with my friends, aren't you?"

Julie couldn't pass up the opportunity.

"That didn't take her long to figure out!" the Coloradoan blurted, forgetting the probation rules Liza had set minutes earlier.

"Actually, I was thinking about the night we met," I said, dipping my head a bit as I looked directly at Liza, smiling. "But since you brought it up, are you always this chatty with your friends or is Julie a bad influence?"

I had succeeded in nailing both of them with my question. They actually were speechless – for a moment, anyway.

"Julie's definitely a bad influence," Liza retorted. "Always has been."

"Always will be," Julie chimed in as she slid behind the steering wheel of the Subaru.

We headed west on I-70, soon passing downtown with the Rocky Mountains stretching before us. Julie and Sue lived on the near northwest side of Denver, not too far from Mile High Stadium and historic Union Station. As we neared their neighborhood, my curiosity about Sue escalated. High energy was needed, I imagined, to keep pace with Julie. We pulled into their driveway and parked behind a dark blue Ford Explorer, a late-90s model.

"Sue beat us here," Julie said, already stepping out of the car. She began warning me that their dog, Cappie, would single me out as the stranger in the group when we entered the house, but that I was not to be frightened. At age 11, Cappie was well past her psycho years of harassing newcomers. Julie reached for the glass storm door, but it swung out toward her before she'd touched the handle.

"Hello!" an excited voice called as a woman charged out the door, taking the shortest route to Liza. Sue, an emergency room doctor, looked as fit as Julie, though her thighs were not those of a cyclist. Nylon canoe shorts gaped around the top of her legs, but her curved hamstrings and diamond-cut calf muscles were proof of her fitness level. Though long, there was nothing lanky about her arms. Either she does a lot of lifting in the hospital or she exercises her upper body in other ways. Feeling like I was caught admiring her physique, Liza finished hugging Sue and, still holding her hand like a tight grip in "Red Rover, Red Rover," pulled her along the sidewalk until they were mere inches from me.

"Isn't she gorgeous?" Liza said. I first thought she was asking me about her friend Sue.

"Exactly as you described her," Sue answered, moving toward me for a hug. "Cate, it's so good to meet you."

We went inside and, as accurately warned, Cappie sauntered into the living room and kissed my bare leg with her investigating wet nose.

"Good girl, Cappie," Julie laughed. "Cate, if you don't like strange dogs sniffing around on you, we can put her in the bedroom."

Liza and Sue's conversation paused about the same time, leaving the room completely quiet while Julie awaited my reply.

"No, she's fine. I love dogs, particularly Siberian Huskies," I said, allowing Cappie to smell the back of my hand, then stretching my fingers to scratch just behind her ears. "Where did her name originate?"

"Sue *and* Cappie were born in late December, making them Capricorns," Julie answered. "We sort of played around with that and came up with the name. We think it's cute."

"I would agree," I said.

Sue took charge in the kitchen, asking Liza to grab dishes from the cabinet and set the table. It was obvious Liza had spent quite a bit of time in this home. She didn't have to hunt for anything. Sue and Julie did not strike me as the Fiesta dinnerware types, but Liza pulled a variety of pastel, cobalt and cinnamon-colored bowls and plates from the maple cabinets and placed the menagerie on what looked like an old butcher's table in the dining room.

"How do you like your Fiestaware?" I asked, making pointless conversation.

"They do what they're supposed to," Sue answered, starting to laugh. "Go ahead, Jules. I know there's something you want to say."

"Thank you, dear," Julie said. "Cate, we have Fiestaware because Sue's sister overheard us talking about getting new dishes a couple of years ago when we were with her family for Thanksgiving. She decided to surprise us that Christmas and the family all went together and got us a complete set."

"That's great," I said, still uncertain why Sue was laughing.

"It is?" Julie asked. "Would you like our Fiestaware?"

I was catching on.

"We had found an incredible ceramics artist in Santa Fe and we were contemplating having a set custom-made," Sue said, dropping a wad of sprouts onto a sandwich. "It was really sweet of my family to do what they did, but the dishes weren't exactly what we had in mind. We didn't *need* new dishes to begin with; they just overheard us having that discussion and, voila, we have Fiestaware!"

Julie and Liza joined Sue's laughter and I found myself entertained by watching the three of them.

"We've gotten a lot of funny looks from our friends when they first see it because they know our style is more the campfire blue tin dinnerware or a mish-mash of ceramic pieces we've picked up over the years," Julie explained. "Don't misunderstand, we both actually really like Fiestaware, but we just wouldn't have picked it for our home."

"So why do you keep it?" I innocently asked.

Sue and Julie's eyes met. They both grinned.

"Sue's family was so proud of themselves for coming up with that gift," Julie said. "And although we have been together for eighteen years, it has taken a long time for some family members to fully accept our relationship. So, we're keeping the Fiestaware. Right, honey?"

Sue didn't answer aloud, but nodded her head in agreement while walking toward the table with two full plates. Liza followed her with two soup cups. They each made one more trip between the kitchen counter and dining table, then Sue summoned Julie and me.

"Consider the dinner bell rung," Sue said, claiming the chair nearest the kitchen.

In front of me rested a mint green cup of yellow tomato gazpacho, large flecks of fresh cilantro floating on top. Veggie sandwiches on nutty, grainy bread crowded the sliced kiwi and banana fruit composition on my plate.

"Tell me you eat this healthy every day," I said, looking first at Sue, then over to Liza for a facial response.

"Yeah, pretty much," Julie said, nodding her head. "Sue does a lot of the creative cooking. I'm the shopper and simple-meal chef."

"That's impressive," I said. "Most people think it's too much trouble, too time-consuming to plan healthy meals."

"Most people don't take good enough care of themselves," Sue said, smiling before taking a sizeable bite out of her sandwich.

"They are constantly harping on me to pay more attention to what I eat," Liza said to me, knowing she was about to get a response from one or both of her pals.

"It's only because we love you, Liza," Sue said, rising from her chair. "Can I get anyone more water?"

Lunch lasted only 30 minutes, but the edibles and conversation were satiating.

"Let's sit outside for a while," Julie said, coercing us to stay and talk a little longer. "We don't get to see you often enough, Liza, and Cate, we have a lot of questions for you."

"*Julie* might have a lot of questions for you," Sue quickly added. "She has a tendency to say 'we' when she really means 'I.' Would anyone like hot tea? I'm making some for myself."

Liza and I both accepted the offer. Within a few minutes, Sue entered the backyard with a boysenberry-colored Fiestaware plate piled full of oatmeal, raisin and walnut cookies.

"Moosewood Cookbook recipe?" I asked as she sat them on a teak TV tray next to me.

"You guessed it," Sue replied. "Do you have some of Mollie Katzen's cookbooks?"

"Only two, so far," I said, "and I love just about everything I've tried in them."

The four of us found plenty to discuss, including Julie's interrogation into my past, my interests, my aspirations. When she would delve too closely into the relationship category, I successfully steered her in another direction. I wasn't about to tell Liza about Sarah while sitting in the company of two women I'd just met. Liza blatantly checked her watch.

"I know," Julie said. "You think you need to leave now."

Liza chortled. "You know I'd rather stay here and spend the entire weekend with you, don't you Julie?"

"Sure, uh-huh," she answered, looking toward me in some sort of acknowledgement.

Liza got up from her chair and held her hand out to me, escorting me out of my chair as if she had just asked me to dance. We hugged our hostesses, thanking them for a tremendous lunch, and passed back through the house to exit from the front. Julie walked behind us carrying a large forest green and white cooler. She shuffled a few things in the back of the Subaru and slid the cooler into an opening.

"I think you're going to like what you find in here," she said, patting the top of the cooler.

"Do we need to stop and get ice or anything?" Liza asked.

"Nope, you're all set," Sue assured her. "Cate, it was a pleasure to meet you. We'll see you on Sunday."

We packed ourselves into the Subaru and drove away, waving to Liza's friends. An anxious nervousness crept through my body again, accelerated when Liza reached over and laid her hand on my lower thigh. Liza drove north, then west on Highway 36 toward Boulder. About a half-hour into our trip, I had a perfectly clear view of the Flatirons, the cluster of flat-faced rock formations that are part of what draws rock climbers from all over the country to the edge of Boulder. Our conversation had evolved (or digressed) from Liza describing her Oregon outings to what I was like in elementary school.

"Are you serious?" I asked, squeezing the hand that still rested on my thigh.

"Yes!" Liza exclaimed. "I want to hear about the parts of your life I've missed out on … all of it."

Although she was driving, her eyes managed to secure mine into a brief staredown, encouraging me to answer her question.

Childhood background material would be safe conversation. I could stop my revelations somewhere around age 24. Talking about past lovers and relationships would have to wait until we were out of the car, in a private place, at a time when we could be looking at each other.

"I can see you now," Liza said, "dashing around the track with a fierce, determined look on your face."

I was telling her about my days in Amateur Athletic Union (AAU) track and field, the weekends mom spent hauling her three daughters and several other kids to out-of-town meets. The coach had started me out as a sprinter, but soon identified my potential as a quarter-miler – the 440-yard dash, as they referred to it back then.

"Those are some great memories for me," I said, looking out the car window to my right, witnessing how Boulder had joined the rest of urban America with its own Home Depot. "Okay, I believe it's your turn."

"What d'ya want to know?" Liza asked. I got a profile look this time of her brilliant smile.

"Where were you raised?"

"How much time do I get to answer that?" she replied.

"Moved around a lot, huh?"

"Quite a bit," she answered, slowly rocking her chin up and down. "My parents both were in the Navy. That's where they met. We lived in Maryland, Texas, Florida, California, Hawaii, England and, very briefly, Colorado, which is where my mom's parents were living when she had daughter No. 4."

"Wow," was all I could think to say at first. Once my mind had absorbed everything my ears had just heard, I requested more detail. "*Both* parents were in the Navy. That seems unusual, particularly when there are four children involved. Why did you have to move so often?"

Liza explained how her parents each were specialists in their own fractioned pod of the United States Navy, making them intrinsically valuable to naval bases everywhere. Because they were willing to relocate when needed, her parents earned even greater respect among the military patriarchy.

"What were their specialties?" I asked.

"I think that's *still* classified information," she said, smiling, but her vague answer was closure on that topic. "It wasn't that bad, really. I have some truly wonderful friends all over the world and that's solely because of the childhood my sisters and I had. Kids of military families in which both parents are on active duty are sort of a subculture. We developed strong ties with one another in a short period of time. We all needed friends we could trust and we never knew how long any of us would be in one location, so it was like an unspoken code: assume you could trust each other from the start without having to prove it first. Every once in a while, someone would violate the code. They had a hard time from then on, wherever they went."

As I learned more about Liza's adolescence, my picture of her took on more colors. The oldest of four girls, Liza spoke with motherly instinct about her little sisters, the way they took wildly imagined adventures without leaving the confines of their fenced-in yard. In true Navy form, Admiral Liza appointed her sisters captain, commander and lieutenant commander. They'd sit in a circle on the linoleum kitchen floor, planning an attack on enemy vessels or discussing the possibility of spies within the ranks. They also played with their Barbie dolls, baked cookies and challenged each other at "Queen of the Mountain." Babysitters most often were Naval officers' wives, women who lived in a world of black and white. In other words, there was no negotiating with them in any shade of gray on any topic. Rules were rules.

"Except for one woman who watched us when we lived in London," Liza said, starting to grin. "She was raised in N'Orleans, the daughter of a U.S. Congressman, and the world in her eyes was everything *but* black and white. Abby Hebert Henderson. She could make us laugh while we were washing dishes or raking leaves or doing homework. If one of us would do something we knew we weren't supposed to do, she'd call all four of us together and we'd have a forum about why the wrong-doer would do such a thing. It's my earliest recollection of peer review."

We both laughed.

"She also made it crystal clear to me that my sisters would be looking to me as a role model, regardless of how I felt about that responsibility. I could become whatever or whomever I choose, she'd say, but always remember there are three pairs of precious eyes watching me, learning from me."

"That's a heavy burden for a young girl," I said. "How did you feel about that?"

"Honestly," she said, "I liked it. And I think it helped me make the right decision sometimes when I was faced with the temptation to do things I shouldn't be doing."

"Are you emotionally close to all your sisters?" I asked.

"I am now," she answered, then paused. "Over the years, there certainly have been times when we were on opposite ends of the spectrum on certain issues."

"Was your being gay one of those issues?" I asked.

"Actually, they were fine with that," she said. "I was never a person to make drastic changes in my actions or how I dressed – never tried the 'radical dyke' scene, for example – so nothing about me has really caught them off-guard. When I *finally* started dating, it was never an issue. The family would meet whoever my date might be and carry on like it was perfectly normal for me to be introducing a woman instead of a man."

"You mean you never formally 'came out' to them?" was my next question, asked in near amazement. "I imagined this conservative military household where 'gay' was a dirty word."

My comment tickled Liza.

"*Disrespect* was the dirty word in our house," she said. "And that included our parents showing disrespect toward us girls. I worked hard to make my parents proud of me AND to be a good example to my sisters. I would have been gravely disappointed had they acted any differently than they did."

Every gay child should be so lucky, I thought to myself. As Liza talked more about her mother and father, sisters, Abby from New Orleans and Liza's sluggish progression toward intimacy, the fascinating puzzle of her character began falling into place. Her family's frequent moving had taught her to build friendships that could withstand the challenges of distance, time apart and change. Bene, for example, a grade school pal, has remained in contact with Liza despite the split paths their lives took. (Bene married a Republican accountant, has three kids and lives in Nashua, New Hampshire.) High school cross-country teammate Lisa married a computer geek who struck gold starting a dotcom, then divorced him when she discovered he actually *believed* rich men were entitled to more than one woman. Lisa introduced him to the phrase "took him

114

to the cleaners" and now is taking glass-blowing lessons in Santa Fe. She keeps a home in Laguna Beach, CA.

Past girlfriends – the intimate kind – were not mentioned that day, which was good because I was not quite ready to broach the topic.

We passed road signs for Peaceful Valley, then Ferncliff. Imagery of living in small towns with those names claimed my thoughts for a moment. As we continued north on a scenic route that leads along the eastern edge of Rocky Mountain National Park, Liza said we were getting close to the campground she had in mind. I reached over and lightly brushed back the hair hanging between her right cheek and me, exposing her angular jaw. My fingertips continued to the nape of her neck, and the silky dark strands now completely draped the back of my hand. Liza's eyes stayed focused on the road while I sat in my passenger seat watching her, my eyes tracing the length of her forehead, around her nose and lips. I loved looking at this woman. I had the urge to snuggle up next to her like I might if we were sitting in the bleachers watching a football game on a cold fall night. Refraining from doing so might ensure safer driving, I thought, so I stayed on my side of the Subaru and enjoyed my view.

"You're missing the scenery," Liza eventually said, grinning as she spoke.

"No, I'm not," I answered.

The park campground Liza had chosen looked small – few enough sites that there was no staffed office where we would check in. The protocol was to drive through the area, find a campsite we liked that was not already occupied and that did not bear a "reserved" sign at its entrance, set up the tent and then return to the help-yourself paying station to fill out our registration form. Rolling slowly through the campground, we passed a couple of sites where people were in the process of pitching tents, and other sites where it appeared the campers had settled in a few days earlier, their shirts and socks dangling from thin string pulled taut between two trees. Liza lightly applied the brakes and started pulling into a site marked "reserved."

"This is our spot, if it meets your approval," she said, turning off the ignition.

Trees blocked our view of the Rocky Mountains and I couldn't initially determine where a tent would comfortably rest without first clearing some brush.

"Come on," Liza said, looking over at me before getting out of the car.

A few steps away, she reached out to me with her right hand. I grabbed it with my left and immediately felt the warmth of her fingers wrap around the back of my hand. A lightly worn trail emerged before us. Liza led me several yards past the brush, then made a hairpin turn that took us behind the aspens. One more sharp turn led us to an opening that left me breathless. Like an Omnimax theater screen, the white-capped mountains rose in front of me with a pale blue sky and its cloudy patches wrapping above my head and to my sides.

"Unbelievable!" I uttered.

Still holding my hand, Liza pulled me into her and began kissing me, tenderly until passion poured through both of us. My chest pounded and I pressed my body as close to Liza's as I could get. She ran the palms of her hands along my cheeks, to the back of my head and down my shoulders, never taking her mouth away from mine. Somehow – it's still a mystery to me – I soon found myself lying on top of her on a bed of golden leaves, consumed by her affection. We carried on in our own little world, unconcerned with inhibitions.

"Right now I feel like I'm 23 instead of 43," Liza said, her voice easing into the silence.

My head rested on her shoulder, my arm draped across her abdomen and my inner thigh remained snugly against her leg.

"Is there an instant replay button I can press?" I asked.

As we both laughed, our bodies finally realized the lightly cushioned ground was beginning to feel more like concrete.

"Should we set up the tent, then go for a hike or something?" Liza suggested.

"Sounds like a plan," I answered, prying myself away from her.

Julie and Sue's tent added a golden splash with a hint of purple on the rain fly to our campsite. Easy to erect, we had the tent up and full of sleeping bags and pads in no time. When I lifted my backpack out of the car, the idea occurred to me that maybe I had packed a bit too much for such a short trip. I hadn't noticed until Liza dragged her purple and teal Osprey Finesse pack from the back of the car that it was identical to Sarah's climbing gear pack. A twinge darted through my stomach. When Liza began describing our hiking options, I forgot all about the Osprey.

We chose a five-mile trail that left from a trailhead in our campground and involved a variety of elevations, nothing strenuous enough though to make us feel like we were on a Stairmaster. We were here for enjoyment, not a workout. With a goal of returning to camp by 6 p.m., we readied ourselves for the hike and headed out. Exposed tree roots and a multitude of mushrooms added a graphic dimension to the path, periodically intriguing me enough to stop and take a closer look. Liza was amused by my interest in such simple gifts of nature.

"I'll bet when your parents took you to a museum, you dawdled for hours," she said.

"Dawdled implies I was wasting time," I playfully corrected her. "We didn't go to museums too often, but I definitely linger longer than a lot of folks."

We crossed the path of several hikers who had gotten an earlier start than we did and exchanged an obligatory greeting with most of them. While we were taking a water break at a spectacular vista right along the trail, a man and woman cautiously approached us.

"Are you Liza, a friend of Sue and Julie's?" the man asked, directing his question to my companion.

"Yes, hi, how are you?" she answered, stepping toward them. "I met you at their Christmas party last year, didn't I? I'm sorry, though, I've forgotten your names."

"That's all right," the woman said. "I'm Colleen. We remembered your name was Liza because you were the only person we didn't already know that night."

"That works," Liza said.

"And I'm Colin," the man said, initiating a handshake.

"How could I have forgotten your names?" Liza said, starting to laugh. "When I met you that night, I remember thinking 'Colin and Colleen are a couple. I won't forget that.' Obviously, that mnemonic device didn't work."

"I work with Sue at the hospital," Colin said.

"I *do* remember that," Liza answered.

"And I keep tabs on Julie while Sue's at work," Colleen said, making all four of us chuckle. "Actually, we cycle together quite a bit. She really pushes me and I need that on long rides."

"I'm glad to hear someone's keeping tabs on her," Liza said. "Sue needs all the help she can get in that area. Let me introduce you to Cate. She met Julie and Sue for the first time today when they fed us lunch."

Both of them shook my hand.

"Are any ER docs working today?" Liza continued.

Colin grinned. "It's unusual for Sue and me to have the same day off, but yeah, I think they have us covered."

"I can't believe we ran into each other here," Liza said. "That's too wild."

"Sue told me about this place," Colin said, "and we've been up here a couple of times this summer."

"That explains it," Liza replied. "The entire hospital staff will be hiking up here before long."

Our conversation lapsed.

"We should let you guys continue your hike," Colleen said. "Have you been on this one before? You're about halfway in if you started at Margo's Passage."

"That's good to know," Liza said. "You're right, then, we should get going. It was great running into you. Thanks for coming up to us."

"We really enjoyed meeting you at Christmas and hoped we would get to see you again sometime," Colin said. "Sue and Julie think a lot of you."

"That's nice to hear," she replied. "Take care. Maybe we'll see you over the holidays."

Another chalk mark in the "positive traits" category for Liza, though I truly wasn't keeping a tally. As we traipsed on, I learned how much Liza adored Colorado and heard colorful stories of vacations visiting her maternal grandparents when they lived on the south side of Boulder. Back at our campsite, the stories continued.

"My grandmother couldn't sit still," Liza said. "When I was six or seven – we girls and Mom were living with them at the time – Gramma would dress me in a pair of blue jeans and a sweatshirt and tell Mom we'd be back in a little while. She took me hiking all around the Flatirons and, when I couldn't walk anymore, she carried me."

"Is she still alive?"

"No. She passed away three years ago."

"I'm sorry."

"Me too. I miss her a lot. What about you? Are any of your grandparents still living?"

Family tales unraveled through dinner and into evening as we rocked in our camp chairs near the soothing fire. Finally, at a pause in that conversation, I asked Liza how often she had camped at this spot. She peered at me and let loose one of those smiles.

"I've never camped here before and I've never done *that,* not out in the open air, anyway, in a national forest," she answered. "When Julie, Sue and I were scouting around last summer, we found this place. We were just driving around, exploring. I think they've camped here and I've been wanting to come back ever since I saw it."

"So that's something we both did for the first time together," I said, leaning over to lightly kiss her. I felt we were headed for a second similar experience and coaxed her into the tent.

When we emerged, later, to brush our teeth and visit the pit toilet nearest our site, the tangerine coals were fading. Liza dumped dirt over everything orange to smother the fire, then followed me back into the tent. Both of us lying completely still, we could hear chipmunks scurrying around under the trees. That hypnotizing "whisp" of the wind passing through the treetops eventually sang us to sleep.

Once we'd finished coffee and hot oatmeal the next morning, we took off on foot to further explore the trails in our area, taking with us sandwiches and snacks Julie graciously had prepared. The weather could not have been more perfect, the midday temperatures peaking near 80 degrees, I guessed, and overnight lows dropping to around 50. Our campground included a shower house that Liza and I were anxious to try out Saturday afternoon, complete with individual shower rooms, each accessed by its own door. That made it possible for us to share without imposing on strangers. My soapy hands ran along Liza's arms, her neck and breasts. I moved slowly along the rest of her body, studying every inch of her beauty. When I awoke the next morning, it was from a dream in which we were still standing in the steam of that shower.

Those were the first two weeks of our relationship.

Chapter Eight

Vulnerability and letting go of the past are mental battles I have fought for years, yet this woman rolled her Trojan Horse inside my world and I felt safe and finally began fully living in the moment..

"Why don't we take a cab to my place," Liza said, "then I can drive you home."

We walked out of O'Hare's baggage claim and got in line at a taxi stand. When she told the Wolley cab driver we were going to the St. Ben's area, his demeanor transitioned to overly pleasant.

"Very nice neighborhood," he said, his thick Middle Eastern accent causing us to strain to dissect his comment.

Settled into the backseat for the half-hour ride, I reached over to lay my hand on Liza's leg, my pinky resting against her hip bone. This was one of those cabs designed for high-crime areas with a sliding bullet-proof window between the driver and us, though the window remained open during our trip. I guessed he couldn't see my hand. It was a muggy August evening in Chicago, high humidity and heat oozing back into the air from the city's plethora of pavement. The crowded Kennedy Expressway unrolled toward the downtown skyline as we neared the Irving Park Road exit, our driver maneuvering to the far-right lane.

"You sisters?" he asked, after probably spending the first 20 minutes trying to guess the connection between us.

Needless to say, Liza and I look nothing alike. Different facial features, different hair color, different physiques …

"Yes," Liza blurted out, keeping a straight face. "We're twins, but she's older than I am by several minutes."

"Several," I added.

Liza directed him down Hamilton and, once he'd pulled away, I stared at her until she looked over to me. We burst into laughter without another word. The "twins" topic came up again on the way to my place.

"You see?" Liza began. "We're already starting to look like each other."

Luckily, we found a vacant parking spot not far from the two-flat – a rare find on a Sunday evening. When Liza and I reached the front porch, I glanced into Amy and Claire's living room where Amy sat on the couch reading. She looked up and smiled at me as we passed. I knew she'd be anxious to grill me for information tomorrow, but tonight she simply winked and went back to her book.

This was Liza's second visit to Farragut and I was a little nervous about more detailed questions she might ask about the place. Soon, I needed to talk with her about Sarah. Soon.

Once we were inside my place, I dropped my backpack in the office, out of the way. We both left our sandals by the door.

"Are you hungry?" I asked.

"Yeah, a little bit," Liza answered. "Can we have something delivered?"

I smiled.

"That was going to be my suggestion," I said. "How does Thai sound?"

The restaurant from which I order on North Clark Street celebrates the widespread reputation of fast delivery; a main reason, no doubt, they thrive in Andersonville. Our stomachs full of pad woon sen and pad thai, we gave up our dining chairs for the living room couch.

"I should go home and unpack," Liza said, sitting to my left, facing me, "but can I stay a while?"

"I'd like that."

What we talked about, I don't specifically remember. What I *do* remember is consciously keeping the conversation on the present, further delaying a discussion about past lovers and my current relationship with Sarah. I felt a bit guilty, but I knew I had to be in the proper frame of mind when that inevitable topic came up. Now was not the time. We both were tired from the camping and traveling, so my guilt began to subside.

"I have an idea," I said.

"Let's hear it," Liza replied, her bright eyes showing a little fatigue from the past two weeks.

"How would you feel about a long soak in a hot tub?"

"I want to explore that feeling," she said, grinning while she arose from the couch and pulled me with her.

122

Although it had been my idea, Liza carried on as if we were in her home, leading me upstairs into my bedroom. We walked hand in hand toward the Jacuzzi, then I let go to lean over and turn on the water. Liza immediately lit the patchouli candle and pulled two plum-colored bath towels from a shelf, setting them near the tub. I pushed the bathroom door closed so that the room would get warmer. Steam began clouding the large mirror above the sink and, as Liza pushed her shorts down over her hips, I watched the foggy reflection instead of looking directly at her. It was almost surreal. She slowly, seductively, lifted her shirt and pulled it off, dropping it on the tile floor. This was my cue. I started to take off my shorts, but Liza came toward me and took over that responsibility. Her hands were warm and smooth trailing down my legs. My shorts now on the floor, her palms followed the slight contour of my calves and hamstrings, then ran along the sides of my torso as she removed my shirt. She carefully slid her fingers under the elastic of my athletic bra and gently lifted it over my breasts and head.

"Should we get in?" she asked, lightly kissing me, dropping my pale blue bra onto the white bath rug.

The water was on the cusp of being too hot, but we eased in and immersed ourselves up to our necks. Liza scooted around until her back was toward me, then reclined so that the low of her back brushed along my pubic bone. Her head laid back, cradled in the curve between my clavicle and shoulder, and her cheekbone rested against my jaw. When I was certain my hands had warmed, I wrapped my arms around her with my hands settling on her abdomen. Liza's firm stomach was the envy of women in their 40s, maybe even most in their 30s, I imagined. She swore genetics was the reason she stayed lean, though I already knew she regularly ran and frequented a gym. My body definitely was less fit – thin, but not firm like Liza's. Sitting in the tub, the skin on my stomach folded into shallow creases like lifelines on the palm of my hand.

I reached for the bar of sandalwood soap and lathered my hands. Liza remained still as I first caressed her neck and shoulders, then curled my fingers under her arms.

"You know that tickles, right?" she asked.

"I thought it might."

I again lathered my hands, this time letting them slope down her chest and over her breasts, the hardness of her nipples stimulating the center of my palm. With that, our bathing became love-making, touching each other and entwining our bodies in ways I'd forgotten, in some ways I'd never known. The combination of heat from our bodies and the water made me wish I'd left the bathroom door open. At one point, I finally stood up and Liza followed. We stepped out of the tub, water running down our bodies onto the bath mat and bra. Liza continued touching me, exciting me. I glanced toward the sink and caught the reflection of our bodies in an area of the mirror that had not steamed up. Intimacy with Liza that first night had reawakened me to those carnal feelings and her spontaneity in Colorado enhanced each sexual experience, but this intensity went beyond that. Her touch, her kisses, her body dancing against mine worked like an orchestra's crescendo. Liza's body shuddered within seconds after mine and I smiled, realizing she also reached orgasm. We stood there, tightly holding each other.

"Look," I said softly, motioning with my eyes toward the mirror.

Liza loosened her hold on me and looked back that way.

"I want your view the next time," she said, chuckling. "There will be a next time, right?"

"One can only hope," I replied, pulling her back into an embrace.

We knew it was getting late and Liza was intent on unpacking at her house. I completely understood. She'd been out of town for two weeks and, despite how desperately we wanted to fall asleep next to each other, she had things to take care of at home. I went to the bedroom closet for a robe, then grabbed a long-sleeved T-shirt and the laundered Michigan gym shorts she had loaned me two weeks earlier.

"If you'd like, you can put these on and leave those here for *the next time*," I said, handing the clothes to her and placing emphasis on my last three words. I succeeded in making her give me one of those incredible smiles and was tempted to try to coerce her to stay the night.

"It's going to be hard waking up in the morning to find you not there," she said, getting dressed. "Have we really only known each other for two weeks?"

"I know, that's hard to believe, isn't it?"

"I can't promise I won't call you when I get home," she said.

124

"That's okay with me. I'll be here, thinking about you."
Liza grinned.

"You're as mushy as I am," she said.

"You have a problem with that?"

"No, no problem."

As soon as she left, I retrieved my backpack from the office and emptied its contents onto the kitchen floor. The odor of campfire smoke emanated from my clothes, so I gathered everything dark and put a load in the washing machine. I sat on a bar stool in the kitchen and crossed one leg over the other, the front of my robe parting and exposing my knee. The way the ceiling light hit my skin, I noticed short nubs protruding from my kneecap. Liza had seemed oblivious.

"Welcome home, Cate," Sarah's voice wafted into the kitchen. "You really shouldn't worry so much about shaving your legs, you know."

Her attempt to humor me worked, though I suddenly realized that while Liza and I were upstairs, thoughts of Sarah never surfaced. That was something that had inhibited me since her death. I had wondered if I ever would be able to make love with someone else in this home Sarah and I had created together. As usual, Sarah was reading my mind.

"I knew when you found the right person," she said, "that you'd get past that."

I was unsure of what to say, of what I wanted to say. I was unsure of how I felt, of how I wanted to feel.

"Cate, tonight you took an enormous step forward in your life. Please try to understand how important that is to me and how happy I am for you. I know you're sitting there worrying that I'm going to disappear because you are falling in love with this woman. I will *always* be with you, in your heart, in your memories. The happiness and fulfillment you feel when you're with Liza is what I want for you. Do you understand what I'm saying?"

Tears crawled down my face, falling on the collar of my robe. I wasn't sad, nor was I happy at the moment. The crying was more out of confusion and intense emotion, a physical release of everything brewing within me.

"Yes, I understand." I sat quiet, thinking, then posed the question, "If she makes me so happy, why am I crying?"

"Things are changing, Cate, and change is scary for some people. You used to invite change, roll with it, challenge it, but right now you're trying to stiff-arm it away. Let it come. It's okay. There *is* something you have to do, though, and you have to do it very soon."

"I know," I said, blurting out like a sarcastic teen-ager. "I'm sorry. I didn't mean for that to come out in that tone. I'm afraid of how she's going to respond."

"I know you are," Sarah said. "And you know what? However she does respond, you can handle it. Invite her over, tell her, and if the worse-case scenario comes true, she'll leave and I'll still be here. You'll be stuck with just me again!"

I laughed, meeting Sarah's objective, and our conversation lightened. We talked about the weekend camping trip, Liza's friends Julie and Sue, and reminisced about our own Colorado adventures while I messed with the laundry and got ready for bed. I pulled back the sheet and set my alarm clock.

"This week, okay?" Sarah asked, a final encouragement to tell Liza about her.

"Maybe," I answered, smiling. "Good night, Love."

After turning out the light, I rolled onto my side and looked out through the glass of the deck door, thoughts racing across my brain like a pinball game gone mad. The phone rang.

"Helloooo?"

"I wanted to say good-night," Liza's voice practically whispered through the receiver.

"Does that mean you're not coming back over here?"

She tittered.

"Not tonight, unfortunately," she said. "Can I have a raincheck?"

"You can have several." We hung to a few moments of silence. "Are you unpacked and settled back in?"

"For the most part," she replied. "I have a lot of mail to open, bills to pay … but I'll do that tomorrow or the next day. Speaking of tomorrow, what do you have going on?"

"A 7:30 breakfast meeting downtown for starters, then the rest of the day might depend on what happens at that meeting. And you?"

"I'm going for a run around 6:15 and I'll probably be in the office by 8:30," she said. "I should let you get to sleep."

"I'm glad you called."

When I sat the phone on the nightstand, my mind seemed clearer and my body relaxed. The next thing I knew, the alarm was ringing at 5:45 a.m.

The meeting with Cynthia Pruitt at West Egg Café felt more like a social hour than business, though we did review logo combinations and potential marketing routes. Cynthia's main concern seemed to be Leslie Carvalho, whose chemotherapy treatments were taking a toll, physically and mentally, on the human resources director.

"I think she needs to take time off until she's through with her treatments," Cynthia said. "I know you said the normalcy of working probably is good for her, but I wonder if she couldn't recuperate more fully from those treatments if she didn't have the stress of work."

"Is there anyone at Baxter she would talk with completely openly?" I asked.

"If there is, I don't know who it would be," she said, obviously frustrated and worried.

"If you don't mind," I said, "I'll call Leslie later today and check in with her."

Cynthia did not know that Leslie had called me to get in touch with a support group and I would never reveal that to others, particularly people with whom she worked. Offering to contact Leslie myself seemed to soothe Cynthia's mind.

"I'd really appreciate that, Cate," she said. "Let me know if there's anything I can do to help, will you?"

I arrived at the office before Michelle, but I didn't beat her there by much. Mondays normally are busy for us, responding to weekend emails and returning phone calls. I was at my desk, making the day's list of tasks, when she came in. A simple "good morning" at my door, then she was back at her desk retrieving voicemail. Around 11:30 a.m., a transferred call rang in my office. My first thought was that it must be Liza since I hadn't heard from her all morning. I was wrong.

"I'm calling to see how Cate the camper enjoyed Colorado," Lindsay said in a very playful voice.

"That's impressive use of alliteration," I responded. "How are you?"

She made an impromptu invitation to lunch, trying to convince me that she needed to hear every detail of the trip. I'm sure she would *not* want to hear every detail.

"I'm going to gracefully decline," I said, waiting for her objection.

"I thought it was a long shot," she replied, "but I tried."

"How was your weekend?" I asked, shifting the conversation.

"The Air & Water Show was a thrill, as usual, but the crowd was almost unbearable," she said. "The weather was ideal, warm with clear skies, and the lakefront was packed between Oak Street Beach and Montrose Harbor. Next year, I'm going to try to find someone who will take me on their boat and watch it from out on the lake."

"That would be nice," I said. "Let me know when you meet that person."

Lindsay laughed.

"Does that mean you might come with me?" she pried.

"You are relentless."

"Yes, well, if you're not going to have lunch with me, I'd better start going through my little black book," she said. "Are you sure you won't reconsider?"

"I can't today," I said. "I will talk to you soon, though. We have board business to discuss."

"You know where to find me," she said. "Have a good afternoon then. I'll talk to you soon."

Lindsay. Who would have thought? If someone had suggested a year ago that Lindsay Cuvier would be pursuing me, I would have laughed them out of the room. Like Sarah said, it *did* boost my ego to have two women interested in me at the same time. My self-esteem had been needing that.

At 12:20 p.m., I started thinking about ordering lunch to be delivered. Not a minute later, I heard Michelle greeting someone. When I looked up, Liza was standing just outside my office, gazing in at me. She wore tan dress pants and a black, sleeveless, scoop-neck blouse. A silver chain glistened around her neck, complementing silver and onyx earrings and a silver bracelet. My heart rate increased and I felt a blush run up my neck and cover my entire face. She just stood there, looking in, smiling, pleased with surprising me.

"Hi," I said, experiencing that same giddy feeling I had the first night we met at the Fairmont.

"Do you get a lunch break?" she asked, stepping through the doorway of my office.

"I do now. What a pleasant surprise."

I got out of my chair and neared her, close enough to make her think I might hug or kiss her, but containing myself.

"If it weren't inappropriate, I *would* kiss you right now," I whispered as I brushed by her. "Come here. I want to introduce you to Michelle."

When I made the formal introduction to Liza Aplington, Michelle quizzically cocked her head, then smiled.

"Would you also go by the name Applelady?" she asked Liza.

"I don't have a clue what you're talking about," Liza answered, guilt written all over her expression.

We all found it amusing and the laughter gave me a good opportunity to initiate our departure.

"Ms. Aplington and I are stepping out for lunch," I said. "If you need me, call me on the cell."

"Nice to meet you, Applelady," Michelle said, chuckling.

Liza and I exited the north doors of the building and stopped on the sidewalk.

"Do you want to sit in a restaurant somewhere or walk over to the lake or what?" I asked.

"I'd love to just walk along the lake with you," she said, "but I skipped breakfast and I'm starving. Is it okay if we go to a restaurant?"

"Right this way," I replied, guiding her west toward Blackie's, a nearby well-liked pub that serves tasty lunches.

In the midst of our meal, it seemed Liza had something on her mind.

"Is everything okay?" I posed.

Liza looked up from her plate and appeared, as best as I could conclude, embarrassed.

"Last night, I wanted to be next to you," she said. "I don't want that to scare you away, or make you feel smothered or anything like that, but the feeling was almost overwhelming."

I stared at her intently, enjoying the words I was hearing. My lips curved into a smile, a sign that must have relieved Liza's apprehension.

"Will you come over for dinner and stay the night?" she asked, locking her eyes onto mine.

"Do you honestly think I could say no?"

When we got up to leave, more than an hour had passed, and Liza quickened her pace after glancing at her watch.

"We have a staff meeting at 2 o'clock," she said. "I need to run. I'm sorry."

"I'll be at your place by 7:30, okay?" I said as she headed toward a taxi. She nodded and waved as the driver pulled out and headed north on Dearborn Street.

The first thing I wanted to take care of when I got back in the office was calling Leslie Carvalho. Cynthia had given me Leslie's cell phone number to make sure I could reach her. When she didn't answer at home, I tried her cell.

"This is Leslie," she answered.

"Leslie, hi, it's Cate McGuire."

"Hi Cate, how are you?"

"Just fine, thank you," I said. "I've been wondering how you're doing."

"Today's a good day. Thanks for asking. I have my last treatment on Friday, though, so it's going to be a slow weekend. Cynthia's been keeping me posted on our progress with your organization. It sounds like she and Francois are pushing this thing into gear."

"It's under way. We might announce the partnership to the public by the end of the month, but that's not firm yet. Hey, I was wondering if you had luck getting in touch with the support group in Deerfield."

"Yes, I actually met with them that week. There's one woman I bonded with more than the others and we are going to try getting together every Wednesday night for a while. Thank you for giving me that contact, Cate."

"You are very welcome."

130

Through our discussion, Leslie convinced me that she was taking care of herself, spending each day the way she wanted to (excluding chemotherapy) for sanity's sake. Since this week marked her final treatment and she was meeting regularly with another survivor, I wasn't worried about her, and Cynthia needn't be either. We concluded our call with plans to reconnect next week.

Michelle and I rarely spoke all afternoon, catching up on an unusually heavy load of phone and email messages. I left the office a few minutes before 5 p.m. to beat traffic headed north on Lake Shore Drive so I could get home and get my things together for staying at Liza's. Laundry also was not finished and I had hoped to talk with Amy or Claire to make sure everything was fine with them. They weren't home during the two hours I was there, leading me to tape a simple note to their kitchen door in the back stairwell. Then I journeyed to the St. Ben's neighborhood and parked right in front of Liza's home.

Staying there Monday night rated nothing less than overwhelmingly wonderful, prompting us to replicate the episode. Tuesday, I stopped by Farragut after work to get clothes and stayed on Hamilton Avenue again that night. This house-hopping activity is common among young lesbians, not women my age. Then again, I never truly fit any stereotypical mold. When I got to work Wednesday morning, the office was exceptionally quiet. Sitting at my desk, the notion struck me that tonight should be the night I talk to Liza about Sarah. The past two days had further solidified my feelings for her and my confidence that the feelings are mutual. I dialed her work number.

"How about staying at my place tonight?" I asked as soon as she answered.

"Okay, but I need to call Cate and cancel my plans with her," she said, attempting to be funny.

I was humored.

"Actually, that's the best direct line I've gotten in years," she continued. "I accept. Do you want to go for a run with me or should I do that before I come over? I haven't run since Monday morning and I'm starting to feel like a hippopotamus."

"A hippopotamus? Right. You really look like a hippopotamus – an emaciated hippopotamus, maybe. Come over when you can and I'll run with you. I'm a little nervous about that, but I'll do it."

"Don't be nervous," she said, trying to be reassuring. "It will be fun. I promise."

We didn't talk to each other again until she showed up at the two-flat around 7 p.m. She looked quite cute in her bright-colored, Hawaiian-looking running shorts and, of course, a tomato-red tank top. A garment bag hung from her fingertips over her shoulder.

"How far are we going?" I asked, taking the garment bag from her and hanging it on the coat tree by the door.

"I'm leaving that up to you," she said, her facial expression implying that we were talking about something other than today's run.

I led us toward Lake Michigan along the route I'd taken the day after Casey called and asked me to run the Cowtown Marathon with her. This time of evening, the after-work running crowd had thinned, allowing Liza and me to run next to each other along the bike path. She let me set the pace. I tested her a couple of times, picking it up a bit, then slowing my strides. Liza adapted flawlessly. She was rather quiet until I initiated talking.

"Running with you is almost like running alone," I joked, glancing over at her for a reaction.

"I didn't know if you liked to converse while you run," she said. "Some people like to focus on their breathing and not talk."

"And what about you?"

"I like sharing stories with running partners, hearing theirs and telling mine," she said. "Do you have any good stories?"

If she only knew now the story she was about to hear later that night.

"I'm sure I can come up with some," I said, "but you can start us off."

We ran for just under 30 minutes, having talked almost the entire time. As Liza had promised, it was fun. I ordered Italian food from Leona's and we rushed through showering to ensure we were available to answer the door when the delivery arrived. Having been hungry before Liza even got to my place, I now was famished. A few minutes after getting dressed, the doorbell rang and dinner was served.

"Would you mind if we ate in the living room?" I asked. My plan was to sit close to one another on the couch, hoping that setting would be more conducive for the coming conversation. The run had been good for me, wearing me down a little and calming my anxiety. I felt ready to broach the subject of Sarah.

"You know," I began, "you never really ask me about past relationships."

"I figured you would talk about them when you wanted to," she replied. "You haven't asked me much about my past relationships either, so I was waiting for you to bring it up."

I took a deep breath and let it back out.

"There's one specific relationship I want to tell you about," I said. "I was with a woman named Sarah Wickham for six years. She and I bought this place, designed the rehab and lived here together for almost six months."

I thought Liza might step in and ask me something. Instead, she calmly sat next to me, her leg against mine, and waited for me to continue.

"She died in February of '98, five-and-a-half months after we moved in."

Liza sat her plate on the coffee table and reached over to take my hand. Hers was so warm. Her face wore that look people get when they've just received bad news and don't yet know how to respond.

"Cate, I'm so sorry."

She was silent again, primed to hear what else I wanted to tell her.

"I was a basket case, needless to say, and my entire family came to Chicago and made sure someone was by my side at all times, at least until they had to go back to Missouri," I said, trying to give her enough detail so that what I was about to say might be more palatable. "I gave the eulogy at Sarah's funeral. Everyone said I was in shock – they probably were right; I'm sure they were right – but I wanted to be the one to tell people how truly wonderful she was, the amazing things she'd done for other people, for me. And at the end, I spoke directly to Sarah. I wanted to tell her she was the light of my life, that I would carry her with me every minute of every day, and that I would never know love like the love we shared."

As I said those words to Liza, I stared into her eyes, wondering what was going on inside her mind and heart. Her eyes filled with tears and her grip tightened on my hand.

"I can't imagine going through that," she said, her other hand cupping around the back of my head, then sliding down my neck and back.

"I convinced myself I could never feel that way about someone again. I didn't want to feel love like that because I don't think I'd survive losing it a second time."

Liza's beautiful, listening eyes peered back at me.

"Then you came along," I said, unable to continue holding back my tears.

Liza embraced me. She might have thought that was the gist of what I had to say, which would have made the evening much easier.

"Why are you crying?" she asked me. "How you feel about me is a *good* thing. You must know I feel the same, don't you?"

I had to laugh, just a little, and I'm sure that further confused her.

"I sort of thought so," I said, still grinning, "but one can never be too sure."

She leaned in to lightly kiss me on the lips. She still did not know the whole story and I needed to tell her – now.

"Liza, what I'm about to say might sound crazy. I've never told anyone, but I *have* to tell you. Two nights after Sarah's funeral, I was upstairs in the bedroom anguishing over my loss, weeping uncontrollably. And then I thought I heard Sarah's voice talking to me."

"That doesn't sound crazy," Liza interrupted. "I've heard stories of people who think they saw the person who died, sometimes seeing them two or three times after the funeral. It's one of the ways people cope with the loss, a way of letting go."

Liza's exposure to after-life experiences was typical, whereas the story unfolding here definitely qualified as atypical.

"Here's the thing," I began. "She *was* talking to me. She *still* talks to me and I can talk to her."

Stoic at first, Liza's face started moving into looks of concern and query. Her eyebrows drew toward each other creating a crease above her nose.

134

"Please don't think I'm crazy. Sarah and I don't talk every day and we can speak to each other only inside this house. For the past two-and-a-half weeks, most of our conversations have been about you. Sarah is very happy for me and has been encouraging me to open my heart to you. I haven't lost my mind. Please believe me."

I could tell Liza did not know what to say. She remained next to me on the couch, but I sensed her hand easing its hold on mine.

"Liza, you're the only woman I've been with in this house since Sarah died. Before, I refused to invite a date here because I felt like it was, I don't know, sacred ground. But Sunday night, nothing could have stopped what I feel for you. Everything felt right, like *you*, not Sarah, were supposed to be here with me."

"Cate, I don't know what to say. Honestly, it scares me a little that you believe you're having conversations with someone who died more than four years ago. I understand saying things out loud to a loved one who has passed away; I think we all do that now and then. But you're telling me that you can hear her talking to you, as clearly as I'm talking to you right now?"

I brushed the edge of my thumb along Liza's jaw, peering into her troubled, watery eyes.

"I can't explain it, but I can tell you that having her – her voice, at least – here was what got me through that first year after she died. She has been a constant source of strength, the voice of logic when I was thinking or acting unreasonably. She has been here to comfort me, but only to the extent that she could. The day after I met you, she already was telling me what a wonderful life I could have with you."

For the first time since I'd mentioned how I communicate with Sarah, Liza broke into a grin.

"She doesn't even know me," Liza said. "I might not be the great catch she thinks I am."

"She *does* know you," I said, "and she knows how I feel about you."

"Did you ever go see a counselor after she died?" Liza gently asked. "I'm not suggesting you need to. I'm just trying to comprehend this and make sense of it."

"Yeah, I did. I went to a grief counselor someone at work had recommended. I started to tell her about my ability to communicate with Sarah, but I stopped short of doing that. I knew I wasn't crazy –

I was depressed, but not crazy – and I preferred she counsel me just as she would anyone else who had lost a loved one. Liza, throughout time there have been people who claimed to be able to communicate with the dead. Everyone assumes it's a joke, that it's not possible. I'm telling you it *is* possible. I don't know how and I don't know how long it lasts, but it *is* real."

Instead of asking more questions or speculating, Liza became serene.

"We can stop talking about this for now, if you want," I said. "Should we finish dinner?"

"Let's finish dinner," she agreed, though I could tell the subject was consuming her thoughts.

I soon got more information on Callie Langston, the Lambda attorney Liza had dated. She was well educated – a Dartmouth grad – and it spoke highly of her that she chose a civil rights career over a potential six-figure corporate job.

"People thought we made the perfect couple," Liza said, laughing. "Callie is a great person, but the seven-year age difference didn't work for me. She's a brilliant woman who will learn a whole lot more about life by the time she's my age."

"So older women are more appealing?" I asked teasingly.

"At least one of them is," she replied, kissing my cheek while I placed leftovers in the refrigerator.

It was after 10 p.m. and I suggested we get ready for bed. Due to the intensity and topic of our earlier dinner conversation, the pheromones were not flowing and as we crawled under the sheets, holding each other seemed to be what we both needed. I doubt either of us fell asleep before midnight, but we lay silent, absorbing the warmth from one another. I didn't set an alarm for morning. As it turns out, I didn't need one.

Chapter Nine

I love the mountains. I love looking at them, hiking them, riding the Rio Grande ski train through them, photographing them ... Life's virtual mountains, the rise and fall of emotions and experiences, can be a different story.

My eyes still closed, I awoke to lips nibbling on my neck. Once she knew I was conscious, Liza's kisses became passionate and she slid on top of me. When she neared orgasm, she backed her head away so she could see my face. Staring penetratingly into each other's eyes, our bodies barely moving, we climaxed together. Then Liza dropped onto my chest and began crying, almost sobbing.

I held her, securely, while some of her tears rolled down my neck and onto the pillow. Although I didn't look at the clock, 30 or 45 minutes must have passed. The room remained hushed.

"Cate?"

"Yes?"

"Cate, I don't know exactly why, but I'm struggling with this," Liza said, her words obviously strained.

"You mean about Sarah?"

"I'm sorry. I wish it didn't bother me and I don't know what to do about it."

"Did you feel this way an hour ago?" I asked, second-guessing one of the most intense sexual, if not spiritual, experiences I'd ever had.

"I have fallen in love with you," she said, her voice beginning to break. "I wanted to tell you that this morning. I wanted to say, 'I love you,' but what you told me last night frightens me."

My self-defense mechanisms began taking over and I found myself pulling away from Liza and getting out of bed.

"I'd tell you that Sarah said you might respond this way and need time to work through it, but you'd think I was crazy." My tone couldn't hide the hurt. I felt I'd been calm and patient the night before, trying as best I could to explain my connection with Sarah. Maybe I wasn't being patient enough. Maybe Liza *did* need time to absorb and dissect what I'd told her. One thing was certain: that horrific hot needle that pierced my heart when Sarah died was back again.

"Cate, the mere idea that your ex-lover is with us right now in this room ... can't you see? I know *you're* not crazy, but that sounds crazy!"

We both were crying, grabbing for any words that might make this all okay. I finally sat on the bed and pulled her into my arms.

"Liza, it's okay. It's going to be okay. I think what we need to do right now is take showers, wash all these salty tears off our faces and get ready for work."

I went and turned on the shower, placing fresh bath towels within reach of the shower door. My beautiful, dark-haired lover sat on the edge of the bed, sadness and tears causing her eyelids to swell. When the water was hot enough, I held out my hand to Liza, inviting her to join me in the confinement of the steaming shower. Our lathered washcloths attended to one another's bodies like a mother bathes her newborn for the first time. I focused on absorbing the tenderness and intense bond we shared for the time-being – however brief or long that time might be. We didn't talk about Sarah. The subject remained at rest.

When Liza called me late in the afternoon to say she thought she needed to spend the night alone, I took inventory of my own needs at that point. I needed to protect myself. Additionally, the Baxter project needed my undivided attention. I would not allow myself to be devastated again. I just couldn't take it. I don't remember what I said to Michelle as I left the office, nor do I remember the drive home. Numbness invaded my torso and limbs like a venomous snakebite. I managed to make my way upstairs and out onto the deck, falling limp into a lounge chair, wondering what would come next. If the Chicago sunset displayed its normal brilliance that night, I didn't notice. When I stared up from my paralyzed position, I could only envision Liza's tearful face. Why couldn't she understand?

Sarah checked in on me that evening.

"I didn't expect that reaction," I told her. "I thought her feelings for me would overcome any problems she has with this, with us, you and me."

138

I fought to keep my composure, though there was no one except Sarah to hear me wail. My chest felt like a hole had been bored through it. My heart ached to be near Liza, but my steel mind was not about to give in and let that happen.

"Cate, she needs time. She really does love you. Why won't you give her some time?" Sarah pleaded with me.

"You think you know the pain that was tearing me apart when I got the call from the police?" I asked her. "When they told me you were dead, I wished I had died, too. I couldn't take losing someone like that again. I can't believe I allowed myself to fall so deeply for Liza, so quickly. What was I thinking? She thinks I'm crazy because I talk to you. No, I was crazy for falling in love again."

In the days that followed, Liza at first left brief messages on my voicemail. She sent benign emails and had snail-mailed a "Thinking of You" greeting card which I received on Saturday. I didn't respond. My energy focused on the collaboration with Cynthia Pruitt's crew at Baxter and updates with our board of directors. While at the office, I kept my mind busy with the tasks at hand. I committed to training for the Cowtown Marathon and, in doing so, began having daily conversations with my little sister. She had told our parents about the impending divorce, which might be finalized around the same time as the race in late February, and she was thrilled I would be running alongside her in Fort Worth. When I wasn't working or running, there was my time at the two-flat conversing with Sarah.

Only a week had passed, though every day of not interacting with Liza felt like an eternity. I was in the front office and Michelle was away from her desk when the phone rang. Without hesitation, I picked up the call.

"A Sister's Hope, this is Cate, how can I help you?"

At first, no one responded.

"Cate, it's Liza."

It took me a moment to reply.

"Hi," was all I could muster as my heart rate began to climb. Optimistically, I wondered if she already had grown comfortable with the Sarah situation. If so, she hadn't been struggling with it as much as I'd thought and I had overreacted.

"I needed to hear your voice, make sure you're okay," she said.

"I miss you, but I'm okay. How are you feeling about things?"

The lag between my question and her answer knotted my stomach.

"Until I come to terms with what you told me about Sarah," she began, "I think it's best for both of us to not see each other. It's tearing me apart to say that, but I don't know what else to do. Over the weekend, that's all I could think about. I'm going to be traveling a lot over the next four months and, if I'm in the frame of mind I was on Saturday, I'm not sure I could do my job. Cate, I wanted to talk with you in person, but I don't think I could say what I needed to say if you were within reach."

I saw Michelle coming down the hallway toward the office and knew that if I didn't get off the phone quickly, I might break down.

"Okay," I managed to utter.

"Okay?" Liza asked.

"There's nothing else I can say."

That afternoon, I tried to keep my mind off Liza and on work. I thought staying at the office would help, but everything I read had to be re-read. When I'd be talking with someone on the telephone, I wasn't fully attentive to what they were saying. Michelle knew something was bothering me and didn't pry when I told her I planned to work from home on Thursday. Being at the house, at least I'd have Sarah to talk to and I could cry if that emotion surfaced. I called into my voicemail Thursday around lunchtime to check messages, finding two from Lindsay: one from 9:10 in the morning and one from 11:45.

"What's new with you?" her first message asked. "Call me when you get some time."

"Thought I'd try again," the second message said. "I went to Knoxville last weekend and wanted to entertain you over lunch with tales of Tennessee. If you get this message before 12:30, that could still happen. Hope to hear from you soon."

I've always made it a rule to return phone calls as soon as possible. As a journalist, that was part of my reputation and sources usually reciprocated the courtesy. Nowadays, it is an uncommon habit that still is marvelously appreciated. Despite hesitations about dialing Lindsay's number, I knew I needed to call her back.

Her name appeared first on the board members directory, alphabetically listed. I ran my index finger from "Cuvier, Lindsay" horizontally to the column of work phone numbers. I didn't quite have all of them memorized – yet. The time on the lower right corner of my computer screen read 12:20 p.m.

"Cate?" she answered, apparently seeing my number on Caller ID.

"Hi Lindsay."

"You're just in time to join me for lunch," she said. "Is that going to happen?"

"You might have noticed on your Caller ID that I'm working from home today, so I guess we'll have to make it another time. I appreciate the invitation, though."

"That's fine," she said, then pausing for a moment. "Is everything okay with you? Your voice sounds different, almost sad."

Her perception caught me off-guard and I nearly started crying. My upper and lower teeth clenched together and I didn't try to answer until certain I could speak "normally."

"It's just been a challenging week, but everything will be fine," I answered, hoping she couldn't still detect sadness in my voice.

"You're sure?"

"Yes. Really."

"If you say so," she said, sounding skeptical. "Are you going to tell me about your trip? Tell me about Colorado and I'll tell you about Tennessee."

This conversation was becoming increasingly more difficult.

"Another time," I answered simply. Although this response likely further intrigued Lindsay, I needed to get off the telephone. She got the message.

"Okay. Another time. I'm going to go ahead and get out of here for a little while, but thanks for calling me back before 12:30. You earn stars by your name for that behavior."

She succeeded in making me chuckle – a timely, welcome emotion – with the way she had said that.

"I'll talk to you again soon," I said, unsure if she heard me before hanging up. Although my appetite level dipped lower than normal, soup or yogurt sounded good right now, so I went to the kitchen for something to eat. It seemed impossible, at least for the time being, to be in that room without recalling my first kiss with Liza. Rather than call upon Sarah for consolation, I snatched a strawberry yogurt from the refrigerator and plopped myself onto the living room couch where sunlight poured through my southeast windows. A half-hour viewing of CNN revitalized me, shifting my focus back onto the future of A Sister's Hope and our need to advertise for temporary event managers who would join us in 6–8 weeks. The afternoon proving to be more productive than I originally thought it could be, I decided to head out on a run around 4:30 p.m., getting most of my mileage in before the after-work running brigades.

Mid-August in Chicago can be frighteningly hot and humid and three miles into today's run I felt like a slice of bacon sizzling over low heat. Spoiled with a user-friendly lakefront path that was dotted with numerous antiquated but functional concrete-based watering spouts, I doused my face and the back of my neck a few times along the five-mile jaunt. Even in this activity, I had to resist thinking of Liza and our shorter route that had been such fun last week. As thoughts of her crept to my forebrain, my strides quickened and forehead wrinkled with red-lined concentration. By the time I turned west up Farragut Avenue, my heart rate had shot well above a targeted range of 150-170. Matters were not assisted any when I saw the figure of a woman sitting on the front steps of the two-flat. I pushed the "stop" button on my athletic watch's timer and slowed to a walking pace a few houses' distance from mine. Finally, the woman looked east down the street and we recognized each other.

"You were right, you look fine," Lindsay said, rising from her seated position where she had been leaning against the handrail. "I decided to stop by and make sure because you sounded pretty unlike yourself when we spoke earlier."

"I really sounded that bad?"

"Yeah," she said, starting to grin. "Why else would I have come over here?"

"Of course, why else?" I offered a mutual grin. "Well, you caught me looking my finest."

142

"You look great," she said. "You look hot ... temperature-wise *and* otherwise. Healthy is attractive, you know?"

"I think you should market yourself as an ego-boosting consultant. You'd make millions."

We both laughed, standing on the front steps, sweat trickling along my forehead and down past my ears. Lindsay's cream-colored silk blouse revealed wet spots down the center of her stomach where the shirt had rested against her while she sat waiting for me. This humidity could make dried fruit sweat.

"How long were you going to wait?" I asked, wondering how long she'd already been there.

"It just so happens that one of your neighbors saw me buzzing your doorbell and asked if I was looking for Cate or the girls," Lindsay answered. "She'd seen you leaving, headed east on Farragut on foot, so I decided to stick around a while. She guessed you'd been gone about a half-hour."

"Which neighbor?"

"An older woman from across the street who apparently saw me over here that morning you and I went to breakfast. She had seen me talking to you and one of your tenants. Is that pure coincidence or does she keep a close eye on this place?"

"It's no coincidence," I replied, smiling.

Mrs. Green, a retired public school teacher, had lived in a Farragut Avenue two-flat for 50 years. When Mrs. Green got married, she and her husband moved into the second floor apartment above his parents, planning to raise children in this extended-family setting. The husband died, however, seven years later from a congenital heart disorder, leaving Mrs. Green with a four-year-old son and pregnant with a daughter. She remained there with her in-laws, who helped with the grandchildren while Mrs. Green taught biology to thousands of Chicago students over four decades. The elder Greens both passed away in 1999, leaving the building to their devoted daughter-in-law.

The temperature as it was, my increasing need for a drink and Lindsay's generous concern for my well-being led me to invite her upstairs. Awkwardly, I started to explain how privileged she, as someone who had kissed me, should feel to be entering my home since I never invited dates into my place. I proceeded to try to

143

expound on how, since we were *not* dating, the rule still applied and that it was okay for her to be here.

"I'm not sure I followed all of that, but that's okay," she said, trailing only a step behind me through the front door of the second floor.

Nervousness jittered through my vocal chords like adolescent vibrato. Lindsay, no doubt, sensed my unsettled state of mind. I handed her a glass of ice and can of Minute Maid lemonade. As she took them from me, her eyes caught mine in a split second of anxiety before I could evasively turn away.

"Cate," she said, securing my attention, "do you want to talk about it?"

Flashbacks from the conversation she and I had the night we'd gone to the Hopleaf popped into my head. Lindsay's open-mindedness about the "sixth sense" had been the impetus for my going back to her townhome for a late dinner that night. It had felt good to hear someone speak so confidently about the possibilities of interaction between the living and those who had passed away. It was like an acknowledgment that I'm *not* crazy. Dare I talk to anyone else about my conversations with Sarah? The urge to open up to someone, to a human being actually standing there looking back at me, felt like a lifeline dangling down to me while I'm mired in quicksand.

"Lindsay, I'm afraid to discuss this with anyone," I said, keeping my back to her, feeling the pressure on my chest beginning to build.

"Does it have to do with the new woman you've been seeing?" she asked.

"In a way, but not entirely."

"Does it have anything to do with your partner who died in '98?"

I swung around to look directly at Lindsay who was standing a non-threatening distance from me. We stared at each other several moments before I spoke.

"What do you know about Sarah?"

"That the two of you seemed to have the ultimate relationship, one found only in the movies. The investigative journalist trying to rid the city of corruption meets the Chicago Public Schools' Sarah Wickham, a soft-spoken government teacher crusading for better city schools. Both of you were trying to make the world a better place and anyone who saw you together could tell you were head over heels for each other."

"You make it *sound* like a movie script," I said, almost breaking into a full smile. "Are you going to reveal your source?"

"I'd rather not say who it was, but it's someone in town who knew both of you well and envied your relationship. This person heard you give the eulogy at Sarah's funeral."

"Our relationship certainly wasn't a secret," I said, acknowledging that any number of individuals could have informed Lindsay about that part of my history. "If it had been, neither of us could have effectively done our jobs. We would have had to worry about people trying to use the 'homosexuality trump card' against us. As it was, there were people who threatened to reveal to the public that I was a lesbian if I didn't drop a story I was pursuing. They were disappointed to discover it was no deep, dark secret being kept from anyone – the Tribune or the public."

"So does what you're dealing with right now involve Sarah?" Lindsay asked.

"If you're going to stay for a while, maybe we should go sit in the living room," I said, leading us out of the kitchen. I sat down in the oversized armchair and Lindsay chose the edge of the couch nearest me, setting her lemonade on a stone coaster on the coffee table. "You asked me earlier today about my trip to Colorado and I didn't want to talk about it because it looks like things aren't going to work out with the woman I started seeing. It has nothing to do with our trip – the trip was wonderful – but last week I told her something about Sarah that didn't go over very well."

"Is this woman crazy or what?" Lindsay asked, partially trying to amuse me. "Are you going to tell me what you told her about Sarah?"

This was the moment when a thousand scenarios flashed before me. If Lindsay had the same reaction as Liza, she could tell others and place my reputation at stake. As a board member, she could challenge my state of mind and disintegrate the foundation of A Sister's Hope. On the other hand, as a woman who seemed genuinely interested in me, Lindsay potentially was the listening ear I woefully needed.

"Lindsay, I'm going to tell you something that, if shared with other people, could ruin my reputation and thwart the future of A Sister's Hope. I'm prefacing what I'm going to say because of the way Liza, the woman I was seeing, reacted when I told her. I haven't committed any crimes or anything like that. It's just that people are slow to accept things they don't understand. With that said, do you remember the conversation you and I had about the 'sixth sense' the night we went to the Hopleaf?"

She nodded, continuing to stare at me.

"You seem to be a staunch believer in the what-if theories of the after-life. Did I gauge that correctly?"

"Absolutely," she said. "I was telling you how people become so close-minded when the subject of past lives or spirits or that sort of thing gets brought up. I love to initiate that conversation with people just to see their reactions and I'm forever amazed by the responses of well-educated, progressive thinkers."

While she talked, I sat fairly motionless in my chair, glancing outside once when the motion of Mrs. Green watering her front yard caught my eye. Lindsay noticed the distraction and turned around to look out the window.

"That's Mrs. Green, eh?"

"In living color."

"Cate, are we talking about an experience you had with Sarah after her death?" Lindsay probed.

Had. Interesting that she would use the past tense. I continued to struggle with sharing this revelation.

"Have you ever known anyone to have on-going dialogue with someone who has died?"

I practically was admitting to that scenario with my question. This approach, however, left me an out, an opportunity to back away from any accusations or assumptions Lindsay might make.

"I haven't known anyone personally, but I believe that's entirely possible," she said. "I would guess that type of interaction would be most common between a parent and child or between spouses who … '"

Lindsay's lips stopped moving and her voice silenced, yet I could see the sentences continuing to formulate through her eyes and facial expressions. After an awkward few moments, she wagered a huge smile.

146

"Can you still communicate with Sarah? That would be incredible!"

The cap sealing pressure around my heart blew off and my torso slumped a little as I relaxed against the back of my chair. Lindsay's reaction to the same information I'd given Liza was the difference between mixing oil with vinegar and oil with a lit match. I no longer worried about her telling other board members I'd "flipped my lid". Then, the realization that someone in the flesh finally knew my secret *and* believed it soaked through me. I had not imagined this feeling of relief, like I didn't have to wear sunglasses anymore to hide my true identity.

"I can," was all I initially responded.

"Tell me about it. When did this first happen? How?"

The story unraveled like a full-length feature film reeling through my mind. Lindsay listened intently, occasionally stopping me for clarification, but mostly enthralled by what I was telling her. The sound of Claire and Amy hammering on a wall downstairs broke my train of thought and I glanced at my Timex wristwatch.

"Oh, my gosh, do you realize what time it is?" I asked.

"I wasn't really concerned," she answered.

"It's after 7. Are you hungry? Do you want to stay for dinner? We could order something to be delivered or, if you wanted to wait while I shower, we could walk over to Ann Sather."

"Why don't we order something," she said. "Then you can go shower and I'll keep myself occupied with one of these *National Geographics*. At some point, can I see the rest of your place?"

I agreed to give her a brief tour after I'd showered and had a couple of minutes to straighten up the upstairs.

It's true that I have dinner delivered quite regularly. That had been the case since Sarah died. We used to love making a grocery list based on the *Bon Appetit* or *Cooking Light* recipes that whetted our appetites. Shopping trips on a Sunday afternoon often surpassed an hour wandering through the aisles of an oversized grocery store. We'd split the preparation responsibilities and enjoy the process of making the meal almost as much as eating it. Cooking for one, however, seemed a waste of time. A chore.

With a stuffed pizza – one of Chicago's specialties – on the way, I excused myself to shower and left Lindsay amidst my collection of about 30 magazines dating back to March/April.

Philosophical rambling about life after death entrenched us as we consumed a small spinach and pine nuts combination and dark beers. Other people had talked about those things around me the past four years, but I hadn't stridden down this corridor since Sarah's appearance to me that night upstairs. I knew she would be pleased that I'd entrusted Lindsay with my secret, happy that I have someone else in whom I can confide. A spontaneous chuckle slipped out.

"What?" Lindsay asked. "Do I have spinach stuck in my teeth?"

"No, your teeth are fine. I was just thinking about my next conversation with Sarah and what she's going to say about you."

"So does she know everything that's going on with you? She can see you at all times?"

"That seems to be the case. At first, that was comforting, then I went through a phase where I was a bit self-conscious, particularly when I began going out on dates. Since this house is the only place where we actually talk with each other, I never brought any of those dates into the house, like I tried explaining to you earlier."

"Now I get that."

"But Liza has been here and now here *you* are, so that rule has changed a little."

"This is *not* a date," Lindsay said, as if she were reminding me. "I don't wear bank clothes on dates."

She certainly thrived on making me smile, catching me off-guard with her dry sense of humor.

The hours passed like a revolving restaurant that you know is in continual motion but simply don't notice. Setting our plates in the kitchen sink, I looked over at the oven clock: 10:15 p.m. Lindsay had been in my company for nearly five hours, carrying on as if the evening had been planned this way when, in reality, she had shown up on my doorstep only to ensure I was okay.

"You've gone above and beyond the call of duty," I said to her, pointing toward the clock. "What's the verdict?"

"You're in perfect mental and physical health, as far as I can tell. A follow-up visit might be in order, though."

Tenacious, wasn't she? I didn't mind the comment. She had succeeded in taking my mind off Liza, for a few hours anyway, and I was grateful for her showing up unannounced. We headed down the hallway toward the front door and Lindsay stopped just short of the coat tree.

"Thanks for feeling like you could talk to me," she said, those chocolate eyes melting in sincerity.

"You're the one who needs to be thanked for checking in on me. I didn't realize I sounded so despaired over the phone."

After showering, I'd pulled on loose-fitting cotton pants, similar to hospital scrubs, and a V-neck blue t-shirt from a ski trip Sarah and I had taken in the winter of '96. One of my favorites, it was starting to thin, but I didn't think about not having a bra on until Lindsay leaned forward to hug me. I felt my erect nipples brushing against her and knew she would notice through her supple silk blouse. The extended hug was caring, not sexual, though having arms around me stimulated my already heightened emotions.

"Will you be in the office tomorrow?" Lindsay asked, reaching toward the doorknob.

"Most of the day," I said, self-consciously crossing my arms. "Thanks again for coming over. That was very thoughtful."

After watching her walk to the corner of Farragut and Clark, I stepped back inside, grabbed a copy of *National Geographic* and headed upstairs for bed. While brushing my teeth in front of the large bathroom mirror, I fought visions of time spent with Liza last week. I glared into my own reflection, no steam this time, just the hardened image of someone burying her emotions. I turned off the bathroom light and, when I did, the reading light beams fell on the "special clock" as if it were a Hollywood legend on stage. Hastily, I scooped it off the nightstand and carried it into the closet, carefully wrapping it in the white Women's College World Series T-shirt.

My outdated clock radio back in action, I set the alarm for 6 a.m. and found a station playing songs of the '70s, hoping something mellow would come on to soothe me into sleep. A trio of tunes by James Taylor, John Lennon and The Commodores worked better than any prescription drug.

Chapter Ten

Life moves on. It always does. The legend that "only time can heal your pain" is based on the belief that, as life continues, the past will fade like an old black-and-white photo, muting the clarity that once was so dominant. Whether time heals pain or previous pain is replaced by newer, greater pain is still up for debate. While the jury's out on that, my life has continued moving on.

Friday night, Lindsay and I dined at La Donna, a woman-owned Italian restaurant in Andersonville. Pumpkin-filled ravioli and red wine accompanied more entertaining conversation with this southern tomboy-turned proper bank vice president, Lindsay retelling humorous adventures of her childhood in Tennessee. We then walked up the street to Los Manos Gallery, also woman-owned, luckily hitting it on opening night of a new exhibit. That's when I began running into people I knew and Lindsay saw people she knew. As one would imagine, rumors hit the streets, despite introducing each other as "this is a friend of mine." A tiny voice inside me tried demanding I feel guilty about being out with Lindsay so soon after the incident with Liza. My justification, however, was that a 44-year-old single woman owes no explanation to anyone about her intimate relationships. Besides, the only people who even knew Liza and I had gotten together were my tenants and Liza's friends in Denver. The whole thing, from start to finish, had lasted less than three weeks. Guilt wasn't about to win this one.

By the way, Lindsay and I were just friends.

When she asked if I was interested in getting together again over the weekend, I didn't even hesitate.

"My schedule is wide open," I replied as we walked along Clark Street toward our homes. "I want to run tomorrow morning and Sunday morning, but I should be done by 10 both mornings. Did you have anything specific in mind?"

"Brunch, for starters," she answered, her accent starting to slip into a fun and lazy Southern twang. "If that's fun we can see how the rest of the day develops."

"Are you going to call me or are you just going to show up?"

"I think it's your turn to come to my place, isn't it?"

"You're right. It is. Should I come over after my run?"

"You can shower first," she said, laughing.

"Yeah," I said, "I planned to."

We got to Farragut and Lindsay started to turn toward my place. Although we had spent hours there talking the night before, inviting Lindsay inside that evening didn't feel right.

"I'll walk you to your place," I said. "It's such a gorgeous night and I'm not ready to go inside just yet."

"Then we can sit on my deck, but it's about one-fifth the size of yours, you know."

"Don't you know size doesn't matter in the lesbian community?"

We giggled and somehow the conversation transitioned into a discussion of dating taller women, heavier women, women with big hands or big hair. Lindsay snatched a bottle of red wine, corkscrew and glasses and led me through the back door onto her conventional, modest deck. Time slipped by me like a smooth pickpocket.

"Are you staying the night?" Lindsay concisely asked, catching me way off-guard. She could tell I was startled. "I only ask because it's already 2 a.m."

"You've got to be kidding," I replied, getting up from the forest green resin chair. "How did it get to be 2 a.m.?"

"Yeah, how did it get to be 2 a.m.?" she echoed, smiling. "You really *are* welcome to spend the night."

My eyes dropped to the cedar decking and I took a few pensive moments to gather my thoughts. Traffic noise from Clark Street had thinned considerably while we'd been on her deck and a lengthy silence was broken only by the hum of a passing CTA bus.

"I think I'm going to go home," I said, looking up at her and gently rocking my head in a "yes" motion.

As I pulled open the front door of her townhome to leave, Lindsay laid a warm hand on my left shoulder, causing me to stop and turn toward her. An apprehensive tremble crept through me as I guessed she was about to kiss me, but those Hershey eyes simply gazed at my face. When she stepped forward, it was for a hug good-night. Her blonde hair, tickling my left cheekbone, smelled like a faint version of Georgio perfume. She started to release from the hug, but re-engaged when she noticed my arms held steady. Her squeeze felt like that of a mother welcoming her child home from a long trip. My eyes welled and I felt tears beginning to stream down my face. Sarah couldn't hold me. Liza apparently didn't want to anymore. Lindsay's arms and shoulders comforted me. Her head nestled against mine allowed me to hide my face as if there were others who would see me crying.

Lindsay reached with one hand to push the door shut, continuing to hold me tightly with her other arm. We didn't say anything for a long time. We stood there by the door, Lindsay sporadically brushing the back of my hair and slowly rubbing my back. When it seemed like I might stand there forever, she backed away from me and grabbed my right hand, leading me to the spare bedroom just 20 feet from us. Without releasing my hand, she laid down on her side and gently pulled me onto the bed. She directed me to lie on my side with my back toward her, then wrapped herself tightly behind me, her forearm across my stomach and her knees cupped into the back of mine.

When I awoke a few hours later, we remained in the same position and Lindsay was fast asleep until I attempted to roll out from under her arm.

"How are you feeling?" she asked, her southern accent masked by morning voice.

"Much better," I said, maneuvering onto my back. "I don't know what that was all about. I'm sorry."

"Why would you say you're sorry? That's totally unnecessary. I'm just glad you weren't by yourself."

"Thank you, Lindsay."

"Anytime."

Recognizing our awkward physical positioning, my pulse started to climb. Lindsay, however, seemed perfectly comfortable. I tried to relax. Lindsay began telling a story about when she would stay at her grandmother's house during the summer while her grandfather was on a business trip. She and "Gramma" would fall asleep on the couch watching late-night movies and wake up early in the morning next to empty popcorn pans and Dr. Pepper cans. We stayed on the bed talking for a solid half-hour. By then, my jitters were gone.

"Can I make you some coffee?" Lindsay asked.

"I'd still like to go for a run this morning and I usually do that before coffee. If you wanted to wait a while, I could run and shower and then we could get a late breakfast somewhere. Can you wait that long?"

"I can wait quite a while," she said, rolling to the edge of the bed and running her fingers through her thick hair. She got up and held out a hand to help me off the soft mattress. "So how long will all that take you?"

"An hour and a half?" I answered, my inflection asking if that time frame would work.

Over the next few weeks, Lindsay and I spent an incredible amount of time together, partially because of A Sister's Hope, but mostly because we wanted each other's companionship. At first, evening plans were masked as detailed meetings to spell out the tediousness of Baxter's sponsorship. Lindsay's financial expertise was priceless. Those soon were splashed with the confetti of walks to Buckingham Fountain, dinners out at some of Chicago's finest (and worst, as we discovered) restaurants, coffee at Kopi Café and lounging time at her place on Winona. We weren't intimate, though the opportunities were infinite.

My discussions with Sarah throughout this period centered on the pursuit of happiness, fulfillment and health. Running became habitual, a morning routine that nursed me physically and mentally. Although I had intended to visit southeast Missouri in the fall, maybe even schedule the trip during the district fair, the developing relationship with Lindsay had altered those plans. Casey hounded me relentlessly about going to St. Louis to see her, but eased off once I mentioned I had met someone. As summer night temperatures began to fall, the potential for new passion flared.

Lindsay asked if I'd be interested in spending a weekend in Michigan, hiking along the lake and hanging out in one of those small, artsy, gay-friendly towns. This previously never had interested me since my entire childhood was spent in a small town, but now I seemed to have developed a curiosity about why so many Chicagoans choose to drive east an hour or two to do this, some going so far as to buy a second home in these tiny, minimally developed, rural areas. Accepting the invitation, I was presented with potential dates, including the upcoming Friday.

"Why wait?" Lindsay asked, nudging my leg with her foot as we sat on the couch in her living room. "C'mon. You know we'll have a great time."

I made a mental check of my day planner and saw no conflicts. The next night we had dinner – her extraordinary vegetarian lasagna – at her place, watching a new episode of NBC's "West Wing." On Thursday, we spoke only over the telephone to make plans for Friday's road trip. I went straight home from work to pack, take time to myself and talk to Sarah. She greeted me as I walked into the kitchen from the back stairwell.

"You surprised me by agreeing to go to Michigan," she said. "I was afraid you were going to pass it up."

"You were in my subconscious pushing me to say 'yes,' weren't you?" I asked her.

"I'll never tell, but I'm really glad you didn't completely shut everyone out after what happened with Liza." Sarah's intonation turned from playful to serious. "You've learned to take care of yourself. You handle your emotions much differently than you used to."

"It's that survival instinct, don't you think?" My response reeked of sarcasm. "Don't let me drop into that 'woe is me' attitude. I've done a good job of avoiding it lately."

"Yeah, you have. Lindsay's great, isn't she?"

I laughed. "You were the Liza fan, remember?"

"Yes, *and* I'm a fan of Lindsay. She's here for you. She cares for you. Not to mention how beautiful and smart she is."

"I guess it's a good thing you're not still around in the flesh or I might be jealous of your attraction to Lindsay," I said, bringing Sarah's laughter into the room around me.

"No, that's one thing you never had to worry about with me," she said. "You filled my heart to the brink. There wasn't room for anyone else, not even a little Lindsay."

Sarah probably knew her saying that would make me cry, but then again, she knew how easily a Kodak commercial could make me cry. That night, I did not have any time to myself, per se, but Sarah's presence was always welcome and much of the evening was silent anyway. We mostly talked while I made dinner and again when I went to bed. I slept so peacefully that I thought the alarm

154

radio, playing Elton John's "Candle in the Wind," was part of my dream.

When I opened my eyes, a Chicago blue sky showed the slightest hint of lavender near the skyline. It was early and I could have stayed in bed another hour, but I wanted plenty of time to piddle around the house before Lindsay picked me up. As the coffee grinder stopped spinning, I heard tapping on my kitchen door.

"Amy! Good morning. Would you like to join me for coffee?"

"Sure," she said, walking in wearing cotton boxer shorts and a T-shirt with "Life is Good" printed across the front of it. She sat down and immediately began the friendly interrogation. "We haven't seen you around much lately. How's everything going?"

"Great," I said, dumping grounds into the filter and turning on the pot. "I've been hanging out at a friend's place quite a bit. How are you two?"

"We're good. Claire has been putting in a lot of extra time at work and she left yesterday for a conference in Boston. She won't be back until Sunday night. Are you around this weekend? Do you want to go to a movie or something?"

"Actually, I'm leaving this morning for the weekend. Sorry."

"Where to this time?"

"Michigan. New Buffalo or somewhere around there."

"Are you going with Liza? That was her name, right?"

I turned on the kitchen faucet and unnecessarily rinsed my hands so that I had time to draw a deep breath and release it before answering.

"No, that didn't really work out," I said, unable to look directly at her when I spoke. "Her name is Lindsay. I think Claire met her out front one day. She lives just a few blocks away on Winona."

"Should I ask what went wrong with Liza?" Amy persisted, knowing as she spoke that she was imposing.

"No, you shouldn't," I replied, giving her a forced grin. "You can meet Lindsay this morning if you're going to be around the next couple of hours. She's picking me up between 8 and 9."

"Yeah, I'll still be here. I don't have clinicals until this afternoon."

"Good. So what else have the two of you been up to? Have you talked to Laney and Tori?"

Amy stayed until I had to run her off so I could shower. We normally didn't go that long without seeing each other and I was thankful for her spontaneous appearance. Around 8:15, the doorbell rang and I walked down the front steps to greet Lindsay at the door. She looked very cute, as usual, wearing a light blue T-shirt under a yellow and periwinkle fleece with faded blue jeans and slip-on leather shoes. In our quick hug, I caught a whiff of her soap or shampoo, a fragrance that surpassed walking into a floral shop.

"Are you ready to go?" she asked, her chipper mood reminding me how fun the weekend could be.

"Before we leave, can I introduce you to Amy, my tenant downstairs? She's the girlfriend of Claire, the woman who was running out of the two-flat that first morning we had breakfast at Svea."

"Sure. I'd love to meet her."

Amy had changed from boxer shorts to stretchy pants and a form-fitting top. She invited us into the living room, asking us to sit down, but we pleasantly refused so we could get on the road. The apartment couldn't have been cleaner unless Mr. Clean showed up in person. The scent of peach candles flickering from the center of the dining table floated to where we stood. The floor rugs looked like they'd just come from the beauty parlor, washed and combed. The front windows wore that Windex glow and I could tell Amy had wiped down the frames and ledges.

"The place looks gorgeous, Amy," I said.

"Thanks, Cate," she replied, quickly turning her attention to Lindsay. "So how did you two meet?"

"I'm on the board of A Sister's Hope," Lindsay answered.

"*New* board member?" Amy asked.

"I joined the board a little over a year ago. Cate thought I was straight and ignored me most of that first year," she elaborated, unable to keep herself from laughing.

"I *did* think she was straight, but I *didn't* ignore her," I explained to Amy, though I knew the psychologist within her was busy processing our body language and everything being said. "This is probably a good time for us to cut out of here. Keep an eye on the place while I'm gone."

"I thought Mrs. Green handles that," Lindsay chimed in.

"Oh, she's met Mrs. Green?" Amy asked, smiling and raising her eyebrows. "No, not much happens here that she doesn't know about. You two have fun. Lindsay, it was very nice meeting you."

The shine on Lindsay's black Volvo four-door bore the reflection of my two-flat and me as I walked toward the passenger side.

"Let's put your bag in the trunk," Lindsay said, taking it from me.

I slid onto the smooth, camel-colored leather seat, noticing the faint odor of Armor-all as I pulled the door closed. The floor mats were immaculate. When Lindsay got into the car, I couldn't help but tease her.

"I'm betting you just came from a hand car wash."

"How much are you betting?"

"You cleaned the car? Inside and out? It looks like it just came from a detailing shop."

"So what are you saying?" Lindsay asked, amused by my insinuations.

"I'm impressed," I answered, trying to wiggle out of my playful predicament.

"No one gets my car as clean as I do," she said, "so I usually wash and wax it myself, except in the wintertime. Besides, I never let it get too dirty to begin with."

That I believed with no problem. She wasn't a "neat freak," but Lindsay's home, car and office always were prepared for company. Maybe it was a southern, proper thing. Or maybe Lindsay's home while she was growing up was messy and cluttered. I could relate to the latter. Our home was never dirty, but there generally seemed to be too much stuff for the given amount of space. I carried the genetic trait of wanting to accumulate "things" until Sarah successfully cured me of that habit.

After she died, I went through all of our pictures and trinkets we'd held onto as keepsakes, battling the temptation to keep everything and store it in the cedar chest. Ever since she began communicating with me, I expected to be chided for not simplifying the stash, but Sarah played mute while I emotionally worked toward that decision. It took me several months, but the collection now could fit into one blue storage tub.

As we drove south on Lake Shore Drive, Mayor Daley's landscape contractors busily redecorated the median area between northbound and southbound lanes with winter-hardy shrubs. Yacht club watery parking lots were beginning to clear as Lake Michigan prepared for frigid months. Lindsay stuck a CD into the car stereo and turned up the volume before the first song came on.

"Let me know what you think of this music," she said, briefly looking over at me.

The bluegrass tune spewed energy through the Volvo like a volcanic eruption. We both were grinning and jamming in our seats while the Museum Campus, Soldier Field and Chicago skyline faded in the rearview mirror.

"Who are we listening to?" I asked above the fiddle and vocals.

"Salamander Crossing," she said. "Aren't they great?"

"Very fun music."

"The sad thing is they broke up," Lindsay said. "Someone told me the band's only woman, Rani Arbo, has started a new group so I need to check into that, but I love Salamander Crossing. I thought you might find it fun."

Within two hours, we pulled onto a newly paved lane cut through acreage of old maples and drove at least a quarter-mile before I saw our "bed and breakfast." It wasn't quite what I had expected, my initial vision of a room within someone else's home where we would share a common conversation area on the main floor and have access to the kitchen. This Cape Cod-style structure boasted a wrap-around porch – perhaps for deer or bird watching – and rocking chairs crafted from young bent tree branches sat near the front door. Lindsay stole a glance my way looking for an initial reaction.

"What do you think?" she asked. "It's bigger than was described to me."

"This is a bed and breakfast?"

"Well, we have to make our own breakfast," she said, smiling. "Don't worry, I'll cook."

We parked and headed inside, leaving our bags in the trunk for the time being. Lindsay seemed anxious as she shoved a key into the deadbolt lock. Stepping into the house, we both took a minute to survey our surroundings before saying anything more. I could tell from her facial expression how pleased Lindsay was with the décor. The furnishings reminded me of a friend's place along the Blue Ridge Mountains, spotted with black-and-white photos of sand dunes, winter along the lakefront and local wildlife. The couch and chairs, oddly enough, were very similar to the ones in my own living room. A built-in wet bar sat tangent to the kitchen and dining area which was basically one huge room divided by a waist-high, pass-through countertop. Wine goblets hung by their stems upside down above the granite.

"Okay, what's the deal with this place?" I prompted. "Don't get me wrong – it's impressive – but whose is it?"

"I wish I could tell you it's mine," she said. "One of the perquisites of my job is befriending people who own second, and sometimes third, homes. A long-time client has been telling me about this house all year and said he only used it four or five times this summer. When I teased him about it, he said *I* should use it. So here we are!"

Lindsay started making rounds, opening the refrigerator, the cabinets and the pantry door. I followed her around like a toddler, mimicking her actions. In addition to an enormous family room and the kitchen/dining area, the first floor included one bedroom complete with full bath. The walls were pale blue surrounding a birds-eye maple bedroom suite. Sand-toned cases dressed two fluffy standard pillows laying atop a white quilt. As I moved closer to the bed, I saw the multi-colored wedding ring pattern in the quilt. The top of the dresser was decorated with old, thin gold-rimmed glasses propped on their leather travel case, an antique men's razor and faded family photos from throughout the century. On the nightstand, a simple, brass alarm clock sat next to a table lamp, its frosted globe a canvas for flowers painted in blue, yellow and rose. The lamp, probably first used in the late 1800s, had been upgraded to 21st century electrical standards.

In the bathroom, a claw-footed white tub stood under a curtained window, the leaves of a silk plant resting on the tub's edge near the spout. A large framed mirror hung over the vanity. The wall opposite the window housed a glass-encased shower – stark contrast to the early-1900s bathtub – and a European flush toilet, the kind where the reserve water tank is attached to the wall about six feet high and you yank a chain from above to cleanse the bowl.

"Cliff told me about this bathroom," Lindsay laughed. "The architect kept telling him the shower didn't go with the rest of the design, but Cliff insisted on having a shower that didn't involve a hanging curtain."

"It still looks nice," I said.

"Not as nice as your bathroom," she remarked, smiling.

I simply grinned and walked out of the bathroom and back into the entryway. Lindsay passed by me and led us to the stairway on the far side of the family room. The stairs were solid walnut with white ash spindles running like teeth of a comb under a walnut railing. When we reached the second level, the glossy hardwood floor spread before us, ending abruptly at the walls to our left and right and at closed French doors 30 feet from us. Intricately etched, beveled glass windows intrigued me as to what lay hidden behind those doors.

"This furniture has been passed down through his family," Lindsay explained, pointing at the day bed and various chairs scattered around the open space.

"He trusts having it here?"

"He's not the kind to worry about the house being broken into," she answered. "Material possessions are just material possessions, he told me. Of course, that's easy to say when your assets are as vast as his."

We laughed as we approached the French doors. Lindsay grabbed the textured, round, aged brass handle and gave it a 45-degree turn. Walking into the obvious master bedroom, we were greeted by intense rays of sunlight piercing the south windowpanes. Thin shears framed the scenery of steep sand dunes and Lake Michigan.

"Now this is a room with a view," Lindsay said, nearing the window.

"Wow. How did they ever find this property? You'd have to walk up and down the dunes, pick your ideal backyard and then track down who owned the land."

"Knowing Cliff," Lindsay said, "that's probably exactly what he did."

The master bathroom closely resembled the one on the first floor, with the exception of the shower. On this second level, the shower was a dual-head setup shooting out from blue tiling – some shade between royal and navy – interspersed with tan tiles that had an uncomplicated sketch of dune grass baked into them. Two sinks in a Corian countertop underlined the huge wall mirror and a basket of plush navy washcloths and hand towels anchored the end closest to the claw-footed bathtub. A dented copper kettle, stuffed with solid tan and navy bath towels, sat on the floor outside the shower. I barely noticed the cork saucer separating the kettle from the tile floor.

"I think that's it," Lindsay said, turning to me. "Will this place do?"

"I'll let you know after I hear about the breakfast menu."

She laughed and headed downstairs. I followed her to the car and, as she reached into the trunk for her bag, sprinkles of rain dotted the butt of her blue jeans, simultaneously hitting the top of my head and nose. The raindrops swelled four-fold, it seemed, before we got back to the house.

"Where did this weather come from?" I asked, setting my bag just inside the entryway.

The drops turned into sheets as a fall rainstorm pounded outside. I removed my shoes, leaving them by my bag, and searched out the most comfortable chair in the living room. Lindsay dug into her suitcase and retrieved a bottle of wine and a handful of music CDs.

"I was going to save this Shiraz for later, but considering the hiking conditions, should I tap into it now?" Lindsay asked. She set the bottle on the wet bar and carried the CDs toward the entertainment center near where I was sitting.

"Sure, I'll have a glass. More Salamander Crossing?"

"No, it's a variety. I don't want you getting bored with anything."

I knew her comment was meant to be applicable to more than the music, but I didn't react.

Waiting for the skies to clear – a three-hour pause in our day – I sipped my half of the bottle of Shiraz while Lindsay and I delved into a discussion about the history of women in business. Having a mother who always had been her own boss, Lindsay owned a different perspective than I about why women do or don't start their own enterprises. I was caught up in the conversation until my hunger pangs sang louder than her words.

"Are you hungry?" I asked.

"I can always eat," she answered. "Cliff suggested a restaurant that's about a 10-minute drive from here. Can you wait that long?"

I leapt from the couch I'd commandeered and bee-lined for the bathroom so I would be ready to leave when she said the word. She chuckled aloud to let me know she found my actions humorous.

Dinner at the local fine dining establishment easily met my expectations. Then again, all I really needed was something in my stomach. Food yields limited praise from me unless the meal involves my grandmother's homemade rolls, cream corn and blackberry cobbler. Lindsay and I both ordered the special: grilled salmon served with tomato couscous and steamed asparagus. Neither of us could finish the hearty portions, so I asked for mine to be packed to go. Lindsay glanced at me across the booth.

"I'll take mine to go also," she said, quickly catching the waiter.

She snagged the check as soon as it lighted on our table and I mildly objected, confident I could pick up our tab at the grocery store or another restaurant later in the weekend. Twenty comical shopping minutes at an outdated IGA preceded our return to Cliff's seldom-used second home. By the time we pulled in front of the house, a million stars had replaced the thick cloud cover that had grayed the day. An anxiousness tapped at my subconscious, uncertainty how the rest of this evening might unfold. I grabbed our leftovers and followed Lindsay, armed with our groceries, inside. Refrigerated items in their place, we deserted the kitchen.

I went toward the couch where I'd hibernated for three hours earlier in the day. Barely reaching a seated position, I realized Lindsay had been directly behind me. I did not have time to process what was happening before it happened. She gently placed her hands on my shoulders and faced me, momentarily pausing, then joined her lips to mine and kissed me passionately. My back rolled onto the couch as she melded her body on top of mine. Lindsay's aggressiveness torched my sexual desires. She was a beautiful woman, her svelt 5-foot-7 body the epitome of perfection for many lesbians (and men, for that matter). Her blonde hair fell to each side of my face and the scent and taste of her minted breath surrounded me. When she slowly pulled my shirt from its tucked position inside

162

the top of my blue jeans, I didn't stop her. Her skin was silky and warm as she rubbed the back of her hand along my stomach, then cautiously over the cup of my bra and breast. My upper body raised slightly from its recline when she squeezed my erect nipple between her thumb and index finger. I turned my head so that her mouth fell on my neck.

Lindsay's hips started dancing against me and I had no intentions of ending the pleasure. With one hand, I firmly pressed her lower back so that her pubic bone pushed along my thigh. My other hand massaged the cheek of her buttocks. Then my hands explored the entirety of her outline, growing more and more curious about the rest of her. Desire emanated from her utterings and actions. The simple fact that she wanted me, physically, sent my self-esteem soaring. That wasn't why I allowed this to continue, however. I enjoyed every second of her hungry lips on my neck, her investigating tongue, her skillful hands and fingers.

"Am I too heavy?" she softly asked, worried about her total body weight rocking on top of me.

"If you are, I hadn't noticed," I answered, running my hand from her buttocks to the back of her head and guiding her mouth to mine.

The couch's width proved satisfactory space for our romping, intense but playful lovemaking. Although Lindsay and I had opened that first door to intimacy during preceding weeks, things had never steamed like this. We had stopped at the proverbial second base. For whatever reasons, I had been corralling my carnal desires and tranquilizing them. Did I truly believe that would last? Along with my roller coaster emotions comes brute cravings for intimacy. Lindsay was satisfying that hunger.

The room temperature surged to sauna levels as nearly every muscle I'd learned to identify in college anatomy class got called into action. With one fluid movement, Lindsay shed her shirt and I slipped my hands along her rib cage to the center of her spine to unclasp her satiny beige bra. Her B-cup breasts titillatingly danced just out of mouth's reach. She yanked on my shirt until it pulled free from under my back and carefully slid it over my head. As she leaned closer to my torso and wedged her palms under my back to release the hook of my bra, her excited nipples brushed along my chest.

"You must be cold," I teased.

"Are you saying you want me to get an ice cube to trace along your body?" she playfully retorted, making the first of many sensual suggestions for the weekend.

We eventually relocated from the couch to the first-floor bedroom, Lindsay flipping the wedding ring-pattern quilt off the bed and pulling me on top of her as she fell to the mattress. It was my turn to aggress, my time to make the rules. For two or three hours, we alternated the role of initiator, the one who placidly determines body positioning and introduces a "plan of action." Our activity seemed almost juvenile, part of the excitement stemming from feeling like maybe we shouldn't be doing this, our energy more comparable to teen-age boys than women past age 40.

When sunlight filled the room and woke us from deep sleep, I had no regrets.

Lindsay and I fell into the dating pattern between September and mid-November. Liza's life bloated with out-of-town trips to Penn State, Iowa, Ohio State, Minnesota – more than one visit to each of the Big Ten campuses. We had not spoken to one another since late August. Each time I was tempted to call her, I instead summoned Sarah's attention to distract me and, basically, remind me of how I felt when Liza told me she needed time to deal with the "idea" of Sarah.

Sharing life with Lindsay was enjoyable, satisfying, easy. Aggressor that she is, few days passed that she wasn't asking me to join her for dinner, a play or whatever other creative venue she could conjure. Still, I took a lot of time to myself.

Running – the mileage on my training program continued mounting – became increasingly difficult as morning meetings with Baxter staff began taking up two or three days a week just before Thanksgiving. Cynthia Pruitt's deadlines for Francois Courteau's public relations team were non-negotiable. Thus, when Francois needed to meet with me, I felt obligated to make myself available at his convenience. Local television stations, including the three big guys and Fox, called to schedule interviews about A Sister's Hope's partnership with Baxter. This required further collaboration with Cynthia and Francois. Sarah assisted in the process by role playing in mock interviews with me. We had a lot of fun with that, not to mention the confidence boost it gave me.

I had planned to spend several days with my family in southeast Missouri during the Thanksgiving holiday, but as Lindsay and I grew closer and she told me she'd be staying in Chicago during that time, I decided to postpone my visit until Christmas. What I felt for her was not comparable to how I'd fallen for Liza or Sarah, but it was powerful, and I couldn't help but think that maybe the connection Lindsay and I shared was enough for a committed relationship. After all, neither of us was getting younger and our skin had begun showing the signs of aging. Lindsay knew how to make me laugh. She liked hearing about my conversations with Sarah. Our time together was exceptional.

Despite my comfort level with this Tennessee blonde, issues still existed. I returned to a modified version of not bringing a girlfriend into the two-flat. Lindsay spent hordes of time with me there, but those hours were not in a Jacuzzi or in bed. Our intimacy took place elsewhere – not on Farragut. When she first initiated affection there, I bluntly halted her.

"I'm sorry, Lindsay, but I'm not comfortable ... with ... not here. Not yet. Do you remember when I tried explaining that several weeks ago, when you came over because you were worried about me?"

"That's okay. It's no problem."

"We can stay at your place tonight," I offered with a counterfeit coyness.

I didn't know it at the time, but the college sports scene kept Liza preoccupied to the point that she had little time to "work through" anything. She discovered through friends of hers who knew Lindsay that the bank vice president had hooked up with the executive director of A Sister's Hope. The friends were totally unaware of Liza's brief love affair.

"You heard Cate McGuire speak at the Chicago Foundation for Women dinner, didn't you?" the one friend asked, knowing Liza regularly attended the Foundation event. "A woman in our investment club is seeing her now, which explains why Lindsay missed the past two meetings. What did you think of the McGuire woman? Was she a good speaker?"

"She must be good at something because we didn't think Lindsay ever would get over that gal she was with for nine or ten years," another friend added. "Even last year when she was dating the woman who has a kid, Lindsay always came to investment club meetings. Not anymore!"

"Maybe she'll come back after the first of the year," the first friend had said. "So, Liza, do you know anything about Cate McGuire?"

Although her face likely told the truth, Liza spoke vaguely about her vast knowledge of me.

"I met her that night," she answered, "and she definitely is a good speaker."

No further information offered, the topic moved to college women's athletics and Liza was allowed to escape into the comfort zone of her work. That night when she recoiled to her safe St. Ben's neighborhood, Liza stood in the entryway of her empty home, remembering the July night I entered her life. For weeks, she had avoided processing what I had revealed, avoided thinking about the woman she'd become engrossed in so quickly. All those emotions now were pouring on top of her like a deathly cold avalanche that slowly suffocates you. Fighting to maintain some semblance of composure, Liza tried distracting herself with mindless house chores. It wasn't working, so she sat down with a pad of paper and began making Christmas gift lists for family members. Once she had written down and underlined everyone's names, her thoughts went right back to me. Her knees curled to her chest, Liza laid on the living room couch – one of several spots we'd made love – and wept like a scolded child. Nothing now, she thought, could reverse the mistake she had made.

She wondered to herself, "Did I think Cate would just wait around hoping that I'd get my shit together and call her to say everything's okay, we can pick up where we left off?" Yet Liza could not deny she still harbored uncertainty about the whole "Sarah issue."

A sweltering shower helped ease the tension in her back and neck. Liza optimistically crawled into bed, her eyes burning as if she'd been swimming eyes wide open in a heavily chlorinated pool. When the restless night gave way to the morning sun, she picked up the telephone.

Chapter Eleven

I later learned of Liza's impromptu trip to Boulder, and the true depth of her friendship with Sue and Julie. Liza wanted me to know every detail of how that all unfolded.

"I'm sorry to call so early," Liza apologized as a voice answered on the other end of the line.

"Liza?"

"Yeah, I'm really sorry."

"Is everything okay?" Sue asked. Liza could hear Julie whispering in the background.

"Not really."

"Liza, what's wrong?"

"I'm such an idiot," Liza answered, her voice starting to break.

"You're not an idiot – we don't think so, anyway – but hold on, Julie wants to get on the phone, too, okay?"

As soon as Julie picked up a receiver, she started settling Liza's turmoil.

"Is this about your health, family, work or love life?" she asked pointedly in an almost light-hearted tone.

"It's about Cate," Liza replied. She knew Julie would sense she was fighting back tears, so Liza let them flow. "I couldn't sleep last night and I really need to talk to someone."

"So what's going on between you and Cate?" Julie posed.

"Nothing. That's the problem. We stopped seeing each other the week after we got back from the camping trip."

"We thought the two of you had a great time!" Sue chimed in. "What happened?"

Liza retold the story of the first three days we spent together back in Chicago, our mutual desire to spend each night in each other's company.

"Okay, so it sounds like things were developing beautifully," Julie said. "Right?"

"It was unbelievable," Liza responded. "But then she told me something that, at the time, I couldn't handle. I tried, but I couldn't get it clear in my mind and I told her I didn't think we should see each other until I came to grips with it."

"What on Earth did she tell you?" Sue asked.

"Cate had a partner for six years who died in 1998," Liza began to explain. "Sarah – that was her partner's name – supposedly still talks to Cate and Cate says she can talk to Sarah."

The phone line was silent. Liza's mild crying intensified as she fought back feelings of guilt for not being more understanding.

"Liza, we can tell how upset you are and I feel horrible that we're talking over the phone. Why don't you come out here this weekend? Do you have football or volleyball or something?" Julie asked, her tone becoming matronly.

"I'm scheduled to go to the Michigan football game on Saturday."

"Can you fly out Saturday evening and stay with us a couple of days?" she pressed.

"I appreciate the offer, but I don't think that's …

Julie interrupted Liza.

"*I* think you should come and see us," she said. "We've been friends for a long, long time, Liza, and I can't remember you ever sounding this down. If you don't want to fly out here, I can come to Chicago."

"No, you don't need to come to Chicago," Liza said. "I'll check into flights and let you know later today. It probably would be good for me to get out of the city."

"Never underestimate the healing power of the Rocky Mountains," Dr. Sue said.

"And the healing power of good friends," Liza added. "Julie, I'll call you this afternoon, all right?"

"Looking forward to your call," Julie said. "By the way, the next time you can't sleep because you're upset, you'd better not wait until the next morning to call me. You're going to hurt my feelings."

Liza felt better when she hung up the phone. The weekend arrived just in time. Julie picked up Liza at Denver International and they drove directly to a Mexican restaurant in LoDo (lower downtown) Denver that Julie swears makes the best margaritas in the country. When they parked, Liza recognized the Cherry Creek Bike Path below and the Larimer Square Historic District a block away.

"Sue plans to meet us here when she gets off work," Julie said, leading Liza to a booth in the lounge section of the restaurant. Traditional Central American music poured into the room through overhead speakers that hid behind bright orange and turquoise piñatas and sombreros the width of a yardstick. Terra cotta ornaments and cotton blankets like those you barter for in Tijuana covered any wall blemishes that might tarnish the image of this place. The décor alone was enough to liven Liza's spirits a little.

"What time is she scheduled to get off?" Liza asked.

"Anytime between ten and midnight, depending on how busy the ER was today," Julie said. "She found someone who was scheduled for a twelve-hour shift today to switch with her so she'd be off tomorrow. Oh, you met the guy, Colin, at our holiday party last year. He's the guy you ran into on a trail this summer. Anyway, we can have as many margaritas as you need because Sue said she's designated driver for the evening."

"How's she getting here?" Liza asked, wondering how two cars would get home with only one designated driver.

"She's calling a cab. I dropped her off this morning on my way to Colin and Colleen's. The three of us cycled seventy miles today; I didn't get home to shower until about the time you were flying out of Detroit."

Liza didn't bring up the painful subject of Cate while she and Julie worked through their tequila libations. They talked about the Big Ten and Julie asked for an update on each of the Aplington sisters. Only when Sue walked in around 11:30 p.m. was the name "Cate" mentioned.

"There she is!" Julie exclaimed as Sue approached. The fact that they'd successfully sipped down three margaritas each during the two-hour wait had made Julie exceptionally jovial.

"Hi Liza," Sue said, hugging her old friend. "Did the two of you get this Cate thing all figured out while I was working?"

Julie passed her a sobering – not sober – glance.

"That's all right," Sue continued. "Tonight we play. Tomorrow we talk. Are you two ready to head home?"

Liza and Julie both knew Sue must be exhausted, though she seldom used fatigue as an excuse for ending a night out. Neither offered resistance as Sue led them out of the Cozumel atmosphere.

On the ride home in the Explorer, Julie took the back seat and let Liza sit up front with Sue.

"So what's going on with you, Ms. Liza?" Sue asked, knowing Liza would tell her if she'd rather wait until morning to unearth the Cate saga.

"Where do I begin?" Liza responded, staring straight out the windshield as if she were mesmerized by the taillights guiding them along Speer Boulevard. "Everything was perfect until she told me about being able to communicate with Sarah. I flipped out. The night she told me, I think I even asked her if she'd seen a counselor or some stupid question like that. My immediate reaction was to assume her grief had driven her over the edge. I started acting like something was wrong with her."

"And what did Cate do?" Sue asked.

"She kept telling me she wasn't crazy and asking me to please not think she's crazy." Liza's margaritas had muted her emotions earlier in the evening and her tongue didn't articulate now as accurately as it normally does, but the meaning of her words and expressions could not have been clearer. "I used to pride myself in being open-minded and receptive to people who had different experiences than I. What's happened to me?"

Although Sue had labored through a steady pelting of patients in the ER all day, her attention remained crisply focused on Liza as the conversation moved from the Explorer to the living room, continuing well into the wee hours of Sunday morning. Liza wasn't accepting the idea of my actually being able to communicate with Sarah. She struggled with it, wrestling the possibility with a winner-take-all fury. Then Julie said something that changed everything.

"Every day on this earth," Julie began, "we learn more and more about our past and the possibilities within each of us."

This was a Julie – her expression fixed, serious – that Liza seldom saw.

"Who's to say some people aren't able to talk to those who have died? I want to believe what she's telling you is true. Do you have any idea how much I'd like to talk to my big brother again? To hear his voice? If you ask me, Cate's the lucky one. You should be envious, not afraid of the fact that she can communicate with this person she loved so much. I'd give almost anything to have another day with my brother."

Julie's tears overcame her, and Sue, like the caregiver she was born to be, immediately slid across the couch to embrace her. The brother to which Julie referred, Jacob, had led a mountain rescue team the previous February in search of 14 skiers trapped on the Rocky Mountain slopes by an avalanche. A second wave of crashing snow rolled down the mountain as Jacob coordinated evacuating the last three skiers. Two somehow survived. But Jacob, 46, and a 35-year-old father of three both were dead when the rescue team found them.

Being proud that he died saving others did not ease Julie's loss. Jacob had been not only her brother, but her mentor.

"I'm sorry, Liza," Julie said, pulling her head from Sue's shoulder and trying to force a smile. "This isn't supposed to be about me."

"And it shouldn't be about me either," Liza replied, shaking her head. "I *am* an idiot. You're right, Julie. Cate's the lucky one. And I seem to have forgotten a lesson I learned as a little girl, that you seldom can view life in black and white. Abby would be ashamed of me."

"Who's Abby?" Sue asked.

Memories of that amazing Louisiana belle led Liza into sharing stories about the days Abby cared for the four Aplington sisters. Julie and Sue laughed as Liza compared Abby Hebert Henderson to the starched Navy wives who surrounded her in the military microworld. The more Liza talked about Abby, the more she realized she missed Cate.

Tuesday morning, Liza hugged Julie good-bye along the curb at Denver International Airport.

"Thank you," she said, staring into her long-time friend's loving eyes. "You know, Jacob's probably still keeping an eye on you."

"Yeah, he probably is," Julie said, grinning. "If you patch things up with Cate, maybe she could ask Sarah to look up my brother and tell him to pay me a visit."

The humor assured Liza that Julie was recovering from her grief, though Sunday morning's discussion had reiterated how painful the past several months had been.

"I told you she's seeing someone else, remember? So, I don't know what my chances are of patching things up, but I'll keep that in mind," Liza replied, reaching down to grab the straps of her carry-on bag.

"You do that," Julie said.

Liza's next few days in Chicago presented an unexpected, challenging surprise. The PAC-10 Conference, headed by a man expected to retire within two years, offered her a lucrative position in Los Angeles. Part of the pitch was the enticement that Liza would be a leading candidate for the commissioner's post when he retired. If that came true, Liza would be the first female to hold such a prestigious position in a high-profile conference.

Calls came in from PAC-10 coaches Liza had seen over the summer at the convention she attended in Oregon. Those coaches already had made up their minds in July that Liza would be a powerful asset to their conference. They had been educating their athletic directors and had successfully persuaded the decision-makers to offer Liza the job. It seemed to be the opportunity of a lifetime.

A couple of days (and sleepless nights) went by. The trip to Colorado that cleared things in Liza's mind now seemed so long ago. Why did this offer come now? Was it some sort of sign? Did this promising career prospect symbolize an encouragement to move on with her life, move out of Chicago and away from Cate?

Knowing the conference needed an answer, Liza committed to calling them the next morning.

Chapter Twelve

The Michigan weekend with Lindsay revitalized me, like that first day of spring when you open the windows and allow a crisp, fresh air to sweep in and overcome the staleness from winter. Back in Chicago, our fun affair continued.

Lindsay answered her telephone on the third ring, just before the answering machine kicked into action. I was sitting in her dining room with a bagel, cream cheese and lox on my plate. We'd been up about an hour and had made a second pot of toasted southern pecan coffee to help wash down a light breakfast. When Lindsay returned to the table, I could tell she was upset about something. As she sat down, the snowmen on her flannel pajama pants huddled in creases at her knees and hips. Her eyes locked first onto the sage-colored coffee mug beyond her plate, then lifted slowly toward me. They were blurred with tears.

I reached toward her and she gripped my hand, squeezing it as if she were about to fall off the side of a mountain.

"Lindsay, what's wrong?"

She started to answer, but closed her lips. The small muscle at the side of her jaws bulged out as she clenched her teeth together and swallowed.

"That was Patricia," she said, assuming I'd know she was referring to the woman she'd been with for more than a decade.

Patricia left Lindsay a few years ago for another woman, who in the past year decided to leave Patricia. I was unclear where this conversation was going, but the pain on Lindsay's face kept my concern focused on her.

"Remember when I went with a friend to the doctor a while back?" she asked me.

I nodded.

"Patricia was the friend," she said, again almost starting to cry. "The doctor met with her yesterday and told her she has ovarian cancer."

As she forced those last two words past her lips, Lindsay crumbled. Intense emotions swept over her like a shell on the beach disappearing under a huge wave. I waited until the grip on my hand loosened, however lightly, before asking any questions.

"How advanced is it?"

"Far enough that they're already talking to her about alternative medicine," she answered, battling to speak clearly through her tears so I could understand what she was saying. "She's all alone, Cate. No one's there with her."

"Do you want to go there? I'll drive you. She needs someone to be with her right now. Do you want me to take you?"

At first, Lindsay did not answer me. I'm certain thoughts were racing through her mind, including the worry of what I might be feeling about all of this. I made it clear to her that she need not concern herself with me.

"Would you?" she finally responded, her beautiful brown eyes muddied by the tears.

I leaned forward from my chair and wrapped my arms around Lindsay, her wet cheek pressing against my neck. She started to stand up and I rose from my chair, never releasing the embrace. We stood knotted in each other, her emotional pain stimulating a vise grip on me. I knew she was oblivious to how tightly she was hugging me. That was okay.

When we pulled up in front of Patricia's home, Lindsay sat motionless for a moment, staring blankly forward. She looked over to me only after I laid my hand on her forearm and squeezed gently.

"I'll call you," she said, as if she didn't know what else to say.

Tension between us was foreign, something we hadn't experienced in the time we'd known each other. Lindsay obviously still harbored incredibly strong feelings for Patricia and, honestly, that wasn't bothering me as one might expect.

"If you or Patricia need something, call me."

She peered back at me, the calmest she'd been since taking the call from Patricia, and said, "Thank you, Cate."

Lindsay got out of the car and never looked back. I stayed long enough to watch her disappear inside the house, then headed back toward Andersonville.

"Sarah, are you here?" I called to her as I walked into the kitchen from the back stairs. "Helloooo?"

174

Once I'd set my overnight bag aside in the hallway, I returned to the kitchen to heat water for tea. Rummaging through my rectangular Tupperware tea container, I decided on Mandarin Spice from the primarily orange and black box. From the kettle's mumbling, I knew tea time was near.

"And how are you this late, cold Saturday morning?" Sarah's voice cut in just before the pot's whistle.

"Cold," I said, turning off the burner and drowning the bag at the bottom of my cup. "I'm starting to think it's just going to be you and me the rest of my life, which would be fine with me."

"No it wouldn't and you know it," Sarah quickly retorted. "So what do you project Lindsay's going to do?"

"I'm not sure yet, but it was very obvious to me that she still cares deeply for Patricia. I'd go so far as to say Lindsay is still deeply in love with her. The look on her face when she got off the phone ... she was completely distraught. Even if it is an option, I don't want to be in the middle of that."

"It sounds like you're already counting Lindsay out of the picture," Sarah said.

"You know what I'm going to do? I'll tell you what I'm going to do. I'm going to stop trying to forecast how my life is going to unravel. You'd think I would've stopped four years ago, but no, this summer I fell back into the ridiculous frame of mind that says maybe you *can* plot how everything's going to work out. That's ludicrous. Nothing is for sure. Nothing."

"Cate, I'm having a hard time determining whether you're being cynical or enlightened," she said. "Which is it?"

"Enlightened, my love. Seeing Lindsay the past couple of months has been wonderful, but I don't think I'm going to be gravely upset if we stop dating. I mean, I care for her and the intimacy has been almost medicinal after what happened with Liza."

"Well that's a healthy way to look at it!" Sarah's voice sounded surprised and amused.

"I say I wouldn't be gravely upset. Let me clarify that. I would like to keep seeing Lindsay and would really miss the closeness, in all its facets, if we break it off. She's become a very dear friend, as you know. Being able to talk to her about you and share the joy of that with someone is wonderful. That would be hard to not have – again. But I'm feeling confident about how I'll react, either way."

"I wish you could feel me hugging you right now," Sarah said. "You're amazing."

"You always were biased," I said, making her laugh.

Sarah normally steered away from comments about our touching or seeing each other. She knew those were sensations I begged for the first several months after she died and knew I couldn't have. The years had dulled the pain of such yearning. Now, I simply was pleased by her comment.

Lindsay called late in the evening to let me know she would be spending the rest of the weekend with Patricia. We didn't talk long, ending the conversation with plans to speak on Monday morning when she got into the office. Hearing her voice, I already was missing her.

Temperatures the first week of December fell below normal. Lindsay and I spoke at least once daily, but we didn't see each other again until Friday night, nearly a week after I'd dropped her at Patricia's. She came to Dearborn Station straight from work. From the moment she stepped into A Sister's Hope, I could tell a major discussion was on the evening's schedule. She hugged me, as usual, though slightly guarded, which could have been because Michelle was still at her desk. Once in my car, the heater still blowing cold air, I slowly wrapped my right hand over the top of her left and stared into her already glassy brown eyes.

"The wind made your eyes water, right?" I asked, grinning in an effort to lighten the mood.

"Yeah, that's it," she said, playing along. "What? Did you think I was crying about something?"

I drove us west to Randolph Street for dinner at Ina's, a woman-owned restaurant I liked to support. Our conversation on the way to Ina's revolved around Patricia's health status, her frame of mind and recommended treatment options. I planned to wait until Lindsay initiated any discussions of us. She delayed that topic until the waiter picked up our half-empty dinner plates.

"Not seeing you this week was very different for me," she started. "I think I'd become completely adapted to having you around almost every day."

"I missed seeing your beautiful face," I said, trying to not make assumptions about her use of the past tense – she *had* become completely adapted. My comment made her smile and that gave me a warm feeling inside.

"Could we get the check, please," Lindsay quickly blurted to the waiter as he passed by.

"Do you want to continue our conversation at your place?" I asked, offering a pause on what might become an emotional evening.

"That might be a good idea," she said, again smiling. "None of these people here want to see me cry."

I wasn't sure what would be behind the tears, but I didn't worry about it either. Within a half-hour, we were sitting on the living room couch close enough so that my leg brushed the edge of hers.

"You've been on the verge of tears since you got to my office," I said gently. "You can talk to me. You know that. Whatever you're feeling, you can tell me."

"Cate, when you and I started dating … actually, it was way before that. When I first started thinking about asking you out, I had already worked through this terribly long process," she said. "Patricia leaving me was the most painful thing I've ever had to deal with and I wanted to make damn sure I had recovered from that before trying to crack into your life."

"You dated others before me, though," I inserted, specifically remembering the woman who had a young child.

"Yes, I did, and I certainly wasn't over Patricia at the time, nor did those women have your allure."

I felt my face blush from the unexpected compliment.

"Being with you, I felt cleansed of those memories," she said. "I stopped dwelling on how happy I'd been with Patricia and began enjoying a personal life again."

The hesitancy before she spoke another word led me to believe there was a huge "but" about to strike. My instincts can be trusted.

"But Cate … " her voice dropped off, almost as if she'd forgotten what she was going to say. "Patricia needs me. She hates herself for leaving me, for throwing away what we had. She didn't ask me, but I found myself telling her I'm still in love with her and that I want to be there to take care of her."

Lindsay continued looking directly at me, wet trails streaming down both her cheeks.

"I wish I knew what you were thinking right now," she said, a not-so-subtle way of asking.

"I'm thinking that Patricia is a very lucky woman to have someone who loves her as much as you do," I responded, feeling tears well in my own eyes.

Lindsay leaned over to hug me and I met her halfway. We remained embraced as she whispered in my ear.

"Sarah was a lucky woman, too."

The break was clean. Lindsay took a leave of absence from A Sister's Hope, so we didn't see each other socially or for board business. She'd call every few days – she needed to talk to someone who could let her cry, allow her to flush out the sadness that would creep in. Our friendship was solid.

I reclaimed the morning, evening and weekend hours we'd been spending together and invested some of them in physical conditioning, mindful that my sister Casey was counting on me to be by her side in February for that marathon. I hadn't stopped training, but the icy weather and time with Lindsay definitely had altered my schedule.

On the morning of December 15, I called big sister Ruth to confirm my visit for Christmas.

"Have you told Mom yet?" she asked. I heard a school bell ring in the background. "Sorry about that. It's the end of first period. Did you hear me? Have you called Mom?"

"No, I called you first. Will you tell her today or do you want me to call her?"

"No, I'll call her. That's fine. What about Casey? Do you know when she's planning to come down?"

For a moment, I couldn't answer. Guilt raced through me because I hadn't called Casey in weeks. Normally, I kept her in the loop about my "love life," but we had lost contact with each other. Worse yet, I had no idea what was going on with her pending divorce.

"When's the last time you talked to her, Ruth?"

178

"A couple of weeks ago, or maybe 10 days ago," she answered, "but she didn't know yet what her holiday schedule was going to be. I thought you might have talked to her."

"No, I haven't, but I'll call her and try to find out."

When I hung up the phone from talking to Ruth, I decided to try reaching Casey right then. It must have been my morning.

"Hello?" a sleepy voice answered.

"Casey, it's Cate. Am I waking you up?"

"No, I don't think I was asleep yet, or maybe I'd just dozed off. I got off at 7 this morning. How are you?"

"I'm good. And I'm sorry I haven't talked to you for so long."

"That's okay. I know you're busy. I'm busy. We have a couple of guys from our firehouse on medical leave, so we've all picked up some extra shifts. What's going on?"

"I talked to Ruth this morning and she asked if I knew what your plans were for Christmas. How's it looking? Probably not good with those guys on leave, huh?"

"Actually," she said, "they both are expected back next week and already said they're working Christmas Day, so it looks like I'm going to have four days off starting Dec. 24. When are you heading down there?"

"Either the 22nd or 23rd. I might stay a full week."

"That'll be fun. I'm looking forward to seeing you."

"How's everything else going, Casey?"

"You mean with Tom?"

"Yes."

"I haven't seen him or talked to him lately. My attorney is working with his attorney and said she'll let me know if there's anything I need to know. I'm not worried about him trying to take more than his share of what we own. His having a girlfriend prevents that from being a problem."

She giggled.

"We'll catch up on everything when you get to Mom and Dad's, okay?" I responded. "I should get to work."

"Yeah, you'd better. It's going on ten o'clock."

Getting to talk to both sisters made my morning. This was going to be a good day.

Chapter Thirteen

The holidays bring all sorts of surprises.

It was Friday. Michelle wouldn't be in the office today. She would come in next Monday (Dec. 18) and work three days straight, then I wouldn't see her until January 8. What I really needed to accomplish was making sure I had certain projects ready for her to finish before she left for the holidays. With our special events team members mostly working from their own homes, office solitude was mine.

A productive morning, though it started late, called for a second dose of caffeine from the coffee shop downstairs. Walking back into the office, I heard my phone ringing and jogged around the corner of Michelle's desk, sloshing coffee onto the hardwood floor in my path.

"Happy holidays and thank you for calling A Sister's Hope," I answered. "How can I help you?"

"Cate, it's Cynthia Pruitt. Happy holidays to you, too."

"Hi Cynthia. It's good to hear your voice. What can I do for you today?"

"I thought I'd take a stab at seeing if you had an open day for lunch – my treat – before Christmas."

"That's very nice of you," I replied, dropping napkins on top of the coffee puddle. "The only day I think would work for me is Wednesday, though. Is that a possibility?"

"It sure is. Am I pushing it too late if we say one p.m.? That way, I can come back into the city and stay the rest of the day."

"One o'clock is great. I can tap into the volunteer snacks Michelle keeps around the office if I get hungry any earlier. Where would you like to meet?"

"How do you feel about sushi?" she asked. "I'm partial to Kamehachi in Old Town."

" I know the restaurant well. I'll meet you there at one next Wednesday then."

"Cate, I also wanted to let you know Leslie Carvalho had to go on medical leave this week."

"Oh no. What happened?" I feared horrible news.

"She's actually laughing about it, which amused the rest of the senior staff," Cynthia said, already taking the edge off my concern. "Leslie took a long weekend trip with her family in south Florida and, since it was warm weather, they all decided to rent bicycles one day and go for a ride."

"Don't tell me she was in a bicycle crash."

"Someone had their dog off the leash and it ran across the path in front of her. The dog was fine, but Leslie broke her wrist when she fell."

"Which wrist?" I asked, worried it might be on the side of her body where lymph nodes were removed.

"The other one," Cynthia answered, knowing what had sparked my question. "She's fine, at least she says she is, and she finally decided to take some time off, which I'm happy about."

"She'll probably be happy when this year's over, don't you think?"

We both laughed, though Leslie's health problems were not taken lightly.

"I'll see you next week, Cate," Cynthia said, ending our call.

One of the projects Michelle would be completing before her holiday departure was packaging gift boxes for key individuals at Baxter. Our idea was to make them clever and classy, but not extravagant. After all, sponsorship dollars are not meant to be spent on expensive presents for the sponsor. Now I could plan to hand Cynthia her gift when we had lunch next week.

The normal lunch hour had long passed and I still had no desire to eat. It's like I didn't want to pass up any of these calm hours alone in the office, the perfect setting for me to stay busy and remain focused. At my desk, I was immersed in reviewing our special events budget when I heard a subtle tap on the frame of my office door. Slightly startled by the sound, I was more shocked when I looked up from the paperwork.

Dark pants and a dark top were offset by the thick red sweater draped over her arm. My heartbeat skipped like an athlete's steps in the triple jump as I stared into Liza's confident face. I had envisioned this moment, but it was supposed to happen months ago. I honestly thought I had erased it from my mind because it was never going to happen. Yet here she stood, a few short steps from me. My body seemed bolted to my chair. My mouth wanted to speak, but I was afraid to say anything. I felt the intensity draw my eyebrows into an inquisitive look and quickly tried to relax my face. As she continued to stand there, those dark blue eyes began to rain. Her confidence faded as she wondered why I hadn't moved, why I hadn't said a word.

"Cate?"

The way she whispered my name, that's all Liza needed to say. I rushed over to her in the doorway, embracing this woman with every ounce of my being. The familiar smell of her hair comforted me as I buried my nose in the darkness at the nape of her neck. She was trembling, repeating the same thing over and over.

"I'm so sorry, so so sorry. Please forgive me. Can you ever forgive me? I'm sorry, Cate. I'm so sorry."

"Shhh." I made the extended, soft sound as my fingers pressed firmly against her upper back and waist, trying to let her know I'd just forgiven her. My arms padlocked her against me.

"You can't believe how happy it makes me that you're here," I said, continuing to hold her tightly. "When I looked up and saw you in the doorway ... I didn't want to assume anything."

"I know," she said. "I wouldn't have blamed you if you had told me to get out. I didn't really know what to expect when I came in, but I couldn't stay away from you anymore."

"We have a *lot* to talk about," I said, tentatively and reluctantly drawing my head back to where our eyes could see one another.

"I took a chance coming here in the middle of the afternoon, I know, but I wanted to make sure I found you," Liza said. "Do you have plans tonight? When can we talk?"

For a few moments, I tethered her attention with my stare. Then I smiled.

"We can start right now," I said, sliding my hand down her arm and taking hold of her hand. "Although, I might need to come back to the office over the weekend. That can wait for now. Let's go to Farragut."

As I cruised around the office to turn out lights, lock closets and filing cabinets, Liza's eyes stalked me like a paparazzi. A couple of times, I stopped almost mid-stride and glanced over to catch her in the act. When I did, that smile of hers I find so amazingly radiant would beam toward me. Pheromone nervousness crept from my chest and abdomen throughout my extremities as I pulled my private office door shut and led Liza past Michelle's desk. Her red sweater, now laying on top of the royal blue ski jacket I'd worn that day, blended into the dull office palette when I flipped off the last overhead light. Afternoon sunrays reaching into the reception area were dim enough that everything around us reflected shades of gray. I could feel Liza close behind me and, when I reached the front door of our office, instead of passing through to the other side I grabbed the thick edge of the door and slowly pushed it shut in front of me. As I did, Liza ran her hand along the top of my shoulders.

I turned around to face her, gently closing the gap between us, letting my eyes trail from her eyes to her nose and cheeks and finally her lips. My gradual advancement, meticulously, ultimately led my lips to hers but, in the meantime, she stood still, attentive, in the same vertical plane. It felt as though she wanted me to be completely in control, fully responsible for what was about to happen. So many seconds – it could have been a full minute – had passed between the time I faced her and the moment we kissed that the actual contact almost startled us. As my mouth and tongue determined the velocity of our actions, Liza followed like a dance partner who knew my every move.

We did not make love in the office, as exciting as that *might* sound to some. We did, however, stand there engrossed in each other for a while. We then realized we should try to get out of downtown before traffic became sluggish on Lake Shore Drive.

"Am I going to find you this hard to resist in 10 or 20 years?" I playfully asked.

"I'm planning to find out," Liza answered, smiling, creating those beautiful defining crow's feet around her eyes.

"Is this yours?" I asked, picking up a black satchel-style briefcase near the door.

"Yes," she answered. "I took a cab here from O'Hare. I had a meeting at Penn State this morning."

I paused to look at her intently.

"You *were* anxious to see me."

"You have no idea," she said, nudging me out the door.

A mild December day, I was comfortable walking to the car with my jacket unzipped. Liza said it had been in the 50s on the

Nittany Lions campus. It could have been 30 degrees in Chicago, but I think we both were oblivious to the weather. Although we didn't get snarled in typical Friday afternoon traffic, the drive to my two-flat seemed to take longer than usual. I wanted to be there. I felt like I needed to be there. As I said earlier, Liza and I had a *lot* to talk about and some of the conversation – the part about Lindsay, for example – would be difficult.

After backing into the garage and poking the garage door button remote, my thumb and forefinger grabbed the ignition key, rotating it back toward me. Our surroundings now dark and silent, Liza simultaneously grabbed my hand and spoke.

"Cate … we're meant to be together."

Every facet of the world around me froze at that moment. Her words rang clearer than any I'd ever heard.

"I know."

She leaned over and sealed the moment with a kiss before we got out of the car. We had exited the garage and I was locking the side door when I heard someone say something. I turned to Liza. She simply motioned toward the two-flat.

"Cate! Where have you been lately?"

It was Amy, standing at the back door, wearing a T-shirt and sweatpants covered in dust.

"I'm a busy woman," I replied, planning to harass her. "That's the way it is when you have a full-time job."

"You just wait, Ms. McGuire," she started. "One of these days you'll read in the headlines that I'm the lead psychologist for the U.S. Olympic team."

We all three laughed, though Amy quite possibly would hold that title one day.

"Hi, you're Liza, right?" Amy asked.

"I'm sorry, have we met?" Liza answered, looking perplexed that Amy seemed to know her.

"She and Claire, her partner, saw you leaving here the day I took you to the airport," I quickly chimed in, "and they asked about you."

Passing Amy a solid glare, I think she got my message to not pursue a conversation at this time. She politely and quickly excused herself to the basement where she'd been sorting through their storage area. Liza followed me up the back stairs to the door leading

184

into my kitchen. As we stepped inside, I knew she was remembering the same thing I was: the first day she had been here. At that time, she didn't know about Sarah and had no reason to hesitate kissing me. That was more than four months ago. Now with her knowledge of Sarah and the connection she and I have in this cherished space, I worried about how Liza would react over the next several moments.

"Am I allowed to kiss you?" she asked. She wore an enormous grin, erasing my concern.

Standing in the kitchen – after she kissed me – I had a flashback of the day Lindsay came over to check on me. Guilt burned through me like fever. I dreaded having to tell Liza about the past couple of months.

"Do you want something to drink? I can make coffee, hot chocolate, tea …"

"Ooh, hot chocolate sounds really good right now," Liza said, walking over to the refrigerator and starting to peruse the photos held to its door with sundry magnets I'd collected on various vacations. "Who are all of these folks?"

My answer would be a legitimate transition into the serious conversations that lie ahead. Among the photos decorating the refrigerator door were snapshots of Sarah and a new addition: a 4" x 6" color print of Lindsay from our weekend in Michigan. I started describing the easy ones: school pictures of my niece and nephew, family holiday portraits, the professionally shot black-and-white 5" x 7" of the Cianfrini mafia, as I always referred to Michelle's family.

"These are my sisters, Casey and Ruth," I said, pointing to each of them as I said their names. "Casey looks like a firefighter, doesn't she?"

"She definitely looks like an athlete," Liza said. "They're both pretty women, just like their sister."

I leaned toward her to dole out a fleeting peck on the cheek before attending to the hot teapot. I made myself a cup of hot chocolate, too, and tried to initiate our mobilization to the living room, but Liza resisted.

"And who's this?" she tapped her finger on the newest photo.

"Her name is Lindsay Cuvier. She is – was – a board member at A Sister's Hope."

Liza stared at the photo, her head making just the slightest motion up and down, yet she said nothing.

"And this is Sarah?" she asked, accurately identifying one of the snapshots.

"Did you do that by process of elimination?" I asked, curious as to why she pegged that woman as Sarah.

"The face is familiar to me, though I don't remember ever meeting her," Liza answered, continuing to look at the photo. "She looks so wholesome. She was a natural beauty, wasn't she?"

"I certainly thought so," I replied. "Thank you for saying that. Should we move into the living room?"

Upon my suggestion, Liza was ready this time to relocate. I chose a spot on one end of the couch and, when Liza started to sit in the chair nearby, I asked her to come sit next to me. A sip of my scalding drink convinced me to set it aside on a coaster for now. Liza placed hers on a coaster next to mine, then adjusted her posture so that she was facing me. She gently dropped both hands onto my leg.

"I don't know what you wanted to talk about first, but I want you to know I know who Lindsay is," she said in an exceptionally calm voice.

Needless to say, I was taken aback. Since I wasn't saying anything, Liza continued.

"Some friends of mine are in an investment club with Lindsay. One night, while we were having dinner, they started talking about Lindsay's new girlfriend – you. They didn't know anything about you and me. All they knew was that I had gone to the CFW dinner and heard you speak, so they were asking me what I could tell them about you."

Without further prompting, I began trying to explain how the relationship with Lindsay developed.

"We're not seeing each other anymore," I said, wanting to assure Liza nothing was going to come between us this time.

"I know," she immediately responded. "I eventually told my friends about the two of us. They were the ones who called me yesterday to tell me about Lindsay's ex and that Lindsay was going to be taking care of her. That's why I finally felt like I could contact you. When I found out you were seeing someone else, I didn't know what to do, but it was my fault that I was out of the picture. If I hadn't acted so ridiculously about Sarah …"

I stopped Liza there. One of my biggest anxieties after seeing her standing in my office was how to tell her about Lindsay. Now

186

here she sat, in my house on my couch next to me, taking responsibility for my love affair with Lindsay.

"Liza, I want to explain how Lindsay and I started seeing each other. A few days after I met you, while you were in California, Lindsay asked me out for dinner. Since she was a board member, I thought it would be a good chance to get to know her better. I had no intentions of it being a date. My God, I'd just met you and my head was still spinning from that. So we met for dinner, then walked over to Buckingham Fountain. It was fun. When I found out she lived just a couple of streets south of me and was planning to take the train home, I offered to give her a ride."

At this point, Liza's facial expression melded into one of curiosity. I think she feared where this story might be headed. I didn't want to keep her in suspense.

"Nothing happened, really," I said. "She *did* kiss me when we pulled up in front of her house. That's when I told her I had just started seeing someone. I can't say that dissuaded her from pursuing me, or at least spending time with me while you were out of town, but she didn't try to be physical."

Liza smiled. I absolutely love to see her smile.

"I don't blame her," she said, referring to Lindsay's pursuit, "but I'm very glad to hear that the two of you weren't intimate."

I'm sure Liza understood that we were talking specifically about the two-week period she was on the west coast when she said that, but I felt it necessary to be crystal clear about the intimacy between Lindsay and me. I cupped my hands over the top of hers.

"We *weren't* intimate then, but things changed in the fall after you and I stopped seeing each other."

Watching Liza's eyes would verify whether or not she had anticipated that piece of information. I waited for a response.

"I won't tell you that's easy to hear," she said, looking down at our joined hands. "I have no right, though, to judge you for anything that happened."

"Liza, I didn't plan on becoming involved with Lindsay. She showed up at a time when I needed someone to talk to and spend time with, and … it just happened. I felt rejected by you and I was hurting. Lindsay's a wonderful woman. She filled the emptiness. As it turns out, that's apparently what I was doing for her."

"So you weren't in love with her?" Liza asked.

"In love? No. I do love her, though, and she'll continue to be a part of my life. Do you feel threatened by that?"

"No," she answered, "because I believe it's fate that we're together."

We leaned toward each other and Liza kissed me, her confidence in what she'd just said showing clearly in the way her mouth moved on mine. I thought our conversation might be on infinite pause, but she subtly pinched my bottom lip with her lips and backed away, her gaze never straying from my eyes.

"Am I right?" she softly asked.

I never dreamed I'd feel this way about anyone after Sarah died. The love I had felt for her and from her constantly amazed me. I sometimes wondered if I deserved a life so rich.

"Well? Am I?" Liza gently prodded.

"Yes, you're right," I answered, squeezing the top of her thigh. "I was just thinking about Sarah and how I knew she was 'the one' from the first night we sat and talked."

I hesitated before going on.

"Yet, I'm sitting here with you and I know this is where I'm supposed to be – with you. Can a person possibly find that twice in a lifetime?"

"If Sarah were still alive, I'm quite sure I wouldn't be planning my future with Cate McGuire," Liza said, smiling as she finished the sentence. "She's gone. Now it's my turn to make you happy."

Liza barely had finished saying the 'py' of happy when Sarah's voice snared my attention, shocking me that she was speaking while Liza was with me.

"I told you, didn't I?" Sarah said, not really asking a question. "I told you she loved you like this. I'm in heaven right now."

I wondered if she meant that last part figuratively or literally.

"Figuratively," she responded to my thought, "but I'm literally pretty close, too."

When I smiled at the comment, Liza perceptively guessed that Sarah was present.

"Is she talking to you right now?" Liza asked.

Liza cast a look around the room.

"I'll take good care of her," Liza said, her face and voice directed toward the ceiling.

Grappling with the temptation to cry, I took an enormously deep breath and regained my composure. Liza, who initially could not accept the fact that I communicate with Sarah, now was talking to Sarah herself.

"Can she hear me? She can hear me, right?" Liza asked.

"She hears you."

With that, I grabbed Liza by one hand and led her off the couch and upstairs. When I slipped my feet out of my shoes, Liza copied my actions and followed me onto the bed.

"I want to hold you," I said, drawing her into my arms.

We nestled into a comfortable horizontal position and lay silent for a few minutes.

"Can I ask you about Sarah?" Liza's voice broke into the stillness.

"What do you want to know?"

"You never told me how she died."

Soon it would be five years passed since that phone call was transferred to my desk at the Tribune. The police officer knew only that I was listed as the emergency contact on a card in Sarah's wallet. Had he known our true relationship, maybe someone would have shown up at the office to tell me in person.

"You might have read about it in the newspaper or seen reports on television," I began. "It was in February of 1998. Since Sarah was a schoolteacher, the superintendent and several of Sarah's colleagues were interviewed. "

"What was her last name?" Liza asked.

"Wickham."

When I had mentioned the name in August, no bells went off in Liza's memory. Instead of delving into details about what had caused Sarah's death, be it illness or whatever, our conversation that evening had gone directly into my continuing communication with Sarah.

Liza's body shuddered and she rolled onto her side to look at me.

"I *do* remember seeing it in the newspaper," she said. "That's why her face looked familiar to me. Cate, *that* was your Sarah?"

She looked shocked, no, horrified. Liza brushed her fingertips along the hairline of my forehead and down my jaw.

"I am so sorry the name didn't register when you said it this summer," she began apologizing. "Cate, I'm really sorry."

"You've been saying that a lot today," I replied, a mild grin lightening the heaviness in the room. "I'm okay. It was brutally difficult to handle at the time, but life goes on. Now can I ask you something?"

"Anything."

"What was it that finally helped you accept the relationship I have with Sarah?"

"When I called you that day and said we shouldn't see each other for a while, I hung up the phone and fell apart. I honestly didn't know what to do. So instead of trying to understand and work through it, I took the easiest way out. I stopped thinking about it so I could do my job. And that worked fine until I had dinner with my friends that night when they talked about Lindsay and her new lover."

Liza's voice quivered and tears trickled from her blue eyes.

"That night, I battled with the saddest feelings of my life. I had lost you."

"But what changed your mind?"

"I still was struggling with what you'd told me because I hadn't dealt with it. I guess I thought it would just take time and things would work out, but when I found out about Lindsay, reality set in. Early the next morning, I called Julie and Sue and they convinced me to fly out there and spend a couple of days with them. Julie said she'd never seen me so depressed, so upset."

"Hold that thought," I said, rolling off one side of the bed.

Securing a box of tissues from the bathroom, I returned to my spot on the still-warm down comforter and handed a tissue to Liza.

"Thank you," she said, wiping her face and nose. "Anyway, while the three of us were talking, I remembered those days when Abby – the woman who used to babysit me and my sisters – would give us her perceptions of the world. I loved that woman. She fascinated me. I think she was one of the most progressive minds I've ever met. She'd be disappointed by how I responded to what you told me. She always said the gray areas of life are the ones from which we learn the most. I started looking at what you told me the way Abby would have looked at it.

"I've missed you so much, Cate. I can't imagine not having you in my life."

"You're going to make *me* cry," I said, running my fingers through the hair hanging to the side of her face.

"I need to tell you something else," she said, slightly worrying me. "Right after I got back from Colorado, I got a call from the Pacific Athletic Conference offering me a job in L.A., a lateral move with the potential of becoming the commissioner in two years."

I simply stared at her, waiting for further information, becoming anxious not knowing what transpired.

"There currently are no women commissioners of top conferences like that," she said. "I had to give them an answer several weeks ago."

My heart dropped into a pressure chamber.

"Are you taking the job?"

"Are you crazy?" she replied, stroking my cheek with the pad of her thumb. "Had I accepted, I would've been required to be in L.A. weeks ago. It was an attractive situation, but I couldn't do it. I couldn't leave Chicago and give up the possibility of us."

There was no need to try to suppress my joyful tears anymore. Liza had made an enormous sacrifice to stay in Chicago with no promise that we'd be reunited. She had put her faith in fate.

We remained planted on the bed for another hour or so, disturbed only when hunger roars from both our midsections finally succeeded in getting us out of the bedroom. Reassuring me that she had no need to return to her house until morning, Liza took the lead in ordering Thai food for delivery. We spent the rest of the evening talking, learning more, falling deeper.

"What are your plans for Christmas?" I asked, pouring each of us a cup of coffee the next morning.

"Well," Liza began, dragging out the word, "I fly to New Orleans Monday afternoon. The women's volleyball national championship is this week and we have a school, Penn State, in the Final Four."

I glanced over at her, raising my left eyebrow. I couldn't help but laugh.

"So this is your modus operandi? You drop into my life for a day or so and then you fly out of town?"

"Welcome to the world of college athletics," she said, approaching me. "Why don't you come with me?"

"Oh, that *is* tempting, but I haven't seen my family for months. I talked to both sisters yesterday morning and told them I'd be home on the 22nd or 23rd."

"You'd only be delaying it another day or two," Liza persuasively rebutted. "I'll buy your airline ticket. You can join me down there as soon as you can get away from the office this week."

"And where were you planning to spend Christmas Eve and Christmas Day?"

"Part of my family will be in Florida, but two of my sisters won't be there, so I currently have a flight back to Chicago on Sunday morning. I could always catch a flight later that day out of Midway if I decided to go see my parents. I don't know. I hadn't really decided. Can you tell?"

"How about coming to Jackson, Missouri?"

Startled at first, Liza quickly created a bartering chip.

"I'll go with you to Missouri if you'll come to New Orleans."

For a moment, I thought of Lindsay and her persistence in getting what she wants, but I didn't share that thought with Liza.

"Going to Jackson isn't as simple as booking a direct flight from New Orleans," I said. "We'd need to fly into St. Louis, then rent a car because it's a two-hour drive from there."

"The logistics will work out if we decide that's what we want to do," Liza said, sliding her hands around my waist and narrowing the gap between us. "What do you want to do?"

"Okay," I conceded.

"Okay? You'll come?"

"Let's see if those logistics really will work out. Let me see you work your magic."

She hugged me as if I'd just given her the present she'd always wanted. Her unbridled enthusiasm invigorated me. When the oven clock caught my eye, displaying 9:30 a.m., I remembered what was on my schedule for the day.

"I told my little sister I'd run the Cowtown Marathon with her," I said, broaching the subject, "and my training program calls for a ten-mile run today."

"You committed to it, huh? That's great. How's it been going?"

"Good, I guess. I'll know for sure these next four weeks. The long runs increase from ten to eighteen miles."

"You can take me home anytime you need to," Liza said. "I don't want to throw you off schedule."

"You've already done that," I playfully accused. "I'd like to spend the rest of the weekend with you. I feel like it's been an eternity since our trip to Colorado. Can I come over after my run?"

"That would make me very happy," Liza said.

We found her a pair of my worn blue jeans to wear home, along with a T-shirt and thick cotton, bright yellow sweater. It caused me to reminisce about the canary yellow envelope she'd given me before she left for the west coast. The card's handwritten text, "Beginnings offer exploration of the unknown," scrolled through my mind.

"Our exploration of the unknown has begun," I said, catching her attention from across the room.

Cast my way came one of my Liza's insurmountable smiles.

As promised, Liza proved her logistical expertise by obtaining airline reservations from Chicago to New Orleans to St. Louis and back to Chicago. I often wondered what my ticket cost her, but I never asked. It was one of those things she wanted to do for me and, whatever the cost, it ended up being worth every cent.

At the national tournament Liza was somewhat of a celebrity, people constantly nabbing her attention as we tried maneuvering through the crowded hallways of the coliseum the two days there were matches. At the host hotel, she took me to numerous receptions and introduced me to dozens of people. I was reminded of the night we'd met at the Fairmont and the fact that she knew more people at my table than I did. The Penn State Lady Lions lost in the volleyball finals Saturday night, but having a national runner-up in the conference was a feather in the Big Ten's cap. Since my arrival late Wednesday, Liza and I had experienced much of the New Orleans flair, complete with spicy crawfish jambalaya, jam-packed Bourbon Street, a women's bar that had been around for decades and, finally, southern-style brunch at the hospitable and infamous Commodore.

We were fatigued – an understatement – when I pulled up the driveway of my parents' home in Jackson. As we stepped out of the car, I heard a bawling calf and chickens gossiping in a pen about 30 yards from us. Coming here always refreshed me, though I never forget the small-town drawbacks.

"Hello there," my mother called to us, tromping out the front door.

My family couldn't have been sweeter to Liza. Each of my sisters had, at the last minute, picked up "a little something" for her to open during our gift exchange on Christmas Eve. At my suggestion, Liza and I decided to skip getting gifts for each other. For two days, we ate and visited with family and ate and visited with more family. The smells of nutmeg, melting butter and fresh-baked bread kept my salivary glands amused. I occasionally asked Liza if she felt uncomfortable or ignored, but she insisted she was having fun. We took time to ourselves, investigating county blacktop roads I'd never traveled, shopping in the new Cape Girardeau mall and, on one sunny day, walking along the Mississippi River near the bridge that runs between Missouri and Illinois. On the day of my 15-mile training run, Casey and I decided to start at Jackson City Park and make a loop around town, past the old hosiery mill and Yamnitz Auto Body toward where the A&W Restaurant used to serve us miniature frosted glass mugs of root beer. Our mileage wouldn't be exact, but close enough. Liza rode with us to the park and ran the three miles back to my parents' place on her own. The longer route gave my little sister and me more than two hours to catch up on things. I wanted to know more about Tom and the divorce. Casey wanted to know more about Liza, which would include learning about Lindsay. The therapeutic benefit from that training run might have overshadowed the physiological gains for both of us.

The week passed too soon. It always does. Since Liza had come with me, we had agreed to return to Chicago on the Friday after Christmas so we would have the weekend and New Year's Eve to ourselves. With a promise to make my visits more frequent, I backed out of the driveway while Mom and Dad both waved from the edge of the garage. Liza noticed my cheerless expression.

"You hate leaving them, don't you?" she asked.

"Yeah. And the older I get, the harder it seems to be."

"We'll just have to come back often," she said, lightly squeezing my right shoulder, then resting her warm palm there.

A light snow welcomed us back into the city as our taxi sailed toward St. Ben's. The plan was to stop at Liza's so she could round up a few items, then we'd drive her Jeep Liberty to Farragut where we'd spend the next three days. Within a half-hour, Liza was ready to go to my place and seemed overly anxious to get there.

"What's up with you?" I asked. "We're not in a hurry, are we?"

"I am *so* ready to be where I can hold you and touch you," she said, "and run around naked if I want to."

With that comment, she took off in a light run, circling the dining table and lifting her arms into the air. A goofy grin on her face, Liza ended her routine right in front of me.

"Was that too bold?" she whispered, trying to appear bashful.

"*What* am I getting myself into?" I responded, igniting her laughter. "I guess we should get going then."

Bitter wind chills tried discouraging me from going on the 16-mile run I was slated to complete over the weekend, but when Liza offered to run part of it with me, I was inspired for the challenge. She peeled off at the seven-mile mark, breathing as smoothly as when we had started, while I headed out for a second loop. It was another mile back from there to the two-flat. Liza was waiting at the kitchen door with hot chocolate in hand when I finally got back to the house.

"How was it?" she asked, handing me the steaming cobalt blue mug.

"I could've used your companionship on those last four miles. It seemed much shorter last week when I ran those fifteen with Casey, probably because we were talking the entire time."

The Jacuzzi soaking party we threw ourselves that night would be repeated the next evening in celebration of New Year's Eve. Each of us had been invited to different parties, but the newness of being together convinced us to stay at my place for ringing in the new year. Liza already was in the hot tub, candles lit and noisemakers lying nearby for the stroke of midnight. I walked into the bathroom, hiding a small package under my robe.

"The water's going to be cold before you get in," Liza teased. "Come in. Please?"

I pulled the package into view and tossed her a towel to dry her hands.

"What's this?" she queried. "We agreed, no gifts."

"It's not really a gift," I said, setting it on the edge of the tub. "You'll see."

She peeled away the red glossy wrapping paper, then dug at the bubble wrap and tissue paper I'd taped around the object. When she realized what it was, Liza grinned.

"I wondered why this wasn't on your nightstand anymore," she said, holding the stainless steel travel alarm clock she had sent me from California.

"It spent a few weeks in the closet, I have to admit, but it was safe to come out again," I explained. "You can have it back now so when you're on the road, you'll think of me when you look at it. Right?"

"Will you do me a favor and bring my leather overnight bag in her?" Liza asked instead of answering me.

I retrieved her bag from the bedroom and set it within her reach.

"Close your eyes," she commanded. "Hold out your hands."

"The rule was no gifts," I retorted, obeying her request.

She placed a wrapped item in my hands and gave me the okay to open my eyes. It was rectangular, slightly heavy, and I guessed it would be either a book or a picture frame. The flashy Disney wrapping paper fell next to the tub and I opened the end of the cardboard box, verifying its contents to be a picture frame. When I pulled it out, I saw that Liza had made a 5" x 7"enlargement of a photo taken of us in Colorado.

"This goes on my nightstand," I said, leaning over the edge of the tub to kiss her.

"Are you ready to get in here yet?" she prodded.

"In a minute," I answered, running downstairs.

When I returned carrying two flutes and our bottle of champagne, Liza grinned. Within seconds, I was submerged to the chin, allowing the jet bubbles to massage my lower back and between my shoulder blades. Liza started inching toward me, as if I wouldn't notice. She took her sweet time, effectively inflating my anticipation until I thought I would burst. Her hands landed on each side of my hips and her hip bones wedged between my legs. As she moved in to kiss me, her breasts floated into mine. A beeping noise distracted me.

"What is that?" I finally said.

"It's midnight," Liza answered, reaching for her runner's watch.

She filled the champagne flutes and returned to my side of the tub. We toasted love and life.

Sliding under the sheets that night, the room felt different to me.

I initiated our love-making by massaging Liza's hand, working my way up her wrist and forearm, tickling the sensitive crease at her elbow. By the time I reached her shoulder, she was writhing next to me. The arrival of the new year indeed was celebrated and my heart was content, knowing Liza would be lying next to me when the sun broke open a new morning.

Chapter Fourteen

The marathon was quickly approaching and I felt prepared for what was coming.

Liza traveled a tremendous amount over the next six weeks. The special events team for A Sister's Hope moved full-time into the office right after the holidays and Baxter's public relations team began promoting our fifth annual cross-country run. Between work, my own marathon training and time with Liza (when she was in town), I didn't notice the fewer conversations I was having with Sarah. In early February, she picked a night Liza was gone and paid me a lengthy visit.

"How are you, Cate?" she asked as I walked into the upstairs bedroom to change clothes.

"Sarah, it's good to hear your voice. I haven't talked to you in a few days."

"Three weeks, to be exact," she replied.

I sank onto the bed and sat there for a moment, wondering how it could have been that long since we'd spoken. We had never let that much time pass without a conversation.

"You seem very happy, the Cate I used to know," Sarah continued. "I've waited quite a while to see you like this."

"I *am* happy, Sarah. Liza is incredible. It's like she's the missing piece in a puzzle I've been trying to put together the past few years."

"Do you remember, on that first night I spoke to you," Sarah asked, "when I said you can carry me in your heart for as long as you need me?" Sarah asked.

"Yes, and you're not going to say I don't need you anymore, are you?" I responded, my voice becoming defensive. "You said you'd be with me *always.*"

I felt the warm rush of blood to my face.

"I *will* be with you always, but there will come a time when it won't be like this. I've stayed with you all this time to make sure you fully recovered, that you were going to be all right."

"Sarah, I will never fully recover from losing you. I'll be happy with Liza, but I'll never fully recover from your death."

She knew what I meant and could not deny it.

"I shouldn't have said it that way, Cate. I'm sorry. You know what I mean, though."

Yes, I knew exactly. One day, probably soon, Sarah would speak to me for the last time.

We talked all night, even when I should have been sleeping, stopping only for my phone conversation with Liza when she called from Iowa. We reminisced. We laughed. And for the first time in five years, Sarah cried. It reinforced my memory of the bond between us, of how much she loved me. That memory filled me with joy. Although she physically was not there, I imagined Sarah curled around me as I finally closed my eyes for a while. I felt protected and at peace.

"You come in here every morning with a twinkle in your eye these days," Michelle said to me as I sauntered into the office the next morning. "Anything you want to share?"

"It shows, huh?"

"Anyone I've met?" she asked.

"Remember Applelady?"

"I sure do," she answered. "So that's been going on a while then, since last fall?"

"No, since just before Christmas. It's a long story. Listen, I'm supposed to go out to Baxter this afternoon. Do you know if Ann got the run update put together? Francois wanted to have a look at it."

"I'll check with her," Michelle said. "She's meeting with Matt O'Reilly at the Mayor's office this morning. She thought she'd get into the office around eleven or so."

"Perfect."

"That's a beautiful brooch," she said, noticing the pink, jeweled ribbon on the lapel of my blazer.

"It's a Patricia Locke, the same designer who made a lot of the earrings I wear. She created these in honor of her former partner, Hollis Sigler, who passed away from breast cancer. Cynthia Pruitt gave it to me."

"That woman has good taste," she said. "Very nice."

I rummaged through the previous day's mail piled on the corner of her desk.

"I'm happy for you, Cate," Michelle added as I started toward my office.

"Thank you, Michelle."

A grin stayed with me all day. I hadn't realized my bliss was that evident.

Time had soared since the first of the year. I hadn't talked to Lindsay for several days and felt I should call to check in on her and Patricia. When we last spoke, Patricia was at a plateau – not getting better, but not losing ground.

"Good morning," I greeted Lindsay as she answered her office phone.

"You have tremendous timing," she replied, letting out a measurable sigh.

"How are you?" I asked.

"Better, now that you called. Patricia has been depressed the past couple of days and I'm running low on energy, but hey, there are a lot of people out there in worse shape than we are."

Lindsay was up to date with the Liza story and had been gracious in saying how pleased she was that things worked out, but we sort of came to an unspoken agreement to not allow our conversations to dwell on Liza or Patricia. How does that happen, you wonder? My friendship with Lindsay was deep enough that we read between the lines of what was said. My goal for the time being was to pump her with emotional support, be positive and not add any more stress to her already overloaded life.

"How have you been?" she asked.

"Busy. The marathon is in two weeks, so my training mileage started decreasing this week. It'll be good to have free time again after the 22nd."

"When will you head to Texas?"

"On the 19th because there's an expo on the 20th and something else is taking place on the 21st. Casey wanted to do it all."

"You'll have a great time. Have you been to Fort Worth before? You have to take cowboy boots, you know?"

For a woman low on energy, Lindsay retained her ability to make me laugh.

"Yeah, I know. I'm running the race in my boots."

"Oh, I'd love to see that!" I'm quite sure her secretary wondered what Lindsay found so funny. "Make sure someone gets pictures, will you?"

Hearing Lindsay's laughter refreshed me. I did miss her. I also worried about her and the responsibility she had taken on with Patricia. She's a very strong woman, emotionally, and I had no doubt she could handle it. Still, I worried.

"I miss you, Cate," she said, brashly interrupting my motherly thoughts. The words caught me off-guard, but were pleasure to my ears.

"Now who has the good timing? I was just thinking the same thing. Maybe we should get together. Do you want to?"

"If it wouldn't cause any problems in your life, I'd really like that. I think I'm experiencing latent withdrawal from you. When this all came up with Patricia, I sort of blocked out everything else. Now that she and I have settled in, I'm starting to address those parts of my life that got put on hold. There are things I want to say to you."

My emotions were starting to waver. Not wanting to cry at the office, particularly this early in the day, I closed out the conversation.

"Then let's talk the week I get back from Texas, okay?"

"I'll look forward to it," she said. "Thanks for calling, Cate, and good luck with the marathon."

February through the end of April the past four years had become hectic for A Sister's Hope because of the cross-country run. Volunteers who packed around the conference table mid-day at least three times a week powdered the office with enthusiasm and involvement. These were ordinary people making an admirable commitment with their free time. The special events team, though an exemplary self-sufficient pair, met with me a minimum of twice weekly to review details and challenges. The partnership with Baxter had reached a point of auto-pilot for now. Francois's public relations gurus had plastered the Chicago Transit Authority trains and buses with posters advertising the run. An agreement with signmeup.com, an online event registration company, had lightened the excessive load of processing registrants. Volunteers who used to open that mail and do data entry now spent time calling people who had signed up simply to say "thank you" for supporting A Sister's Hope.

Liza returned from her Iowa trip in time to run with me that night. We skated through an 8-mile run as if it were three, warding off the chilly winds striking us from the east.

"I think you're ready for Cowtown," she said as we walked past the two-flat to Clark, monitoring our heart rates and cooling down in the 30-degree dusk darkness before heading upstairs. "What do you think?"

Admittedly, I felt more fit than I had in years. The supple, padded layer that insulated my abdomen muscles had thinned over the past six months. I wondered how vividly Liza remembered the first time she had seen my stomach and if she noticed a difference between then and now. I didn't want to seem conceited or self-conscious by asking. Maybe this was more apparent and important to me because I compared my leanness to Liza's. With her 43-year-old "abs," she still could model hip huggers and tube tops.

"Yeah, I think I am. I just hope my pace isn't too much slower than Casey's."

"You never know," Liza said, "you might be ahead of her."

"Always the morale booster, aren't you?" I laughed, guiding us into the house.

Since New Year's Eve, the aura throughout the two-flat had transformed. Before, even when Sarah's voice bounced off all the walls, I sensed a cavity of emptiness. I had become comfortable with that feeling, as if that's the way a home is supposed to feel. As Liza followed me through the living room, I hardly could detect that hollowness. My mind shifted to Sarah, wondering if she could pay a visit again tonight, but I stopped myself. Liza had been gone most of the week and deserved my undivided attention.

The first year of a relationship generally falls into a category of those days that never will be duplicated. Liza and I were making the most of ours. Everything we did together for the first time was cause to celebrate. Each time we made love was reason to experiment and explore. Our intense involvement kept me so engrossed, I didn't have time to miss the conversations with Sarah. And I no longer needed the emotional strength she had provided me the past five years.

Liza and I alternated where we'd sleep every few nights. The house on Hamilton Avenue offered more square footage and much higher quality electronics: surround-sound stereo, big flat-screen television, DVD player, etc. Farragut, however, had the favored master bathroom and upper deck view, though February wasn't the best time to appreciate that part of the house. The home rotation was back to Farragut the week before the marathon. Liza and I stayed up late the Wednesday night before race weekend, packing for our five-day adventure that held no promise of predictable temperatures. Chicago's high for the day had been 15 degrees, below average for this time of year, and Fort Worth had hit a record 55 degrees the past weekend. I packed my thickest tights, which actually were designed for cycling, and I added the turquoise runner's shorts that Liza had verbalized she thought looked good on me. Thrown in were a couple of other options that could suffice if the weather turned ugly – specifically, cold rain. I carefully folded a pair of blue jeans, navy casual dress pants, a V-neck black pullover and some Oxford cotton shirts for touring around the Dallas-Fort Worth area. When it came time to pack shoes, I discreetly grinned as the Justin Ropers "cowboy boots" caught my eye. Lindsay had gotten so tickled when I said I'd be running in them.

"I'm going to be outclassed," Liza said, snapping my train of thought. "I don't own any boots like that."

"Well, we can take care of that in Fort Worth," I responded, chuckling. "These are made there. Then we'll have to find a place to 'scoot the boot'. Know what that means?"

"I *did* see Urban Cowboy," she said, playfully acting as if she were insulted. "John Travolta and Debra Winger, right?"

I laughed and Liza seemed equally entertained by our dialogue.

Our flight the next morning didn't leave until 11:30 a.m., so I fried eight strips of bacon, scrambled four eggs and peeled a perfectly ripe mango for breakfast. Liza, who had been on the phone and computer for nearly an hour getting some last-minute work issues resolved, surrendered to the smells emanating from the kitchen and joined me at the high-top table.

"Are you about finished?" I asked.

"Almost," she said, tearing a piece of bacon and slipping it past her lips. "I can make the rest of my calls from the airport. What time is the cab coming?"

"In about thirty minutes. I'm going to take a quick shower to get the bacon-and-eggs smell out of my hair. Care to join me?"

"You can get started and I'll clean the dishes," she answered, smiling. "I'll be up shortly."

When I walked into the bedroom and began to undress, I hailed Sarah. I wanted only to hear her voice briefly before leaving for Texas, but she didn't show. Opening the wooden jewelry box I'd gotten as a graduation present more than 25 years ago, I honed in on a sterling silver pinky ring Sarah had given me when we first got together. I slid it onto that finger of my right hand.

I was almost ready to turn off the water when Liza finally climbed into the pulsating rhythm of the showerhead massager. She dropped her head back into the hot stream and let it flow down her forehead and off the edge of her angular chin. I squeezed a quarter-sized puddle of shampoo into the palm of my hand and held it in front of her until she opened her eyes.

"May I?" I asked.

"By all means," she replied, cocking her wet head toward me.

I massaged the slick gel into her hair and gently kneaded her scalp, the way an attendant might carefully wash the head of a fragile, aged woman. It was one of the simple ways I tried to show my love to Liza.

"I feel so special when you do that," she said, using one hand to squeeze the excess water from her locks before we stepped onto the bath mat. "Thank you."

"You're welcome."

I used my towel to dab water from the lean area between Liza's shoulder blades and gently nibbled around the back and side of her neck. Leaving her wanting, I hoped, I dashed into the bedroom to get dressed.

"You just wait," she teasingly scolded.

Both of us grinning, Liza slipped her trim legs into the blue jeans she had laid out for the flight.

The taxicab arrived five minutes early. I saw it stop outside and started toward the front door when the telephone rang. A recorded message asked if I wanted the driver to wait and, if so, for how long.

"That's irritating," I said, punching three on my phone's keypad to designate the number of minutes I wanted the driver to wait.

"What's that?" Liza asked, coming down the stairs from the bedroom.

"Oh, I'll explain when we get in the car. The cab is here."

Liza grabbed her suitcase and our shared garment bag and headed outside, leaving me to lock the door. I heard the front door slam shut behind Liza and I hesitated, double-checking that we had all the necessary items for this trip. Standing in the second-floor doorway, I began to sense the slightest emptiness in the house. I hadn't felt it all morning, but it definitely was present now. Then the front door opened and Liza called up to me.

"Cate, do you need help with anything?"

While she stood at the base of the steps, the emptiness subsided.

"No, thank you," I answered. "I'm on my way down."

I was pretty sure I understood what was happening. The locks secured, I maneuvered my over-packed suitcase down the front stairway and porch steps, knowing that this "sacred space" of mine had changed – forever.

Casey's wide grin easily garnered my attention as Liza and I patiently shuffled through the gateway behind an obese young woman and her out-of-control toddler. She welcomed me with a firm firefighter's hug, then shifted to Liza for a lighter version of the same. She looked thin – even thinner than she was at Christmas – but I waited to say anything until later that day.

"How was your flight?" she asked, directing the question to Liza.

Casey had always been very good at trying to make my significant other feel a part of the family. Sometimes it felt as though she paid them more attention than me, a practice for which I harassed her on occasion.

"Smooth sailing," she answered. "How about you?"

"My seven-fifteen a.m. flight didn't end up leaving until nine," Casey replied. "Anytime there's snow, Lambert Airport delays flights. It's like they never can seem to start plowing the runways in time or maybe they need more plows."

"You got snow?" I interjected.

"About four inches is all, but apparently it came down pretty quickly early this morning. Did you get *any* in Chicago?"

"Not a flake," Liza answered. "Do we know what the temperature is here today?"

"Yeah, I went outside before coming to your gate," Casey said. "You're going to be pleased. It feels like about fifty degrees."

All three of us were grinning ear to ear now as we made our way to baggage claim. Casey already had retrieved her backpack before meeting us and it rode firmly on her strong broad shoulders. Kudos to the baggage handlers, our luggage came winding on the carousel toward us within a couple of minutes.

"As you probably already figured, I didn't get the rental car yet," Casey laughed. "Since I got in so much later than I planned, I decided to just wait until you guys got here. The reservation is with Hertz. This way."

Liza passed me a golden smile, then took off trailing behind Casey. I'm quite sure she had no idea how much those impromptu smiles meant to me. Garment bag over my shoulder, I wrapped my fingers around the handle of my wheeled luggage and fell in line behind Liza.

Casey had made all the arrangements for this trip, including tourist options if we found ourselves with free non-marathon time. As we drove west on Highway 183 from DFW airport, she gave us a brief rundown of what she'd discovered. There was Billy Bob's dance club, featured in the movie "Urban Cowboy," and Casey needed an explanation as to why Liza and I were hysterically laughing. If that didn't appeal to us, we could hang out in the Stockyards section of Fort Worth where there's live music nightly at several bars.

"One of the bars down there has saddles instead of barstools to sit on," Casey said, attempting to sound more southern than she already did. "A guy I work with said to make sure we go to the White Elephant Saloon. Supposedly, there's a lot of history to the place."

She listed barbecue restaurants that were "not to be missed," a college bar/café hangout called The Hop, the museum district and a bus tour that reportedly was one of the best history lessons the West had to offer.

"Aren't we actually in the South?" Liza asked in a playful, sarcastic tone.

206

"Did you know that Fort Worth is known as the city where the West begins?" Casey replied. "I think a lot of people classify every state west of Louisiana as 'the West.' That's weird, isn't it? And people always say I'm from the South, but Missouri's not in the South."

"We just talk like we're southern," I chimed in, making both of them laugh.

Casey pulled into the semi-circle driveway of the Radisson Plaza-Fort Worth where we'd be staying the next four nights. Like most Radissons, this one was an upscale, still moderately priced hotel, especially considering its location in downtown "Foat Wuth," as some locals pronounce it. We were a block away from the huge, white, historic courthouse building that marked the seat of Tarrant County. The landmark structure, built in the late 1800s at the top of a hill, can be seen from miles away in all four directions. The Radisson was one of several host hotels where shuttles would swing by on race morning to pick us up and transport us about two miles north to the start/finish area.

Our plans were set for that night: an unofficial welcoming party "Texas style" for participants and those who came to support them, sponsored by Shiner Beer Company in honor of the race's 25th anniversary. Friday night's pasta dinner would place us among the thousands of other carbo-loading individuals who would tread alongside me like a herd of Texas longhorns during Saturday's marathon. We planned to rest and recover on Sunday, maybe take that bus tour Casey mentioned.

We had a blast at the "Shiner" party, emptying several Shiner Bock bottles and befriending lots of other runners. Liza and I identified a group of lesbians who had no inhibitions about taking over a large section of the dance floor when a great two-stepping tune filled the room. We meandered in their direction when Casey became enthralled in a conversation with a square-jawed, handsome brunette who had been poured perfectly into his tight Wrangler jeans. When Liza and I were ready to call it a night, Casey decided to stay out a bit longer and said she'd catch a cab back to the hotel. Although she's the baby of the family, at age 42 she gets to do whatever she wants, so I didn't argue. Besides, the guy seemed very nice and Casey was all smiles. I was too tired or inebriated to be intimate when we got to the hotel, so Liza massaged me to sleep.

Casey came in about three hours later, carefully and quietly getting ready for bed. Being a light sleeper, I woke up and tiptoed to the bathroom for a glass of water and two Advil.

None of us appeared conscious until 8:30 the next morning. I felt Liza roll onto her side and cup her body behind mine, so I reached back and laid my hand on her hip. We lay still only a few minutes before Casey stretched out her arms and legs and turned her head toward us to see if we were awake.

"I'm sorry I woke you up when I came in," Casey half-whispered in a coarse morning voice.

"That's all right," I answered. "I needed some water anyway. Did you have a good time after we left?"

Casey sniggered. "I had a *great* time."

"Way to go, Casey," Liza cheered.

"What was his name?" I asked, sorry I'd forgotten the introduction at the bar.

"Hunter," Casey replied. "Hunter Davenport. He's from Austin."

"Is he going to the pasta dinner tonight?" I asked.

"He wasn't planning on it until I told him we were going," she answered. "Would you two mind if he hooked up with us tonight?"

Now Liza and I snickered.

"I'd love to see Hunter again," I said. "Wouldn't you, Liza?"

"Only if he promises to wear those same jeans," she said, sitting up from her horizontal position to give Casey a raised eyebrow and smile.

The three of us wandered around Sundance Square all morning, settling down for a sandwich in a quaint café near the impressive Bass Hall, a performance arts center that opened in 1998. The Bass family, of shoe company notoriety, is among the wealthy pillars who began revitalizing Fort Worth in the early 1990s. Over lunch, we agreed to check out the newly renovated and expanded "T" – the city's public transportation system – as a means of getting to the museum district. We spent most of the afternoon there, even taking in an Omnimax feature shot in the Great Barrier Reef. Around 4:30 p.m., Casey suggested we return to the hotel for a shower and, maybe, a brief nap before dinner. It didn't take us long to get back to the hotel and Casey plopped onto her bed as soon as we were in the room.

"Since we showered this morning, I think Liza and I are going to check out that Caravan of Dreams lounge around the corner," I said. "We'll meet you back here about 6:45. Okay?"

"Have fun," Casey said.

She probably was sound asleep by the time Liza and I stepped into the elevator on our floor. We nursed our mixed drinks at Caravan of Dreams and shared a small order of vegetarian nachos, loaded with pico de gallo, guacamole, beans, corn and two types of cheese. A three-piece country band started playing at 6 o'clock, drawing people onto the small parquet dance floor. We sat people-watching until it was time to go.

Casey finished blow drying her hair while we caught the end of an "Everybody Loves Raymond" rerun. We arrived at the pasta dinner on time and Casey began scouring the crowd for Hunter.

"Let him find you," Liza suggested.

"Oh, you don't know Casey," I said. "She never waits for anything she wants. She always goes after it with full force."

"You make me sound like a self-centered nightmare," Casey said to me, lightly slapping my upper arm.

"I mean it as a compliment, little sister, and it works quite well for you."

Gentleman Hunter, as I eventually referred to him, proved adept at interacting with a lesbian couple from Chicago, contributing his opinion and knowledge about domestic partner benefits at the University of Texas-Austin. His comfort level with us contradicted the rumors about homophobic Texans. I had to ask.

"Hunter, you seem completely comfortable sitting here talking with us about lesbian and gay issues," I said pointedly. I needn't worry about Casey's reaction. She would expect such a comment from me.

He broke into a Texas-size grin.

"My mom and her life partner, Nora, own the ranch I live on," he said.

Casey glanced over to catch my reaction.

We stayed on that topic all through dinner, learning that Hunter's mother raises show horses and her partner is an economics professor at UT-Austin. When we'd exhausted the topic and the pasta on our plates, Liza and I excused ourselves and returned to the hotel. Casey promised to be in by a decent hour since tomorrow was the big day.

"I'm thinking about running the 10K tomorrow," Liza said, squirting toothpaste onto the edge of her toothbrush.

"You should," I replied, taking the toothpaste from her.

"If I do, I won't be at the first check-in spot we planned," she said between brushing strokes.

"That's fine. Remember, I'm going to be with Casey. If I start dragging, she'll keep me going."

"Then, I'm going to do it," she said. "Being around all these runners has me pumped to really start training again."

"Oh no, does that mean I'm going to be a runner's widow?"

"No, you're going to run with me," she said, smiling. "I'm not talking about marathons, necessarily. We could do some of those fun 5Ks and 10Ks around Chicago. There are a ton of them."

"Let's have this conversation again when we get back to Chicago. I'm withholding further comment until then."

We had just cuddled under the sheets when someone knocked on the door. Then I heard a key card slide into the door slot and the handle turn.

"It's me," Casey said softly.

"I didn't expect you back this early," I said.

"Hunter's going to look for me at the finish line," she said. "I want to get plenty of sleep before the race."

"Good idea," I replied. "I requested a wake-up call for seven. Do you think that gives us enough time?"

"I think we'll be awake before then anyway," Casey answered. "Nerves, you know. I'm just hoping I can actually fall asleep."

She was right – we were wide awake by the time the automated wake-up system rang our telephone. By 6:55 a.m., all three of us had showered again to invigorate our circulatory systems and loosen our muscles. The morning news included a pre-marathon special edition during which they reported conditions for weather, traffic, the route and viewing spots for supporters.

"It's forty-eight degrees," Casey said aloud as current temperatures popped onto the TV screen. "Clear skies, expecting a high of fifty-seven. Whoohoo!"

210

We all dressed in running shorts and short-sleeved wicking shirts. Casey zipped up her windbreaker and stuffed a handful of Jolly Rancher candies into the pocket. Liza and I donned our fleece pullovers and she grabbed the small backpack we'd stocked for post-race activities. When we reached the lobby, an announcement was being made for the 7:30 a.m. shuttle to the Stockyards (a.k.a., race start). It wasn't even 8 o'clock when we piled out of the bus, but thousands of participants and spectators already had gathered.

Liza needed to sign up for the 10K, so we found the registration tent and stood in line about 10 minutes before she was handed her bib and race packet. The next stop was gear check-in where we could leave our backpack and jackets. At 8:20 a.m., we filed into the barricaded starting area behind the last 5K runners who were straggling out onto the course. Casey and I stayed at the edge of the crowd where we could communicate with Liza until actually beginning the race. Although the conversation classified as small talk, I liked having her near me before this endeavor. She had not mentioned the pinky ring, yet I'm sure she noticed.

"I'm summoning a little extra energy for this adventure," I said, holding up my right hand and touching the ring with the tip of my right thumb.

"I saw that in the cab on the way to the airport," Liza responded. "Does it hold hidden powers?"

"I hope so," I answered, grinning. "Sarah gave it to me right after we got together. I figured if I start struggling, say around mile thirteen, maybe she can channel some energy through the ring into me."

Casey joined the conversation at that point.

"Cate always doubts how good of shape she's in," she said, turning to me. "You won't need the ring, but it's kind of cool imagining Sarah might be with us on the route."

"You're ready," Liza said, peering intently into my eyes.

The announcer's voice blasted out: "Runners, are you ready?" I grabbed Liza's hand and lightly released my grip, allowing my fingertips to trail her palm and fingers. We didn't say another word and, as the starter's gun fired, Casey and I peeled away through the barricaded chute with the masses. The weather could not have been more accommodating, a mildly cool breeze mediating the morning sun. The goosebumps wrapping my arms and legs while we'd been standing still dissolved before the end of the first mile. Casey, as expected, began talking as soon as the crowd of runners around us had thinned. Most of our dialogue originated from her, requiring me to respond with only an occasional "uh-huh" or "then what?" I felt good. No threatening side stitches. No struggled breathing. Thirty minutes into the race, my thoughts temporarily left the conversation with Casey and focused on Liza who was at the starting line of the 10K. She was a strong, natural runner with an even stride. Liza defined running as her course work for a doctorate in organizational thinking.

"Did you hear me?" Casey's voice cut into my daydreaming.

"I'm sorry. No. I was just thinking that the 10K should be starting about now. What did you say?"

"I asked you if this pace is okay," she, apparently, repeated.

"It's good for me. Is it all right for you?"

"Yep," she answered. "I was just checking. How do you think she'll do? What pace does she run?"

"I don't really know, but I think she's pretty quick. We can ask her when we see her at water station seven. That's the first place we're supposed to look for her."

As the number of miles and boisterous spectators we passed grew, I became more anxious to see Liza's marvelous smile amidst the crowd at our rendezvous point. Casey and I snacked on her Jolly Rancher candies along the early part of the course. We neared the rendezvous mile marker and a cheery volunteer shoved a small paper cup of water toward me. Another volunteer, probably no older than 12, offered a doused yellow sponge. Grasping it with my free left hand, I rubbed it around the entire circumference of my neck, cool water streaming down my cleavage and between my shoulder blades. I crumpled the cup and tossed it and the sponge toward a plastic-lined cardboard garbage box. The cup shot was short, but the sponge hit the target dead center. When my eyes lifted from the box to scan the line of cheering faces, they fell immediately on Liza standing about 15 yards away. She had retrieved her fleece jacket and was waving her arms like Tom Hanks in the movie *Castaway* when he tried to catch the attention of a passing ship miles out at sea.

"Do you see Liza?" Casey asked, veering us toward her.

"Ha! How could we miss her?"

We slowed our pace enough so that I could ask how she'd fared in the 10K. The hairline along her face was soaking wet and she had zipped the fleece so that it stood up around her neck.

"I ran a 47:31," she called to us as we passed. "How are you feeling?"

"Proud of you!" I said over my right shoulder. I cranked my head around enough to see her beaming face.

Casey guided us away from the edge of the route, which sometimes is plagued with hazards like trashed cups and slick energy bar wrappers.

"Wow, she *is* quick," Casey said, having figured a rough estimate of Liza's pace in the 10K.

The plan was to look for Liza again at mile marker 22 and the finish line. Although the sun fanning over us and the paved road made it feel hotter than the expected 58-degree high for the day, my body thrived in this setting. Seldom did I feel overheated during outdoor athletic activity, even if temperatures reached into the 80s or 90s. Casey seemed happy with her surroundings as well. She talked almost non-stop the next eight miles, giving more detail about her divorce from Tom and sharing with me some of the advice she'd been given by her "brothers" at the firehouse. They were a tight, entangled group there, similar to soldiers in a platoon. What affected one of them indirectly affected the rest of them. Casey loved that interdependence and loyalty, just as she had experienced it in team sports.

The marathon route directed us past a high school where svelte teen-agers proudly wearing their track and field or cross country team sweatshirts handed out sports drink, water and inspiration. "We want to be like YOU!" read one of the poster board signs strung to a tree near them. Elderly spectators waved from their nursing home recreation room through windows decorated with several 8½ " x 11" colored sheets giving the same simple message: "GO!"

Casey and I began a guessing game as to what Liza might hold in store for us at mile 22, the last time we'd see her before the finish. When my little sister began listing possibilities like Oreo cookies and chocolate-covered peanuts, I had to make her stop before my stomach caught whiff of what she was saying. We sighted

Liza long before we got to her, and Casey accommodated my slowing to a near walk when I was within reach of her.

"How's it going?" she asked, her hand momentarily meeting mine.

"Pretty good," I answered. "Remember, I'll look for you on the left at the very end of the refreshment chute."

"I remember," she said, grinning, handing Casey and me each a plastic medallion on a ribbon. "I'll see you there."

We dropped them over our heads and around our necks, letting the plastic disk bounce against our chests. I steadied the medallion between my thumb and forefinger to read what was embossed on it: "I'm somebody's hero." A surge of energy and joy rushed through me. We faced a mere 4.2 miles lying between us and the finish banner that hung across the road in the heart of the Stockyards. I often cupped that medallion during the next 30 minutes or so, reminding myself how blessed I was to have Liza in my life. With slightly more than a mile to go, I realized I'd been running with the tip of my right thumb resting against the pinky ring Sarah had given me. It had been subconscious, yet now that I had noticed, it's as if I couldn't pull my thumb away. Casey had grown quiet, probably to mentally absorb this final leg of our journey. All that seemed to fill my mind was the many times Sarah had visited me over the past five years, sometimes to boost my morale or help me think through situations. More often, her visits provided the extraordinary companionship I so deeply missed, even though it was only her voice.

The lines of spectators thickened as Casey and I caught a glimpse of the finish line banner. She reached for my hand and clasped it like a firefighter would hold onto her axe, raising her hand and mine into the air as we covered the final 60 yards of the marathon. Happy tears rolling down my salty face, I glanced over at Casey.

"Thank you for asking me to do this with you," I said.

She squeezed my hand even tighter, then let go as we coasted over the ramp that recognizes the timing chips attached to our shoestrings. Volunteers offering Kevlar blankets greeted us at the staged area where other volunteers collected our timing chips. Casey saw Hunter milling around the yogurt tables and quickly headed in that direction. I thought I heard someone calling my name and looked to my left to see a familiar face walking toward me.

The twinkle in her hazel eyes made me think two stars had dropped from the heavens. She wore that faded mint green shirt I loved and her beautiful complexion was as tan as ever. I started feeling light-headed, doubting what I was seeing. Just when I thought I might faint, her arms wrapped around me. They were strong. Her hold was firm. She was real.

"I am so proud of you," Sarah said, resting her head against mine, continuing to hug me. "I wanted to be here, *really* be here, to tell you that."

I couldn't speak at first. I didn't know what to say. I still wondered if I was imagining this.

"You *are* here," I said aloud, rubbing my damp hand up and down her back. "I'm the happiest woman in the world right now."

Letting the moment sink in, I hesitated before asking what needed to be asked.

"What's happening?"

Remaining physically connected to my body, Sarah pulled her head away from mine to look me in the eyes. She was gorgeous, a true natural beauty, just like Liza had said.

"You're leaving –for good, this time – aren't you?" I asked.

"I have some other things to take care of now, things that had to be put on hold until you reached this point," she answered. "Cate, I *will* always be with you, but not the way it's been. You and Liza have a life together now and that's where your happiness lies. She's the reason I can move on."

"Will we ever talk again?"

"I don't know. I don't know what else lies ahead for me, but it's time to find out. I hope my coming here this way won't cause you pain. For five years, I've wanted to hold you again so that you could feel my body against yours. I wish I could put a lifetime of hugs into the one I'm giving you at this moment."

"I'll make it last a lifetime," I replied, running one hand tighter around her waist and the other up her back to the base of her skull, feeling her fine hair tickle the back of my hand.

To me, it felt as though we stood there embraced for an eternity. In reality, only a couple of minutes passed.

"I love you, Cate," Sarah said, "more than you'll ever know."

"But I *do* know," I replied. "That's why you're standing here holding me. I seem to remember you explaining that to me about five years ago."

Sarah lightly laughed.

"You're right," she admitted. "I did say something to that effect."

Grinning, her eyes shining like reflections from the face of a diamond, Sarah gradually released her taut hold on me. She leaned her head toward my face and landed her soft, warm lips against mine, holding the pose as if she were waiting for someone to take a picture. That sensation also would last me a lifetime.

"Thanks for wearing the pinky ring during your race," she said, beginning to turn and walk away. "I always thought it looked great on your hand."

"Maybe I'll keep wearing it," I responded, smiling. "I love you, Sarah."

"I love you," she mouthed the words. Sarah rubbed the fingers of her right hand in a circular motion against her chest, over her heart - a silent symbol we often used during our six years together. Then she disappeared amidst the dozens of runners filing past me.

"Are you okay?" a young male volunteer gently asked as he touched my upper arm. I'm sure I must have appeared dazed or zoned out to him.

"Yes, thank you, I'm fine," I replied, stepping over to the bagels table. As I continued walking toward the runners' exit at the end of the refreshment area, snatching a blue sports drink and two bananas en route, I saw Liza patiently stationed several barricade lengths away from me on my left. When she realized I could see her, that smile opened across her face. My pace quickened. She greeted me with a hug equally as fulfilling (though much different emotionally) as the one I'd just received from Sarah.

"You look fantastic!" Liza said, her fingers brushing vigilante hair out of my face. "How do you feel?"

"Surprisingly comfortable," I said, taking a healthy swig of the azure beverage.

"I saw Casey and Hunter come through a couple of minutes ago and Casey said she'd lost track of you when she saw Hunter,"

Liza explained. "I tried not to worry, but I did start scanning the finishers who were hanging out by the medical tent."

I reached down and took Liza's hand, leading us to a sunny spot on the sidewalk where it was a little less hectic and there was room for both of us to sit.

"The reason it took me longer to come through was because I ran into someone I knew," I began, still uncertain how my words were going to come out. "It was Sarah, as real as you're sitting in front of me."

I didn't give her time to respond. I wanted to explain.

"Liza, you were Sarah's gate, the opening she needed to find before she could leave me. She came here to say good-bye."

Instead of questions at the moment, Liza crawled over to me and took both my hands into hers.

"How are you feeling?" she asked, her face wearing a concerned expression.

"I've been asked that a lot today," I answered, effectively making her smile. "I'm good. I'm happy. I'm with you."